A
MUSICIAN'S
Heart

Books by Sandra Ardoin

Contemporary Romance

Hidden Veil Hometown
A Musician's Heart

Love at Christmas Inn Series
Love in Second Bloom
Leaving the Past Behind
Lost in Winter's Wonderland
Box Set: *Longing for Second Chances:*
Three Second Chance Romance Novellas

Historical Romance

Widow's Might Series
Unwrapping Hope
Enduring Dreams
Rekindling Trust

A Love Most Worthy

A
MUSICIAN'S
Heart

HIDDEN VEIL HOMETOWN
BOOK ONE

SANDRA ARDOIN

CORNER ROOM BOOKS

Let love and faithfulness never leave you; bind them around your neck, write them on the tablet of your heart. Then you will win favor and a good name in the sight of God and man.

Proverbs 3:3-4

With elbow grease and a tenacious focus, Jo Ella Ledbetter scrubbed a corner table in Jo E's Java while grappling for the words to answer her grandmother's question. "Sure, I want to marry again, Gran." She zeroed in on a spot of dried icing from a pastry. "One day."

"I hate to inform you, dear, but 'one day' is passing you by at the speed of a bullet train."

"I'm only thirty-two." She paused at the realization that she'd forgotten about her birthday last month. "Thirty-three. I have time."

Speaking of time, Jo glanced at the clock on the wall and frowned. Six-forty. She had twenty minutes to get home and prepare for her piano lesson with Isaac.

Gran closed the gap between them, her brown-spotted hands clutched in front of her and that "mark my words" look on her well-lined face. "In another ten years, you'll say the same thing . . . at *forty*-three."

Jo resisted the urge to huff and moved to another table with her towel and a spray bottle of disinfectant solution, its potent scent competing with the smell of coffee. "What is the rush?"

Gran followed her to stand at her side once more. "I won't be around forever, not on this ol' earth. We both need to face it."

Jo's arm froze in mid-wipe. She studied the pint-sized frame of her grandmother, a deceptive frame that concealed the strength of the woman's strong-willed personality. "Are you feeling all right? Is there something you're trying to tell me?"

Gran's lips pinched with impatience. "I'm in great health for a woman my age." She pulled out a chair and sat at the table with the grace of a fifty-year-old, not someone with the stiff joints of an eighty-one-year-old. "That could change in the blink of an eye if the good Lord gets a mind to take me home. Why, I could keel over any minute. What would happen to you?"

The subject of her grandmother's mortality had haunted Jo for the past couple of years, ever since Grandpa died. Until then, she couldn't imagine anything happening to either of the people who raised her. Now the anxiety returned, leaving her grief-stricken before the fact.

No. She wouldn't consider it. "Gran, you're too feisty to keel over without a fight."

"That may be true, but I am trying to tell you something, honey."

Jo's stomach fell. "What?"

Gran leaned over the table to peer into Jo's face. "Death is inevitable, and I can't stand the thought of leaving you alone,

Jo E."

The fond nickname her grandfather had given her produced an ache in Jo's chest. How she missed his laughter and the way he made a fuss over Gran. How she longed for someone like him for herself. How she hated the idea of Gran leaving her, too.

Years ago, Jo moved away from her grandparents and the town she loved. She wouldn't leave again. Not on the off chance she'd meet someone who thought of *her* once in a while and not just himself, someone she could trust. "Suitable single men don't jump out of the woodwork in Hidden Veil."

"What about Lane Becker? Now, there's a catch."

Jo continued to clean tables, dismissing the suggestion. "Lane is a nice guy, but there's no spark when I'm around him. Besides, he's focused on opening his equine therapy center."

Gran's lips puckered as she thought. "Okay, then his friend Sutton Vance. A little rough around the edges, but—"

"Sutton is iffy in his faith." She considered both men friends, but she didn't belong on a horse ranch or a farm. "I'm a townie, Gran."

Those red-painted lips pressed together again, the bottom one poking out. "How about that vet out on the highway?"

"Dr. Abbott?" Everyone he knew called him Trey. A sweet guy, but . . .

"Yes. Charles Abbott, the Third." Gran eyed the tin ceiling and smiled. "Good families pass along family names, you know."

"I'm sure Trey comes from a fine family, but everyone knows he carries a torch for his vet tech." Everyone knew but said vet tech.

"Oh, for heaven's sakes." Her grandmother's bumpy nails tapped the table. "What about Gene Locke?"

"Very funny."

The pharmacist was a sweetheart but two decades older and in love with his business.

With a few exceptions, like Lane and Sutton, most young people had moved to cities and larger towns after high school. Few remained who weren't married, spoken for, or good-for-nothings. It hadn't helped that the textile plant, the largest employer in town, closed a few years ago. Afterwards, Hidden Veil began its transformation from a sleepy rural town into a go-to spot for relaxation and charm, all guided by Mayor Hildenburg.

Jo hadn't returned to find a husband. She'd returned to care for her grandparents. Despite her teenage grumbling about small-town claustrophobia, adult experiences had taught her gratitude for the place where she'd grown up. Life was comfortable, filled with people she had known all her years. Filled with those who cared about her and those she cared about, especially Gran. Although her grandmother could take care of herself for now, a day would come when she'd need help. That day would not find Jo living miles away.

She had done her time in the city after landing a management position with a company that owned a small chain of coffee shops like hers. But she belonged in Hidden Veil with her grandmother and people she'd known all her life, people she'd abandoned at nineteen to run off and marry.

How well that had turned out!

Jo stashed the wet rag in the plastic bin with the other laundry she would carry home to wash. "Gran, I love you, but the Lord will bring me someone in His time. Until then, this conversation is over."

Her grandmother pushed out of the chair and mumbled something indecipherable, something that sounded far from an agreement.

Gran stared out the front window at something down the street. She released a wobbly whistle. "Now, there's someone I've never met."

Jo sidled up beside her and peered outside. A man walked away from the pharmacy down the block to cross to her side of the street. Tall. Lean but well-muscled. Long legs in faded jeans. He'd tucked his lengthy, blond hair behind his ears and restrained it with a ball cap. Between the distance and his lowered head, his facial features remained mostly indistinct. Still, the sight tempted Jo to match Gran's whistle.

"Do you know him, Jo E?"

Without a clear, full look at his face, she couldn't say. "I don't think so."

"I wonder if he's a 'townie.'"

Jo scoffed at Gran's mockery. "Don't get too excited. He's probably just passing through."

"Or he could be a new resident."

"Or he could be a serial killer." She grabbed the bin with the dirty dishes, certain she'd put an end to the conversation about her love life. "I'm taking this to the kitchen, then I'll lock up so we can leave."

Gran pushed away from the table. "I'm hitting the ladies' room first."

"But we're going straight home." And they only lived four

blocks away.

Her grandmother shrugged. "What can I say? I'm old."

Jo shook her head and wiped one last table before walking into the kitchen. She placed the dirty dishes on the counter to empty the commercial dishwasher for another load.

After waiting two years for a downtown location for her coffee shop, she finally got a break ten months ago. She'd counted her blessings at finding a lease space already set up as a restaurant.

The space had needed more work than she originally realized. Her landlord had washed his hands of it, saying any repairs short of a caved-in roof and toppling walls were her responsibility. Because of the low rent, she accepted the challenge, and it turned out better than she'd expected.

Although open for six months, Jo hadn't banked much, however, the success of the coffee shop amazed her. Who would have thought a town of less than twenty-three hundred people would support her endeavor to such a degree?

She did. That was who.

If the success continued, soon she'd take home a better living.

Her sneaker made a soft splash. Before she could slow her pace to look down, her other foot hit the puddle and slid out of from under her. The room tilted and pain shot up her leg. Multiple dollar signs plastered on a new dishwasher flashed through her mind on her way to the floor.

* * * *

Kyle Callahan had walked the full west side of downtown Hidden Veil—at least the two blocks that made up the main business district. He'd stopped in at various shops, including the hardware store, pharmacy, and antique store. Each place introduced him to local business owners willing to talk. Every one of them assured him that Hidden Veil received its fair share of locals and out-of-towners, especially on the weekends.

The owner of Yesteryear Antiques and Collectibles, Garnet Clark, was a spry ninety-something with a mean knowledge of history. He spent over half an hour listening to the woman tell the stories behind items like butter churns and printing presses. Inspired, he looked for tidbits to include in a song. Typical of his abilities lately, nothing came to mind.

After leaving the antique shop, he'd entered the pharmacy next door and looked around. The adjoining space was being renovated to become an old-fashioned soda shop. The owner, Mr. Locke, had gone on and on about his plans. Too bad the place wasn't ready for Kyle to sit on a red stool at the counter to eat a sundae and scribble lyrics. Maybe ice cream would help his thoughts gel into something worth singing about. Nothing else had worked.

He'd enjoyed the walking tour . . . what there was of it, but Hidden Veil was no Nashville and for sure no Atlanta, where he'd grown up. Specialty stores, such as a bakery, bookshop, candle and soap maker, jeweler, even the soon-to-be soda fountain and ice cream parlor called attention to the charm of the little town. But where did people go for serious shopping and entertainment? To him, no Walmart equated to no civilization.

The century-old brick buildings with their colorful awnings, reproduction gas-fueled lamps on cast iron posts, and newly planted spring flowers in gigantic pots along the sidewalk lent Hidden Veil that quaint appearance his college friend, Mitch Hernandez, spoke of. Nice, but he'd rent Mitch's house only long enough to get his head on straight before returning to Nashville.

Kyle glanced up and down the street at the short blocks of the downtown area. Nope. He'd decide his next career step and move on.

That familiar, silent voice made itself heard again, prodding Kyle to consider his future with care. *Your suggestion is impractical, Lord.* Kyle preferred to think of it as a suggestion rather than a directive.

For years, he'd fought to make it in the country music business. Why switch to writing contemporary Christian music for a living and struggle all over again?

Sure, he performed an occasional church concert as an offering to the Lord, but it was not his everyday job. And with the way his former band met its end, something about a drastic switch in musical genres now seemed akin to greater failure.

He crossed the street, dodging puddles leftover from the morning's rain. The faint smell of it lingered in the air. Wandering the east side of Main Street led him to the coffee shop he'd seen earlier. A dose of caffeine might prompt his brain to think creatively.

Kyle stood outside and read the name on the door: Jo E's Java.

The early April breeze ruffled the lengthy strands of hair sitting on the collar of his long-sleeved Henley. Only the ball cap kept it out of his eyes. He entered the coffee shop. While inhaling the aroma of brewed coffee, he scanned the interior. The walls were red brick and the tables a light cherry tone. Plaques and prints with cutesy sayings decorated the room, and tin squares painted black covered the ceiling. Bare bulb pendant lights with a soft yellow glow hung in staggered lengths, giving the place a warm, laid-back feel.

A long counter stained the same shade as the tables stretched along the rear of the room. Baskets of teas and chocolates topped the empty, refrigerated display case beneath. It likely held pastries or sandwiches most of the day. Equipment, cups, and various other supplies dominated the back counter, along with bottles of various flavorings. On the wall, a chalkboard provided selections of available hot and cold drinks, including teas and soft drinks.

Trendy, yet cozy, the place seemed more like one he'd find in Atlanta, not a small town like this. It stoked his curiosity about the owner's past.

Kyle thought sure he'd seen someone move inside the place a moment before he entered, but no one manned the front counter and the shop lacked any other customers.

He checked the hours on the door. Jo E's Java closed at six during the week. In Nashville, places like this remained open until well into the evening. Well, that explained the empty display shelves and no customers. Why not lock the door to keep late comers like him out?

A high-pitched screech came from the rear of the shop. He rushed behind the counter and jerked to a stop at the doorway leading into a kitchen. Two more steps and he would have tripped over the woman sprawled on the floor.

Lord, don't let her be dead.

Her eyes were closed, and she didn't move. But that face . . . Even after a year, he hadn't forgotten it.

"Are you hurt?" As Kyle approached her, his boots slipped on the linoleum. He reached for the counter and caught himself before he fell.

The woman opened her eyes and stared at him, her lips parted as though on the verge of a scream.

Seriously? He'd been the one to suffer the last time they met, so if anyone screamed, it should be him.

Two

Honestly, she could just scream! How much would the dishwasher's repair cost her this time?

Jo held in the sound. No sense in scaring the man in front of her any more than she already had.

Treating her body as if it were expensive crystal ready to shatter over a clumsy move, Jo turned her head to see advancing black lizard-skin cowboy boots, the tops covered by the hem of a pair of faded jeans.

He slipped and almost fell. She wanted to call out to be careful, but her mouth wouldn't work. It would have been too late, anyway.

As her gaze drifted upward, it took in a trim, masculine frame, a plain navy Henley, and a ball cap. The tips of blond hair under the hat almost touched the tops of his shoulders.

The man she and Gran had seen earlier.

Her face warmed at the irrational thought that he'd heard and responded to her grandmother's whistle.

Jo's gaze drifted down a notch to take in his face. Rather than another full-fledged screech, she released a groan. Unless the fall had caused her to see things that weren't there—if so, why him?—he was not simply a man. She stared into the gorgeous face and blue-gray eyes of the amazing musician she'd once met, the one who made her blood boil after she'd moaned with pleasure over his music.

"Don't move."

That husky voice could croon a country ballad like nobody's business, and those long fingers skimmed piano keys as though they wore ice skates.

The man was a member of BC's Posse out of Nashville. Why would someone like him come to Hidden Veil, North Carolina? No matter how hard the mayor and business owners tried to put Jo's tiny hometown on the map, it wasn't the concert capital of the state.

Was the band performing somewhere nearby? She hadn't heard, and she heard plenty from her customers during the day.

Defying his command to stay still, Jo struggled to rise, but he placed a gentle hold on her shoulders. "Let's make sure nothing's broken before you move around."

Gran's squeal came from the entry to the kitchen. "What happened, Jo Ella? Are you hurt?"

Jo winced at hearing her first and middle names, only used when her grandmother was angry with her or worried about her. "I'm okay, but don't come in. Water's on the floor. I don't want you to slip, too." With her osteoporosis, there was no telling what bones her grandmother might break.

Gran craned her neck to see over the musician. "How did that happen?"

"Looks like the dishwasher's leaking." Jo tried to brush away the man's hold. "Nothing is broken." She hoped.

He refused to let go until he'd helped her to her feet. For the best really. She leaned against the counter to keep the weight off her throbbing left ankle. Everything spun, and she thought she would lose the rest of her late lunch.

He must have sensed it, because he reached out to steady her. "Do you need a doctor?"

She stifled a groan at the pain that ran like a football team—cleats and all—through her ankle and up her leg. Her muscles ached, and she'd find bruises later, but at least Jo didn't see multiples of him.

"No doctor." She grimaced at the large wet spot on the seat of her jeans. "I'm good . . . more embarrassed than hurt."

Gran skirted the water that had ponded on the floor and eyed the man who stood at Jo's side, ready to catch her if she fell a second time. "Who are you?" Curiosity—and a bit of pleasure?—marked her voice.

"Kyle Callahan, ma'am."

Kyle Callahan. She hadn't imagined his identity. The night they met, she didn't tell him her name.

Her blood pressure soared. It was obvious he didn't remember her, otherwise, he'd say something, right? But wasn't it just like her to have not forgotten him? Hadn't she learned anything the first time a musician crossed her path?

"I came in thinking the place was open and heard a scream."

She should have locked the front door before going to the kitchen. Now it was too late. "I didn't scream. I let out a yelp of surprise."

"Nice to meet you, Mr. Callahan. Thank you for helping

my granddaughter." Gran eyed Jo with a glare that asked if the fall had knocked out her manners.

"Yes. Thank you, Mr. Callahan. I'm sorry to have startled you, but I can manage now."

"You're favoring your left foot."

"It's fine. See?" Jo put all her weight on that ankle. Her eyes misted with the pain. Raising her foot, she turned away from their hovering, determined to walk out of the building limp-free if it killed her.

After inspecting the swelling appendage and moving it around with gentle motions, Gran pronounced her diagnosis. "I don't think it's broken, but we should get you home, wrap it, and put some ice on it."

Home sounded good. "Oh. What time is it?"

Kyle glanced at his phone. "It's 6:51."

"Gran, Isaac is probably already waiting for us at the house."

Kyle backed away as if she'd announced she had a stomach bug. "Why don't you call him and tell him you'll be a little late? I'm sure he'll understand."

"I don't have my phone on me and—"

"Here. You can use mine." He held his phone out to her.

"That's generous of you, Mr. Callahan, but Isaac has no cell phone."

"No cell phone?" He asked like it was the craziest thing he'd ever heard.

"Isaac is only eight, and his mother won't let him have one because he loses things. He's my piano student. We only live a few blocks away. We should make it in time." Why had she provided such detail?

"You teach piano?"

"I limit my students to five." Between running the coffee shop and providing piano classes, life could turn hectic some days. However, she enjoyed teaching, and the extra money went into a fund for more renovations to the shop—like a new commercial dishwasher and, one day, flooring for the kitchen, something newer than the clean but cracked and chipped 1960s-era linoleum.

"I bet you're great at it."

The grin on his face ramped up Jo's heartbeat and coaxed a tiny smile from her, despite her determination to remain unaffected by him.

He shrugged. "I started lessons when I was about the same age as Isaac."

"Then you play, too, Mr. Callahan?" By the satisfaction in her voice, Gran's keen interest in him heightened after finding something this man and her granddaughter had in common.

Jo waited for him to reveal his true occupation. Not only did he skate across the ivories, but he could pick guitar strings with the likes of Keith Urban or Brad Paisley.

"I play a little."

Jo snorted, then covered it with a cough. If he chose not to out his talent, she wouldn't either.

"You and my granddaughter should play together one day."

Gran! Before Jo could tamp down her grandmother's enthusiasm and excuse that embarrassing invitation, the woman pointed to her left ankle. "You can't walk four blocks with that swelling, Jo E."

She was right. The day started with sunshine, so they had left the cars at home this morning, not prepared for the deluge during the afternoon.

No one said anything for several seconds. Then Kyle exhaled. "My SUV is down the street. Let me give you a ride." That long-suffering puff of air sounded as though the offer came from duty rather than a genuine desire to help. Typical big city, self-centered musician.

"That isn't necessary." Jo glanced at her ankle. It was looking and feeling like she'd taken a bicycle pump to it, and the sneaker squeezed the skin. She needed to get the shoe off as soon as possible.

"Your grandmother is right. You could do more damage walking, especially if you cracked a bone. Maybe you should have it and your head checked at the clinic."

Jo's eyes widened. "There's nothing wrong with my head."

He drew back and held up a hand. "I didn't mean it like that. I just meant—"

"Enough." Gran folded her arms over her chest. "You will let the man help you home, Jo Ella Ledbetter."

The out-and-out complete name. Even worse than using Jo Ella. And now their guest knew it. Not that it would make any difference regarding his memory of her.

Jo drew on every ounce of civility she could muster, knowing defeat when faced with it. "We accept your offer, Mr. Callahan."

"Kyle. Please."

She'd heard that line from him before, accompanied by the smooth voice that once tempted her to give in to his offer to buy her dinner. Considering that he didn't seem to remember asking a year ago, she was doubly glad she'd declined. "We should leave."

"Let me wipe up the water. Then I'll move my car, so you don't have to walk far."

Jo froze. Why put himself out like that?

"You go, Kyle," said Gran. "I'll take care of the water."

After he disappeared from the kitchen and the front door of the shop closed, her grandmother sighed. "You are too independent for your own good, girlie."

In this case, independent was far better than brokenhearted. And Kyle Callahan had "Heartbreaker" flashing from those blue eyes.

He was a professional musician, and she'd had her fill of those.

* * * *

Jo Ella Ledbetter. So that was her name.

Kyle ran it through his mind several times as he parked his car in front of the coffee shop. His gaze lit on the white letters emblazoned on the black and green-striped awning out front. Jo E. The name of the coffee shop made sense now.

As soon as he saw her lying on the floor, he'd recalled her sweet face and those milk chocolate eyes. Eyes that turned to dark chocolate as soon as she got a good look at him.

Her brunette hair with its coppery highlights was longer than it was a year ago. That night, she'd sat with friends at a table in the venue where BC's Posse played most weekends. He still couldn't determine why he'd picked her out of all the moony-eyed women there—and there were plenty. It wasn't even like him to hit on females in the audience. He'd witnessed too much trouble come to other performers. No, he preferred to take the time to get to know a woman, rather than chase after groupies.

Until he saw Jo Ella.

His definition of Jo Ella Ledbetter as moony-eyed that night came because of her delight over the music, not the band members and definitely not him. She'd sat enraptured while they played, but as soon as a set ended, she ignored them, keeping her seat while her companions strutted up and down past the stage, laughing and flirting with his bandmates.

So, yeah, his attraction to her hadn't come from a boost to his ego. Her love of music drew him in. To learn she's a piano teacher? A surprise, but it made sense.

Back in Nashville, she'd turned down his dinner invitation and walked away. A little more small talk before asking her out might have brought him success. He could have least gotten her name. Maybe he'd deserved the rejection.

He could have said something about remembering her a few minutes ago, but along with the pain in her expression, alarm had mixed with annoyance. The emotions scrolled across her face like individual frames from a reel of film and prompted him to keep his mouth shut.

What would he have said, anyway? *Hey, what a small world. Remember me? You stomped on my heart a year ago.* That would go over well.

Did she even remember him? He wished he knew what about him turned her off that night.

"Dinner with you? I don't think so, Mr. Callahan. Good night."

Her words, along with the image of her rushing out of the

honky-tonk, ransacked his memory. He'd stared after her, too stunned to feel anger or disappointment.

As the ladies exited the shop, Jo Ella hopped on one leg. Her hand gripped her elderly grandmother's arm to steady herself. If she'd waited, he would have carried her out. She couldn't weigh much, even with that willowy frame.

Kyle moved to the passenger side of the vehicle, opened the door, then strode to the sidewalk to assist the grandmother. "I have her." He slipped his arm under Jo Ella's legs and swept her off her feet, eliciting a gasp from her.

"What are you doing? Put me down." Her gaze darted around. Checking to see who watched?

"Just relax and hold on so I can get you home for your appointment." When she'd first mentioned Isaac, he'd backed away, sure she spoke of her husband. Learning Isaac was a kid and that Jo Ella lived with her grandmother brought him a strange satisfaction.

With the purse of her lips, Jo Ella crossed her arms. She smelled of roasted coffee beans and sugar and lavender. The odd combination heightened his conflicting emotions of attraction and animosity. She had shown no interest in him a year ago—quite the opposite. Was he nuts to still find her appealing?

If she stopped scowling at him long enough to talk to him, they might find they had nothing in common but a love for music, and that would be that.

When she refused to hold on as he'd suggested, Kyle shrugged. His step off the curb jarred her, and she grabbed the material of his shirt to steady herself. He fought it, but a giant smirk lightened his load.

Until he got another whiff of her special scent, one that

reminded him of summer gardens, lazy mornings, and . . . the desire for home.

Three

Once he'd helped both ladies into the car, Kyle slipped behind the wheel and turned the key. The engine purred. "Where to?"

Less than three minutes later, he parked in a short, concrete driveway behind an older model, bright blue Mini Cooper. The bungalow-style dwelling a few blocks from downtown suggested a pre-1950 construction preserved with care over the decades. Nice.

Ready to get the Jo Ella Ledbetter reunion experience over, he'd see her inside and leave.

Rather than carry her this time, he stepped alongside her, assisting her grandmother in getting her to the wide covered porch that spread from one front end of the house to the other. With his arm wrapped around her waist, he did his best to ignore the softness and warmth of her body as she hopped beside him.

A woman sitting on a wicker loveseat on the porch stood

at seeing Jo Ella limping toward them. A child—Isaac, he presumed—remained seated, his legs swinging back and forth, the soles of his shoes brushing the planks under his feet.

"Hey, Lisa." Jo Ella took a breath. "I'm sorry I'm late. You weren't too cool sitting out here, I hope."

"I have my sweater." The woman pulled on the knitted material as proof. "And Isaac is always warm. What happened to you?"

"I slipped at the shop."

Lisa took Gran's place at Jo Ella's side as the older woman climbed the porch steps and unlocked the front door. "I can see you're in pain. Why don't we cancel tonight's lesson?"

"That isn't necessary, especially since you're already here."

Jo rubbed her temple, prompting Kyle's worry over a concussion. "Are you sure you didn't hit your head when you fell?"

"I'm sure."

"Maybe you should—"

"I don't need a doctor, Mr. Callahan." She glanced at her grandmother's back. "But thanks for your concern."

The older woman cut on the lights inside the house. Their glow showed off an interior that kept its old-time charm but with some twenty-first century updates. The home's furnishings were a mixture of antique and new. They reminded him of the same warm, comfortable feel inside the coffee shop.

Kyle helped Jo Ella to the couch in the living area. When he gently lifted her legs to place her feet on the cushion, she sucked in a breath, more from surprise than pain. His action probably reminded her of when he'd carried her to the car.

He removed her shoe without asking and her toes curled. "You know you're in no condition to do more than rest, right?"

Her grimace told him to mind his own business. He raised his arms in surrender.

A fine grand piano faced the front corner of the room, situated between a large window looking out on the street and a side window. How he'd love to slide his fingers along those keys. The last time he'd played a grand was at Christmas during a brief visit to his parents' house.

"What if I give Isaac his lesson?"

Her eyes widened. "You?"

"If you'd like proof of my ability . . ."

Before Jo Ella could say no, or that she didn't want proof, he sat at the piano and played a portion of Beethoven's "Moonlight Sonata." Afterward, he spun on the bench and the heat of triumph spread through him. Jo Ella sat with her eyes closed, a gentle smile playing on her lips. The same blissful expression he'd seen the last time they met turned that triumph into a fire of longing inside him.

Lisa clapped. "That was incredible." She clasped her son's shoulder. "See, Isaac? You'll play like that one day."

Isaac looked unconvinced. In fact, his blank eyes reflected boredom. Unlike Isaac, Kyle was born passionate about music—first the piano, then the guitar, and later writing songs that spoke to his heart.

Jo Ella recovered from her enjoyment of the music and said nothing. He could not lay a finger on why, but she seemed a complicated mix of wounded yet brave, adventurous but timid—similar to how his dog behaved when he saw something unfamiliar and wanted to investigate, but not get too close.

The thought of Davey reminded him he should get home. Instead, he folded his arms over his chest. "Well?"

"Mr. Callahan," she made a half-hearted effort to smile, "I appreciate the offer, but I've taken enough of your time."

"I have no plans for the evening." Besides sitting at the kitchen table, attempting to pen lyrics to a song that refused to be written.

Gran—he didn't know her name—brought in a roll of elastic bandage and wrapped Jo's ankle. As she worked, she peered over her shoulder at Isaac. "You know where you're to sit, honey."

The boy scowled but scooted onto the piano bench next to Kyle. Lisa hurried over, carrying her son's music book. She placed it on the rack and backed up a few steps. "He's been practicing all week." Her steady gaze conveyed her desire for Kyle to act as Isaac's teacher for the night's lesson.

He didn't want to step on the toes of Jo Ella's sore foot. "Jo El—"

"Jo is fine, Mr. Callahan."

Evidently, he'd stepped on them, anyway. "Why don't I sit here and help Isaac while you provide instructions from the couch?"

She hesitated, then sighed. "His lesson plan is in the book on top of the piano. Will you bring it to me, please?"

He placed the book in her hand and returned to the piano bench. Thirty minutes later, Isaac rushed out the front door with his mother hurrying to keep up.

Kyle whistled. "He really isn't into his lessons, is he?"

Her lips tipped up and sent Kyle's head spinning. If she set her smile free, it would light up her face and doom him to eternal infatuation. "Isaac would rather play video games. I've told Lisa she's wasting her money for now, but her mother played at a young age, and so did Lisa. She insists her son will be thankful for the lessons one day."

"Now that's over, I brought cake and coffee." Gran set a tray on a side table. "Is someone waiting at home for you, Kyle?"

"Only my dog."

"Dogs are good company. Such a shame there's only the two of you." She didn't sound as though she thought he suffered from being single. In fact, Kyle saw in her expression a silent demand for her granddaughter to take some kind of action. Jo Ella's frown elicited a huff from the older woman.

The sweet smell of sugar and the tartness of lemon wafted under his nose. Two cups of black coffee steamed and added to the aroma.

At Jo's frown, he sank into the plush, overstuffed chair and accepted his plate. Although an easygoing guy, if someone pushed him too hard, he'd stand his ground. This time it meant staying as long as he wished.

He set the dainty cup and saucer on a side table. "Looks good."

Gran gave the other piece of cake to Jo, who asked, "Where is yours?"

"It's been a long day, Jo E. I'm going upstairs to rest and read."

"Are you sure you're feeling well?"

Jo's concern for her grandmother and her patience with Isaac during the lesson showed a side of her she reserved for others. Apparently, he was the one who sent her good humor to the corner for a timeout.

"I'm as fine as I've been all day." The older woman faced him. "It was a pleasure to meet you, Kyle, and I'm sure we'll see you soon."

If her granddaughter had her way . . . "Same here, ma'am. Goodnight."

Jo played with her cake. Even as moist as it was, she covered the painted flowers on the plate with tiny crumbs.

Kyle could get less silence at home from his dog. "I think Isaac's lesson went well. We make a good duo."

She studied him for a moment. "I appreciate your help, but we are not a duo."

The insane thought crossed his mind that they might be one day.

He placed his empty plate on the table. Time to leave before he humiliated himself.

✳   ✳   ✳   ✳

Did insanity run in his family? In no way were the two of them any kind of pair.

Jo leaned against the piano case, gazing out the front window as Kyle strolled to the SUV. She understood why her friends had flirted with the band during their stop last year at the saloon where BC's Posse played. Most of the members shared the good looks of Hollywood celebrities. Kyle was no exception.

She'd hesitated to return to her hotel room after dinner that night, not wanting to be the one to dampen everyone's joy. After all, she and her friends had met in Nashville for a ten-year college reunion, and she loved country music.

Even knowing musicians were as plentiful in the city as cockroaches in a filthy kitchen, she used the outing to prove to herself she had moved past the circumstances that destroyed her marriage.

The whole time they sat at their table, Jo had remained stoic, keeping her focus off all the men in the band. Then Kyle performed a solo, and her body betrayed her as she closed her eyes and let his voice and the music mesmerize her.

A year ago, Jo had tried to convince herself that her interest resulted from the way Kyle's music made her feel. After all, he could turn a single note into a powerful emotion. She hadn't intended to offend him with her reaction to his dinner invitation, but she'd suspected the truth. Her attraction was more than an appreciation for his musical talent. It scared her then. Tonight, seeing him on her own turf, a bolt of terror had seared her.

What brought Kyle to the rural town of Hidden Veil, anyway? It couldn't have been her when he hadn't even known her name. She gripped the edge of the piano's lid. Had one of her friends told him where to find her?

Ugh. Now she was fantasizing. No more Hallmark movies for a while.

Kyle said his goodbye with a shadowy wave, a sure sign he'd seen her peering out the window. She stepped back, gasping when her weight landed on her injured foot. She lifted it to stand like a flamingo.

Jo hoped the all-too-helpful musician hadn't noticed and thought of her as a hopeless klutz. She rolled her eyes. Did Kyle's opinion really matter?

It would be wiser to ask how she could stop it from mattering.

Once the pain subsided and the headlights disappeared, she turned to find her grandmother watching her. "I thought you went to bed."

Gran entered the living room dressed in a nightgown peeking from under a ruby-colored robe. Her silver hair glistened with the overhead light. "I heard Kyle leave and came down to get a glass of water."

Jo clamped her mouth shut against asking what was wrong with the glass her grandmother kept on the nightstand next to her bed. She picked up her plate and set it on top of Kyle's. Only a few crumbs remained of the lemon cake. A faint pleasure washed over her at his enjoyment of it.

She put the dishes on the tray. "I'll clean these up, then head to bed."

"I'll take this. You shouldn't walk around on that ankle. It's too early for me to go to bed, anyhow." Gran grabbed the tray out of her hands. "I saw the way you looked at him tonight."

"You saw the way he irritated me?"

"I raised you from a toddler, Jo E. You can't blind me by blowing smoke in my eyes."

Her grandmother's choreography of the night's events should upset Jo, but a chuckle slipped past her lips. "You are too much, Gran."

The woman lifted a proud chin. "The Lord and I will get you married off yet, honey. Why don't you sleep in the guest room down here tonight? No sense in tempting more damage to that foot."

Letting the subject of her grandmother's matchmaking drop—for now, Jo nodded. "Good idea." She hadn't looked forward to climbing the stairs, especially since Gran wouldn't be able to help support her weight.

As Jo approached the foyer, alternating a hobble with a hop, Gran said, "I don't know what we would have done tonight without him."

"We would have managed." They could have phoned a dozen people who would have dropped what they were doing to help.

For Jo, the pressing questions were how long did Kyle Callahan intend to stay in Hidden Veil, and how could she avoid him?

Four

Jo limped into the coffee shop's kitchen under her own power, gripping anything she could hold to as a precaution. Her ankle wasn't as swollen this morning, but it still hurt, and the last thing she needed was another fall. Gran had urged her to stay home, but she had too much to do today.

Hopefully, the gray clouds that had rolled in overnight would move on and turn the sky a typical Carolina blue, but she'd driven this morning, in case it rained again.

At a knock on the back door, Jo hobbled across the room. "Coming." She opened the door to her new employee and backed away to allow her inside. "Good morning and welcome to Jo E's Java."

"Thank you, ma'am." Bethany Fellowe's brows scrunched. "You're limping. What happened?"

One reason Jo had hired Bethany was because of the woman's cheerful and empathetic attitude. Both had seemed a natural part of her personality during the interview.

After explaining last night's accident, Jo led her into the kitchen and showed her where to hang her purse in the storage closet. Afterward, Bethany washed up. "You take it easy and let me handle things. Where would you like me to start?"

They went over the early morning routine and, to Jo's relief, her new employee began her work with gusto.

Jo perched on a stool, manning the cash register and taking orders while her new hire prepared those orders and cleaned tables. Time whooshed by as she chatted with concerned friends and explained over and over why she favored her foot. She made light of the accident with only a bare mention of Kyle's help, calling him a passerby. Any further description would plant a grapevine of speculation, producing an ample crop of gossip.

At ten, the front door opened. A middle-aged man walked inside dressed in work pants, heavy boots, and a faded blue shirt with his first name embroidered in black thread above a pocket. He carried a metal toolbox and weaved through tables to reach the counter.

"Hey, Stewart." She'd called the repairman first thing this morning. Unfortunately, he was well-acquainted with her equipment.

"Got here as soon as I could, Jo."

"I appreciate it." She led him into the kitchen.

"You limping?"

"I didn't notice the leak until I hit the water."

He pulled a face. "I keep telling you that dishwasher needs replacing."

"I know. As Gran says, money doesn't grow on trees." One day, the dishwasher would force her to replace it. For now, she'd baby it along.

Before setting his toolbox on the floor, Stewart glanced at the full recycle bin she kept near the back wall. "Broke out the second-stringers, huh?"

Unlike coffee establishments that used paper products, Jo preferred the melamine dinnerware for customers who sat inside or at the two bistro tables out front. But to keep from building up a stack of dirty utensils, cups, and plates to wash by hand—frowned upon by the town inspector—Jo had employed the paper and plastic products meant for takeout and emergency situations like this one. They were the second-stringers, as Stewart called them.

"It hasn't hurt my customers to use disposables today." Though her regulars had commented on it.

He patted the door of the commercial dishwasher, a leftover from the last tenant. "I'll see what I can do for the old girl."

"If anyone can fix it, it's you. I'd better get back out front and help Bethany. This is her first day."

Jo left Stewart in the kitchen to work his miracle and retook her place behind the counter. Once the morning rush slowed, she poured her own cup of coffee and sat at a table along the wall to observe Bethany. The woman bustled around the room, her sneakers sometimes squeaking on the tile floor. She straightened this and cleaned that. Occasionally, she shared a laugh with the group of four elderly men sitting at the long table Jo had placed in the alcove at the back of the shop. The men were Jo's loudest and most loyal customers.

Bethany approached Jo's table, her youthful face shining. "They're a lively bunch."

"They come in at the same time every morning and stay for a couple of hours to play cards or one of the board games I keep on the bookshelf." Jo eyed the men, her heart heavy. "There used to be five, but Harry passed away a couple of months ago."

"How sad." Bethany wiped the top of the spotless table next to Jo's. If she kept up the cleaning pace, the room would sparkle.

"You're doing a wonderful job. No one would know it's your first day."

Bethany straightened. "I got plenty of experience working my way through college."

Jo discovered during the interview that Bethany had earned a history degree. As a young mom needing to supplement the family income, there wasn't much call for a historian in Hidden Veil. Maybe one day they would open a museum to highlight the town's past. Then Jo would probably lose what promised to be an ideal employee.

Over the music that piped through ceiling speakers—an eclectic mix of nearly every genre but rap, Jo's phone dinged with a text message. "Bethany, would you hand me my phone, please? It's under the counter."

"Sure."

As soon as she had the phone in her hand, she tapped the message button and saw the name on the screen. Her stomach lurched with dread. Staring at the phone with her index finger hovering in the air, she weighed the wisdom of deleting the text without reading it. Curiosity got the better of her.

> Hey, babe. Got a concert in Greensboro on
> May 6. Sure want to see u there and will
> leave u a couple of tickets.

Babe, my eye. He couldn't even spell out "you" to show her respect.

Jo had to give Taylor credit. He had nerve. She'd had no communication with him since her move back to Hidden Veil. Why did her ex-husband seek her out now? To rub his musical success in her face?

It was like him to think she'd wait around until he snapped his fingers, expecting her to come running. Not that there weren't times in the past to back up that expectation. She'd run to him too often during their marriage, always with the belief that things would be different. Sadly, the paperwork she kept in a safe deposit box at the bank assured her and the rest of the world that she was no longer obligated to meet his expectations.

Jo deleted the message. If she'd needed something to reinforce her intention to stay away from Kyle Callahan, that was it.

What a waste of his time.

Kyle stared at the yellow legal pad on the kitchen table, the remaining blank pages a stark reminder of his writer's block. He had scribbled two lines in the last hour, and he didn't like them. Lying scattered on the floor and table around him were a dozen balled up sheets of paper, each with lyrics he'd rejected.

His frustration mounted. He'd never struggled this hard to come up with an idea that appealed to him.

Kyle blamed the quiet. The neighborhood was *so* quiet.

Wasn't that why he'd come to Hidden Veil, though, for peace and a time to de-stress after the blow he and his bandmates received?

Kyle hunched his shoulders and stretched, cracking his stiff neck and tight muscles. If he sat any longer, he risked petrification. A wry snort pierced the quiet. The people around here could center him in the town's park, like a granite statue. He could see the engraving on the base: *In Memory of the Songless Songwriter.*

After circling the room a few times, he peered out the window at the gray sky—another day of predicted rain. "How about a short walk before those clouds burst, Davey?"

The bullmastiff looked up from his bed by the wall and lumbered to his feet. He shook his body, dispelling his afternoon nap and jingling the tags on the collar.

Leash in hand, Kyle led Davey out the front door. They strolled down the sidewalk, past neighboring homes in the fifty-year-old subdivision—well-kept residences and larger than his Nashville apartment, but not by much. Even with that, two of them could fit in the house his parents owned in Atlanta.

The school bus had come through over an hour ago, and some of the neighborhood kids ran from yard to yard as they played. Kyle kept a tight hold on Davey, since dogs were often a magnet for kids. Although not aggressive, his boy wasn't used to children.

Kyle chuckled when the elementary-aged boys and girls playing tag down the street took one look at Davey's large, wrinkled head and stout body. They made a beeline for the backyard. "Looks like you're scary, my friend."

Davey snuffled and kept walking.

Kyle's phone rang. He dug it out of his back pocket and answered the call. "Hey, Kels. What's up?"

"Does something need to be up for me to call?"

"I guess not. How are things coming with the wedding?"

"Excellent . . . when I keep Mom from taking over the planning."

His sister had accepted the long-overdue proposal from the software geek they had grown up with, and the couple had scheduled the wedding for August. He'd had his doubts about Justin Strong, but the guy made Kelsey happy, and so far, he'd proven himself steadfast and worthy of her.

"What do you think of country life?"

Kyle's footsteps slowed at the question. Kelsey was one of the few people who knew of the situation with Brian and the band and why he'd come to Hidden Veil. It would do no good to hedge. She would weasel his problem out of him. Besides, of his four Callahan siblings, she'd always been his confidant, closest in age and affection. "It's a little like Hope Creek, except the land is rolling, not mountainous."

"Ooh, it sounds perfect."

Although she lived in Atlanta, his sister had renovated their great-grandparents' cabin outside the little town in the Smoky Mountains of Tennessee as her getaway. He had thought of this town as his temporary getaway, but the oppressive silence of the last few days and his attempt to avoid running into Jo Ledbetter made it seem more like a prison.

"Yeah, you'd like it. It's quaint." Mitch had used that

word as a selling point when he'd talked Kyle into renting his house for as long as necessary while Mitch and his family traveled for his job. "The few people I've met seem nice." With one exception. No, even she could be nice . . . to others. "I could use a little nightlife. This place closes up at six."

But was entertainment really what he wanted? Back in Nashville, he complained about the noise and drunken revelers that roamed from one honky-tonk to another along Broadway.

"It's only for a couple of months, and you deserve a break. Maybe you'll meet someone special."

His sister's words conjured the image of Jo watching him leave last night. Seeing her at the window, her features bathed in the soft ivory glow of a nearby lamp, had stolen his breath.

He could have offered to fix her dishwasher today, but as far as she was concerned, the less she saw of him, the better.

"Says the woman with weddings on the brain. And I met a lovely woman yesterday."

"Really?"

"She owns an antique store and is in her nineties."

"Did anyone ever tell you that you're hopeless?"

"Yeah, you." He grinned at her frustrated growl. "My idea of a country girl is one who likes my music *and* city life, Kels." Jo Ella Ledbetter checked only one of those boxes.

"Nashville should give you lots of women to choose from. Have you even looked for that special someone?"

When Jo's image plagued his mind again, Kyle dodged the question. "How's Goliath?" Davey looked up at hearing the name of his brother.

"You mean, how is Justiath?" Kelsey laughed, accepting his change of subject. "Justin and Goliath are inseparable these days. For someone who feared my dog in the beginning, Justin has taken quite a liking to him. He even takes Goliath to work occasionally."

"You're kidding?"

"Nope. Now I'm wondering if he's marrying me simply to gain my dog."

"We all know better."

"Yeah." Her voice had taken on the dreamy quality of a hopeless romantic. "Any progress on the writing front?"

Kyle had hoped she wouldn't ask but wouldn't lie to her. "I haven't written a word worth singing."

"What's wrong?"

He rubbed the area between his closed eyes and exhaled. "I don't know. I can't seem to get my head in the game."

He waited through the silence, knowing she'd have something to say, something he didn't want to hear.

"Is it possible the words won't come because they're the wrong ones?"

Kyle had confided only in Kelsey about the nagging inside him to pen words of eternal value rather than romantic lyrics. "I'm not ready to change my life because of an impression. My problem could be nothing more than worry over the future."

"Or it could be that 'still, small voice' pointing you in a different direction. You can't ignore God's prompting, Kyle, because whatever you do, career-wise, it won't be His best for you."

And that worried him more than anything. How did he win a game of tug-of-war for his future against God and remain close to the Creator who had given him whatever talent he possessed?

His sister broke into his thoughts. "Okay, I won't hound you like ..."

"Mom?"

"You know she means well."

Raindrops splatted on his head and shoulders. Kyle turned around and hurried toward the house he'd rented. "I'm taking Davey for a walk, and it's raining, so I'd better run." Literally.

"I need to get back to work, too. Go explore your surroundings. Meet new people, and maybe it will spark some creative ideas."

"Maybe." He wouldn't mention that he'd already done what she suggested and now hid in his house.

But why should he let one gorgeous, grumpy woman rule his life?

Five

A warm breeze had fanned Kyle's face during the drive to town, but it died with his turn onto Main Street. He rolled up to the curb in front of Jo E's Java and sat in the vehicle, drumming his fingers on the steering wheel. He'd passed other empty parking spots along the street but chose this space, right out front where Jo could see him. Maybe he should throw the SUV into reverse and head to the Red Dog Diner.

His jaw hardened. Maybe he should stop acting like a scared rabbit and go inside. And he couldn't get the quality of coffee at the Red Dog Diner that Jo served here.

He peered through the front windows at the full tables of cheerful people, talking and laughing in pairs and groups. If this was a normal day for her, she ran a successful business.

Kyle rolled up the windows, shut off the engine, and opened the car door. His sister had a point. Sights, sounds, people, they all fed the muse. And right now, his muse faced starvation. Time to feed it.

The rain had ceased an hour ago, leaving behind thick, humid air, and warm, bright sunshine that dried the sidewalks. He stopped outside the door to read the poster in the front window, advertising a charity event coming up for a local teen who had recently received a kidney transplant. It listed several ways to contribute to the expenses, beginning with a baseball game at the high school, vendors and entertainers in the town's park, and an event called a Bachelor Bid. The organizers had scheduled the fundraiser for the fifteenth—a week from today.

Kyle, always willing to help with a good cause, pulled out his phone and made a note on his uncharacteristically blank calendar to attend. He slipped the phone into the pocket of his jeans and entered Jo E's Java.

Jo leaned against the counter. Two days had passed since her fall, but he figured she'd taken no time to rest at home. He had to admire her dedication. Or was it hardheadedness?

Today, she'd dressed in a knit shirt the same grass green as the stripes running down the awning that shaded the sidewalk out front. Thursday, she'd worn a black shirt to match the other stripes. Both bore the embroidered name of the coffee shop. He decided the green suited her best.

At seeing him standing at the door, she bobbed her head—he couldn't tell if she was pleased or miffed—and leaned sideways to speak to the teen boy next to her. The kid made his way across the room.

He hadn't expected much from Jo, just a smile and a few minutes of conversation. That she sent her employee to speak to him gouged a canyon of disappointment through his mood.

"Good morning. Come on in." The cheery teen smiled at him.

"Good morning." Kyle moved away from the door and scanned the room for a place to sit, finding an unoccupied pair of comfortable barrel chairs in the front corner. He'd head there after ordering.

He followed the boy to the counter. By now, Jo had disappeared, probably into the kitchen to avoid him. "What can I get you? Jo said it's on the house and she'll come speak to you in a few minutes."

On the house? Okay, he hadn't expected that.

He glanced at the board, ordered an iced cappuccino, and waited for it at the counter. Jo still didn't show. With his drink in hand, he settled into a chair.

Kyle had taken his first sip of the coffee when Jo crossed the room, her hobble barely noticeable today. She carried a plate with a pastry. "Here you go."

"I only ordered the coffee."

She waved off his protest. "Consider it a small thank you for the other night. I hope you like cinnamon rolls. Martha at the bakery supplies me with them, and they're amazing." The words tumbled out as she set the plate with the pastry on a table next to the chair he occupied.

On Thursday, Jo had seemed to defer to her grandmother regarding Kyle, so he almost asked if he owed Gran for the pastry. But he kept the question to himself. No sense in stirring up trouble. "How's the ankle?"

She glanced at the injured foot. "It's better this morning, not as bad as we thought. But I canceled my plan to run a marathon today."

With her calm voice and her blank expression, he couldn't

tell if she was serious or joking. He assumed it was the latter. The laugh lines around her mouth proved she smiled often, and the spark that had flashed in those brown eyes promised anything but boredom.

The door opened, and she backed away. "I have customers. Enjoy your coffee and pastry."

"Thanks."

Kyle tasted the cinnamon roll that melted in his mouth. All he would get here today was a sugar high and caffeine buzz. But he would be back. Because despite her lack of interest in going out with him, Jo Ella Ledbetter intrigued him more than any woman he'd met in years.

✳ ✳ ✳ ✳

"What is this, Jo Ella?" Gran picked up Jo's cell phone from the kitchen counter in her house and held it out. The text message Jo had received from Taylor a couple of minutes ago filled the screen. Confusion deepened the wrinkles that creased her grandmother's skin. "Why is he texting you?"

Jo shut the refrigerator, her Sunday supper appetite gone, replaced by a tightness running across her abdomen. She shouldn't have left the message sitting in plain sight. Now she had to explain to her grandmother. "That's the second time he's texted me in the past few days."

"What does he want?"

"He wants me to attend a concert in May."

"Will you?"

Not in a million years. "No. I deleted the first message without answering, so he sent another text today."

"That you haven't deleted." Gran studied the screen and the words that implored Jo to call him. "Do you think he wants money?"

Jo's attempt at a laugh sounded more like the opening of a creaky door. "If so, he's looking in the wrong place. The coffee shop has taken almost all my savings."

"If you had it, would you give it to him?"

"After the way he treated me, I don't owe Taylor anything. Besides, I doubt he wants money. From what I've heard, he's doing well."

Gran's gray eyebrows dipped. "You owe him nothing but your forgiveness, Jo E."

The reproach wasn't a new one. Jo had received it often since her divorce. She used to claim she'd left what happened with Taylor in the past, but Gran saw right through her.

She waited for her grandmother to mention that her attitude toward Kyle reflected her unwillingness to forgive her ex-husband. Jo considered it a matter of self-preservation—a way to prevent an unbearable case of déjà vu.

She'd given Kyle coffee and a pastry on the house yesterday. Didn't that count for something? Didn't it show her appreciation for his help Thursday night?

Gran stepped closer, her expression earnest as she rested a hand on Jo's arm. "Remember that forgiveness isn't only for the person who wronged us. It's for *our* good, too. You'll never move away from the hurt you experienced or get on with your life with someone else if you won't forgive Taylor."

"Move on with someone like Kyle Callahan?" Saying his name produced an odd flutter in her stomach.

"Or someone else."

"I'm fine as I am, Gran." Jo smiled to reassure her grandmother, but doubt thundered through her head.

For years, her ex-husband had remained out of sight, and to Jo, out of mind. Then Kyle arrived in town, and Taylor contacted her. Everything boiled to the surface again, threatening to crush her serenity.

"You can tell me you're fine until the cows come home, honey, but can you tell God the same?" Her grandmother gave her the side-eye. "I probably know you better than anyone on this earth, but I don't know you better than Him."

Jo's neck muscles tensed with the clench of her back teeth. "You want me to respond to Taylor's text as a way of showing forgiveness?"

"I want you to respond in everything the way God tells you to do." Gran handed her the phone and walked out of the room.

Jo stood at the counter in the kitchen, gazing out the back window, seeing but not seeing Gran's yard. Movement within the grouping of nandinas near the birdbath drew her attention to a neighbor's cat. The tortoiseshell feline crept out from among the bright foliage toward a robin sitting on the rim of the concrete bowl. The bird preened its feathers, oblivious to impending danger.

"Look out, Mr. Robin."

As she hurried toward the back door, Jo saw herself during her marriage—going about the business of everyday life, ignorant of the dangers that stalked her relationship with Taylor. But whatever her role in the failure of their marriage, it didn't compare to his repetitive cheating.

She opened the back door, and the bird flew off, ending

the cat's pursuit. The stare of the feline accused Jo of ruining its hunt. The sight brought back Taylor's red-faced scowl when she confronted him with his extra-marital activities, like he'd had the right to be angry with her.

She matched the cat's scowl. "Don't look at me like that. I'm not responsible for your actions."

Jo shut the door, then tossed the phone onto the kitchen table before leaving the room. It was too late to avoid the consequences of Taylor's betrayal, but it wasn't too late to avoid a repeat of history.

Look at the heart. The out-of-the-blue idea caught her off-guard.

She may love music, but she didn't trust herself to seek the heart of any man involved in the music business.

Marriage to Taylor Morris taught her the fragility of trust.

Six

Early Monday morning, Kyle climbed out of bed with yesterday's service vivid on his mind. The church he'd attended met in an old Quonset hut renovated from a feed store into a place of worship. The uniqueness of it drew him inside, and the pastor's sermon convinced him to return next Sunday. The small congregation had taken over the structure after the previous owner moved into a newer, more modern space.

The interior looked the same as most other contemporary churches. Wings added on either side of the metal building housed classrooms and offices. The sweet scents of grain and hay lingered in the air, but the unusual smells did nothing to detract from the songs of praise and the delivery of a powerful message from a pastor not much older than Kyle.

Walk in obedience and *for your own good* still resonated—sentiments he'd heard from his sister and brought out in the tenth chapter of Deuteronomy. Those two phrases had stepped on Kyle's toes until he was sure they were all broken. He didn't make a habit of walking in disobedience, so God should cut him some slack, right?

He rolled his eyes. *Yeah, that's how it works, Callahan.*

He dragged out his guitar and plucked the strings. The exercise to keep his fingers limber produced jarring chords that sent Davey to another room.

After ten minutes, he moved on to play a few of BC's Posse's most popular songs. He might talk to Brian about removing the videos from the YouTube channel, especially since Kyle held the copyright to a few of the songs.

The way Brian Chaplinski had treated his *friends* made it hard to think of him in benevolent terms. Although the other band members held a grudge against Brian, Kyle had realized he could live his life filled with resentment or put the past behind him and start fresh. He chose fresh. What that looked like was to be determined, despite yesterday's sermon.

He set aside the guitar and settled into the hard seat of a kitchen chair. Picking up a pencil from the table, he held it over the yellow pages of a legal pad. Various lines ran through his head, three in particular.

Love lost.

Love found.

Undeserved love.

They'd come to him while people watching at Jo E's Java. Okay, mostly, he watched Jo.

His songs focused on the relationships between people, romantic ballads that expressed the struggles and emotions of lasting love.

Lost.

Found.

Undeserved.

After twenty minutes of staring at the words he'd written, Kyle figured he had gone as far as his creativity would carry him, so he grabbed his car keys. Ten minutes later, he pulled into the parking lot behind Jo E's Java, ready for more inspiration.

Carrying his notepad, he entered the building from the rear this time. A screen door to his right gave him a glimpse of the kitchen. He nodded as he passed a group of four elderly men seated around a rectangular table for six. They talked and laughed over the end of a game of checkers. Coffee cups and empty plates lay scattered around them.

"Hold up, fella."

Kyle stopped and twisted to see the white-haired man who'd called out to him. He looked about eighty, and his sharp gaze reminded Kyle of his late grandfather. "Yes, sir?"

"No one gets through Jo's back door without paying a toll."

The others guffawed. One slapped the table.

Kyle's lips quivered. The fun bunch. He rubbed his chin. "I wouldn't want to be known as someone who didn't pay his dues. What do I owe?"

The man stacked red checker pieces into a pile. "One game oughta do it."

Feeling no rush to get to work, Kyle backtracked to the table. "Just one?"

"We'll see how well you do. Could be I'd waste my time playing more than one with you." The good-humored grin on the man's face and the snickers from his friends said he meant nothing offensive.

Kyle hadn't played checkers since he was a kid. He hoped

he remembered how. "Red or black?"

"You're a stranger. You choose."

"Red."

The previous player got up and moved to another chair, allowing Kyle to sit near the board.

"Name's Bobby." Bobby handed him the red pieces, then pointed to each man around the table. "Ray, Gerald, and Walter."

Kyle acknowledged each with a nod and introduced himself.

As Bobby pondered his second move, the portly Gerald asked, "You new in town?"

"New, but not permanent." Kyle explained his presence in Hidden Veil as an extended vacation.

"Young people got too much time on their hands these days," said Ray. "When I was your age, I worked two jobs to support my family."

Bobby jumped one of Kyle's checkers. "You can't count the honey-do tasks your wife gave you."

Gerald and Walter laughed.

In a matter of minutes, Bobby had suckered Kyle into having no moves.

"What on earth is going on here?" Jo's grandmother walked up to the table. "I hope you aren't letting these buzzards give you a hard time, Kyle."

He turned to look at her and winked. "I let Bobby think he beat me."

"How do you know this young'un, Vera?" asked Bobby.

So, her name was Vera. At least Kyle now knew that much about Jo's grandmother.

"This is the nice gentleman who rescued Jo E when she

fell and hurt her ankle. He gave up his evening to help her."

"I'll bet he did." Bobby chuckled. "He sounds like a real knight in shining armor."

"I'm thinking you could learn a thing or two from him." Vera narrowed her eyes. "He overlooked your cheating, didn't he?"

The other three men grumbled over Bobby's tendency to ignore the rules when it came to playing checkers. Kyle let them grumble. There was nothing to be gained by agreeing, nothing but the satisfaction of seeing Bobby's expression when he learned Kyle had caught him jumping a piece he shouldn't have jumped. Besides, he'd enjoyed the game and exchanges of witty banter, and may want to join in again one day.

Vera tapped Kyle's shoulder. "Come with me."

"Nice meeting y'all." He rose from the table to follow Jo's grandmother.

"You come back when you want another trouncing. I only cheat those I like." Bobby's grin coaxed a laugh from Kyle.

Vera led him to the two comfortable chairs near the front door. "Jo ran an errand, but she'll be back before long. You tell me what you want, and I'll bring it to you."

Kyle opened his mouth to deny he was there to see Jo, but closed it. Of the places he could have gone in Hidden Veil, he'd come here, so he couldn't say for certain he wouldn't be lying to her. "I'll go to the counter and order."

"Nonsense. I'm here for the exercise."

Once he gave her his order and the money to pay for it, which she would have rejected if he hadn't insisted, he sat down.

The place wasn't as busy today as it had been on Saturday. Two other people occupied different tables. A brunette in her early twenties scrolled through something on a tablet, text books spread out on the surface in front of her. She looked up and smiled at him in a friendly, non-flirtatious way. A middle-aged man in a suit checked his phone. With the noise made by Bobby and company, not to mention the music from the speakers scattered around the room, Kyle wasn't sure how either of them concentrated.

He tapped his fingers on the chair arm while listening to George Strait's eighties hit "Amarillo by Morning." Man, it'd be nice to have someone like the King of Country Music to record *his* songs. One day, maybe.

Vera returned and plopped into the chair catty-corner to him. "Are you here to see how Jo E's doing, or to flirt with me?"

"To flirt with you, of course."

"Honey, I hate to break it to you, but you'll need another fifty years on you."

He drew out an exaggerated sigh. "I'm afraid there's nothing I can do about the fifty years."

Vera laughed. "Did a job bring you to town, Kyle?"

"No, ma'am. I'm between gigs right now."

Her brow crinkled. "Gigs?"

"Performances."

"Yes, I know what that word means." Her lips pursed. "You're in a band? What kind of music, if I may ask?"

"Country music. I'm a songwriter and performer."

"At least it isn't pop music," she mumbled.

Kyle tilted his head, taken aback by her frown and the odd statement.

Her forehead wrinkles deepened as she studied him. "How far between gigs?"

He'd picked up on her eagerness to kindle a relationship between him and Jo, so he understood why she would be protective of her granddaughter. "I'm not a deadbeat if that worries you, Mrs.—" Would she consider it impolite to call her Vera?

"Oh my. Did I never introduce myself? My name is Mrs. Bevins, but you're welcome to call me Vera or Gran, if you prefer."

Now he knew where the sparkle in Jo's eyes came from. He nodded but figured he'd play it safe by not treading on Jo's "Gran" territory. "Vera, I'm on a vacation of sorts. After my band broke up, a friend offered to rent me his house here for a time. Figuring the quiet and change of scenery would help me get in some writing, I took it." He shrugged, hoping to make light of a situation which had turned out to be anything but light.

"I see."

A lead ball landed in his stomach. She saw what? That Kyle had no lucrative employment, or that he'd been in a band? And why would the second issue matter?

Vera appeared lost in thought, then twisted on the seat cushion and leaned toward him. "Have you seen the signs advertising the 'Weekend for Ryan'?"

"There's one on the window behind you."

She didn't bother to turn around. "We've all prayed for the boy's health for years, but a few months ago it was push comes to shove, and he needed a kidney transplant. Fortunately, they found a match, but it was very expensive, you know."

He tried to follow her line of thought. "If you're suggesting I contribute a hefty sum of money, I have to tell you, the band did well enough, but not that well. Until last year, I supplemented my income teaching literature and creative writing."

She waved a hand through the air. "No. I'd like you to contribute something of greater value."

"What's that?"

Rather than call his name when his order was ready, Bethany brought him his coffee. "Here you go."

"Thank you." Kyle took the steaming drink and breathed in the sweetness of caramel and whipped cream, along with the robustness of the coffee.

Once Bethany walked away, Vera settled back in the chair. "I believe your something of greater value is yourself, Kyle."

A small sip of the macchiato produced a quiet moan of pleasure before he set the hot cup on the end table between the chairs. "Sure, I can help during an event. Which one did you have in mind?"

"You are so thoughtful." She patted his knee as though placating a child. "Actually, I was thinking about the auction."

He laughed. "When necessary, I can rattle off lyrics at a pretty good pace, but I've got nothing on an auctioneer."

She didn't even crack a smile at his comment. "They're calling it a Bachelor Bid, or some such silly thing." The cautious way in which she'd spoken put Kyle on edge. Vera was not a timid woman. She drew in a breath. "Certain single men in the county are, um, auctioning off dates. It's all in fun, of course."

He gulped more coffee than he'd intended, then

suppressed a whimper as it scorched his tongue and throat going down. He stared at Vera until her words sank in, leaving no doubt as to their meaning. His pain forgotten, his jaw fell a second before a spurt of laughter broke free. "You want me to put myself up for bid?"

Vera glared at Kyle. "Shh. This isn't to announce publicly. Not yet, anyway."

His laughter sputtered as he studied Vera's face. The woman was serious. The Bachelor Bid? That sounded too much like the reality TV shows Kyle had scorned time after time. He lowered his voice. "I'll contribute money or labor, but I won't auction myself off to a stranger."

"You've never been on a blind date?"

"No, ma'am, I have not."

"Then you'll never understand what treasure you might have missed. It's how I met my husband, you know. He never complained." Vera eyed his left hand and the bare ring finger. "I suppose I should have confirmed things first. You aren't married or engaged, are you, Kyle?"

He shook his head. "No, but—"

"Dating someone?"

"Not at the moment, but—"

"Then there's no problem. Unless you're not interested in Jo E. You are, aren't you?"

By this time, his head spun. He still had enough sense not to answer her question. "What does Jo have to do with a bachelor auction?"

The little woman's slim shoulders lifted and fell. "I'd like you to make yourself available to my granddaughter in a way in which she can't refuse."

"I should kidnap her?"

At his quip, a slight smile tilted her lips. "That's a little extreme, don't you think?"

"Good to hear, because it's never been necessary for me to abduct a woman in order to date her."

"I don't doubt it." Vera scooted to the edge of the chair, looked around the room, and in a conspiratorial whisper said, "I have a plan."

Kyle resisted the urge to shake the rattle out of his head. "I'll contribute time or money for a good cause, but there's a big problem with your plan. I'm not auctioning myself."

She settled back in the chair once more, folded her hands in her lap, and struck an attitude of poise. "It's honorable of you to want to help a stranger. It was the thing I liked about you from the start, Kyle. But you won't do it . . . for Jo E's sake?"

The words she'd tacked on at the end of that sentence penetrated. "What do you mean, for Jo's sake? What does she have to do with me entering a bachelor auction?"

Vera sighed. "I guess I read you wrong, and you're not interested in my granddaughter . . . in a romantic sense."

"I never said I couldn't become interested." He clamped his lips shut at the honest admission—a little like closing the barn door after the horse trotted out.

"My granddaughter needs someone like you, Kyle."

"Why me?"

"Let's just say she has something to work out, and I think you can help her."

Not only was he frustrated by the non-answer, but she'd stoked his curiosity about Jo's past.

Hot or not, he chugged the rest of the coffee, choking when the liquid slid down the wrong pipe, as his grandfather would have said. He coughed, and Vera scooted over to slap his back. Great. Now everyone in the place gawked at him, including Bobby.

Kyle cleared his throat. "You saw Jo's attitude toward me. So, I'll tell you now, Vera, she will never bid on me. Your plan will not work."

"Of course, she won't bid on you. She despises you."

He frowned and set the empty cup back on the table with a clatter. "Thanks."

"Let me amend my comment, Kyle. She *thinks* she despises you."

For the life of him, he couldn't follow the woman's thought process. "Did Jo tell you we'd met before last week?" When Vera's eyes flashed with surprise, Kyle related the circumstances of their previous encounter. "She turned me down for a dinner date and walked away."

Vera's brown gaze—so much like her granddaughter's—drew him in. "I'm afraid that isn't a surprise."

"Then you can explain why, because she sure didn't."

"Jo Ella believes she has a good reason. That reason is why I'm asking you to do this."

"I still don't understand." Kyle blew out a harsh breath, knowing he would regret his next words. "But let's say I went along with your idea. How would Jo win a date with me in an auction, when even you admit she wouldn't bid for me?"

"You leave that to me, honey." She patted his knee again and stood, prepared to leave him without enlightenment. Her answer didn't fill him with confidence.

He saw no sense in taking part in something bound for failure. "I didn't say I would do it."

Vera simply grinned and walked away.

He pressed into the back cushion of the chair and drummed his fingers on the arms in a random, tuneless melody. Rerunning the conversation through his mind, he questioned why he'd give a second thought to Vera's request. Enter an auction to gain Jo Ella Ledbetter's favor? Why embarrass himself over a woman who *thought* she despised him?

Kyle opened his notebook and pulled out a pen. He had no time to worry about Jo's opinion of him. He had enough on his plate.

Half an hour later, he shut the notebook and left the coffee shop without expending a drop of ink.

Seven

Kyle had to leave the house, eager to escape repeating the memory of his conversation with Vera two days ago. He also needed dog food and was told Hidden Veil Feed and Seed carried Davey's brand.

The new building—a major improvement on the Quonset hut the owner sold to the church—sat on at least an acre of land on the outer edge of town. Advertising signs hung off the metal siding while racks of small vegetables and stacks of bagged soils and compost reminded home gardeners to prepare for spring planting. Yesterday, Bobby had called it a one-stop shop for anything rural and animal related.

Three days in a row, Kyle had sat in the coffee shop. He'd conversed and played games with the old men he'd met on Monday while trying to get a better read on Jo. She treated him as she did all of her customers. No better, no worse. Every so often, though, out of the corner of his eye, he saw her watching him—more accurately, frowning at him.

He was no player like some of his bandmates. His faith kept him on the—mostly—straight and narrow, despite the surrounding culture. Yet, he'd never been desperate for female attention, either.

Inside the farm store, saddles gave the front right corner of the building a leather smell. Other horse products occupied shelves and wall hooks behind them. The left side of the store contained garden tools, mechanical and electrical items, anything and everything for use around a person's property.

As he explored, looking for the dog food, his body jolted with a slug to his shoulder.

"Oh, hey man, I'm sorry." A customer around Kyle's age, wearing faded jeans, a t-shirt and a ball cap, adjusted the large sack slung over his shoulder. His western boots were the real thing—scuffed and wrinkled, broken in through hard work—not the show boots Kyle wore when performing. "I didn't see you."

"No problem." Kyle rubbed his shoulder. "I'm sure it'll slip back into place. Eventually." His laugh lightened the remark.

A smile crossed the man's face. "I think I saw you in church. New in Hidden Veil?"

"I'm temporary."

"Well, glad to have you for however long you stay. Sorry I didn't introduce myself on Sunday, but I needed to leave as soon as the service ended." One hand held the bag of feed. The other jutted out. "I'm Lane Becker."

"Nice to meet you." Kyle shook Lane's hand and introduced himself. "You wouldn't know where to find the dog food, would you?"

Lane pointed to a back corner. "That way."

"Thanks." He eyed the bag. "You have a horse? My youngest sister, Kara, still owns the mare our parents bought her when she was a teenager."

Visits to the barn where Kara kept the horse were as close as he'd come to the four-legged creatures. The more familiar he became with small town and rural life, the more he recognized that playing country music in a honky-tonk didn't make him "country."

"I'm up to thirty horses right now. With foaling season in full swing, it'll soon be more."

"Thirty?" Kyle whistled. "Are you sure one bag of feed is enough?"

"Not by a long shot." A layer of dust jumped when Lane slapped the bag. "This is special feed for a gelding with a sensitive stomach. I'm taking it up front so they'll know what to charge me. I'll get the rest of my order tomorrow."

"Why keep all those horses?"

"It's my business. I raise and sell Quarter horses."

"And Lane is opening an equine therapy center soon." A perky little blonde approached the two of them, showing off slim hips and long legs in a pair of tight-fitting jeans over western boots. The scooped neck of her bright pink t-shirt hung a little too low. If she wasn't still in high school, she hadn't been out long. Her attention focused on the horseman. "I hear you volunteered for the bachelor auction."

Lane winced. "I want to help where I can."

Kyle sensed her scheme as easily as he smelled the flowered perfume that hung like a curtain around her.

"You're so sweet. I've been saving for weeks." She winked and walked away.

Kyle struggled to hold back the laughter at Lane's dismay

and the deep color in his cheeks. "You plan to take part in the fundraising auction? Why?"

"I've known Ryan McCormack's family for years. They're good people." Lane's brow furrowed. "The auction wasn't my idea, but when they asked for single men to volunteer, I figured it was the least I could do." He glanced over his shoulder at the woman who'd left them. "Thankfully, it's only one date and nothing serious."

Kyle let loose the laughter he'd kept in check, but Lane's words tempered it. One date equaled an opportunity to make a family's life easier. His guilt meter bounced into the red zone. "How many men have they rounded up for the event?"

"Seven or eight, I think. You interested?"

He shook his head. "I'll find another way to donate." And keep Vera's ludicrous suggestion to himself.

"I've never heard of an equine therapy center." It sounded like a fancy term for a horse hospital.

"The official name is Healing Springs Equine Therapy Center. We'll use horses to work with veterans and others suffering from PTSD. We're preparing for the opening in September."

Lane either doubled in size, or Kyle shrank when up against the man's generosity. "I'm impressed."

"Don't be." The way he shook off the praise tempted Kyle to recommend Lane for a Citizen of the Year award. "My place is about five miles northwest of town. Crooked Creek Ranch. If you have time, come on by. I'll show you around."

"Sounds good." The setting and topic might stir his stagnant creative juices. He'd go anywhere and try anything. Almost.

Lane shifted the bag still draped across his shoulder. "This thing's fifty pounds of heavy. Maybe I'll see you at the fundraiser on Saturday."

"I'll be there."

"Great."

Lane left for the cashier, and Kyle continued his search for the dog food. As he passed various aisles, he again compared Lane Becker's altruism with his own plan to attend the fundraiser and donate to Ryan's cause.

"Thankfully, it's only one date."

No one said he had to volunteer for the auction based on Vera's suggestion. He could do it as his own contribution. By the end of next month, he'd say his goodbyes to Hidden Veil and whichever woman won the bid, because he'd return to performing and writing country music. He would return to the life he knew before the band's breakup.

He'd also say goodbye to Jo, never knowing what might have been if she hadn't despised him.

* * * *

Jo and Bethany lugged boxes into the small vendor trailer Jo had borrowed from a friend.

Even at seven o'clock in the morning, the air in the park boasted delicious aromas. She inhaled the tang of barbecue and the mouthwatering scent of fried chicken—foods to be sold by other vendors from towns in and around the county.

Despite the recent spring rains, the weather bore witness to its contribution to the fundraiser for the McCormack family with the promise of a cloudless, azure sky and a moderate temperature—perfect for drawing a large attendance.

The dogwood trees had shed their pale ivory blooms in favor of bright green leaves. Oaks and hickories unfurled their buds to become giant sunshades, which wouldn't fully mature for another few weeks. Colorful spring blooms of iris, Dutch iris, and tulips joined pansies and hyacinths to line the stone paths that meandered through the park. A beautiful setting for a grand event.

Fifteen to twenty additional canopied booths surrounded Jo, set up for non-food merchants. Like her, everyone would add their profits to the fundraiser while promoting their businesses. She couldn't deny that she hoped both residents and visitors to Hidden Veil would discover Jo E's Java and frequent the coffee shop. The priority, though, was to help Ryan's family lessen their debt.

While she and Bethany emptied boxes and arranged paper cups, tops, and small paper plates inside the trailer, Gran prepared the coffee and espresso machines.

"I appreciate you giving up your time at home today, Beth."

When finished with the trailer's organization, Bethany would return to the shop and supervise the two high schoolers Jo hired to serve her regular customers on Saturdays.

"We can't give much money, so I consider this my contribution to the fundraiser. It breaks my heart to think of one of my kids being so sick."

It broke Jo's heart to think of the parents' loss had Ryan not received his kidney. What would she do if a child of hers faced a similar fate? She and Taylor waited to have children until it was too late for them to do so as a couple. Now, with no husband in sight, the possibility of ever having children seemed slim.

She placed her hands on her hips and breathed deep. After two hours of setting up, she'd worked up a slight sweat, even though the temperature hadn't reached the day's expected seventy-plus degrees. "Everything looks great, Gran."

"You've trained me well."

Jo wrapped an arm around her grandmother's waist. "You trained me better." If only she'd realized that earlier in life.

At nine-thirty, people trickled into the town's park. It was early enough in the morning that many sought her out for a plain black caffeine pick-me-up and a pastry sugar high. Every penny she made here today, minus a few expenses, would go to the fundraiser. If the pace kept up, she'd be proud of her donation.

"What do you have that's cold?"

At the familiar voice, the cup Jo filled with coffee slipped, sloshing the hot drink over her hand. She sucked in a breath at the burn.

"I didn't mean to startle you." Regret laced Kyle's smooth voice.

"Are you all right, honey?" Gran wrapped a towel around ice cubes and handed it to Jo.

She laid the cold cloth against the burning skin and whirled, pasting on a smile. "It's fine. I'm good."

Not having seen Kyle since Wednesday, she told herself she hadn't missed his presence in the coffee shop, hadn't missed his laughter when he sat with Bobby and his friends. Not that she'd paid attention to him . . . much.

That lie tasted bitter.

Her eyebrows shot up. Until now, she'd seen him only in

t-shirts and jeans. Today, he wore a blue Oxford shirt—a baby blue that matched his eyes—and navy dress pants. The ends of his hair no longer hit the collar of his shirt in one length. He'd had a barber clip them close on the sides and back, with the top left longer and brushed away from his face. With the style, he looked older, more serious, stylish, and . . . okay, *hot.*

She fought to keep from pulling an ice cube from the towel and running it over her face. "You're awfully well-dressed for attending an outdoor festival."

He looked down at his clothes, as though only now realizing what he wore. "I want to make a good impression."

"On who?" Jo could have bitten her tongue. Whoever he chose to impress wasn't her business.

He shrugged. "On whichever woman buys my time."

As his meaning dawned, Jo wouldn't have thought her eyes could grow any larger. "You've entered the bachelor auction?"

Why did that shock her? Because he was a stranger in Hidden Veil with no ties to anyone here? Maybe. At least it sounded more plausible than the accusation of jealousy from the little voice inside her.

Gran stilled. Even though she stood with her back to Kyle, her grandmother never attempted to disguise her interest in their conversation.

"Someone told me it was a good way to help."

A soft snort emanated from Gran, and Jo could see her grandmother's fingerprints all over this situation. But why? And why should Kyle's plan to auction off a date to some woman with too much cash lying around bother her?

"I suppose spending a couple of hours with a stranger is a

generous exchange. We're not an area populated by wealthy people, but I hear the organizers are expecting the bids to run anywhere from one hundred fifty to three hundred dollars."

He rubbed his chin, the crinkles at the ends of his eyes deepening. "I upped the ante."

"What do you mean?"

"I'm auctioning myself for two dates."

"Two?"

For the first time since she'd met him, he appeared sheepish. "Crazy, huh?"

Jo looked into that sea of blue that stared at her as if he conveyed a silent message to her to save him from his decision. What did he expect her to do about it?

Oh, no. No, no. She had no extra money to bail him out of a fix he'd gotten himself into. "I hope you enjoy your time with whoever wins the dates."

"The second one isn't exactly a date. It will be a private concert."

The line behind Kyle had built while they talked. Two women in their early twenties eyed him, whispering and giggling like adolescents. No doubt they overheard and plotted an amount to bid to have Kyle sing to them.

Pointing to the chalkboard easel sitting on the ground outside the trailer, Jo said, "It's a limited menu today."

He glanced at it. "I'll have an iced Americano."

Jo tossed aside the damp towel to prepare Kyle's drink. Off and on, she cast glances at the whispering young women behind him. Long stretches on the road and the admiration of young female fans like them had doomed her marriage. Her skin crawled, knowing how men like her husband—like Kyle?—responded to them.

Look at the heart.

She handed Kyle his drink, ignoring the advice. He might have a heart of solid gold, but Jo wouldn't risk learning it was only gold plated.

Eight

He really was crazy.

Kyle stood near the small, temporary stage in the park, and surveyed the women gathered in front of it like a pack of hyenas waiting to devour their prey. He'd heard that around fifty ladies paid fifteen dollars each for the thrill of spending hundreds more. At least, he wasn't the only crazy one here today.

He'd slung his guitar behind him, the leather strap digging into his shoulder. When Mayor Hildenburg discovered his profession, she'd talked him into providing a brief sample of his talent before the bid. How could he say no?

Then she hit Kyle with the suggestion to up his contribution by donating a private concert. He'd balked, but she was persuasive.

The laughter and conversation from the crowd would sound like a sweet melody if he were only giving a musical performance. But these women buzzed with a different vibe.

They didn't expect a short musical performance from him, any more than they expected a special talent from the rest of the band of merry bachelors. No. They look forward to emptying their wallets on a fun night out for a good cause.

Kyle hadn't informed Vera of his participation beforehand, not wanting her to put into action whatever scheme she'd hinted at in the coffee shop. So, he was on his own.

What made him think telling Jo would inspire her to place a bid? Since when had he lost his hold on reality? A grunt quaked through his gut. He lost that hold the day he helped an injured coffee shop owner.

Whoops, cheers, and catcalls brought Kyle's attention back to the stage where Sutton Vance, a fit but burly guy in a western shirt and jeans, flexed his muscles, preening and peacocking for the bidders. Lane Becker stood beside Kyle, wolf-whistling in fun at his friend.

"Thank you, ladies," shouted Mrs. Hildenburg. Why shout when she held a mic to her mouth? "Your bids for Mr. Vance have brought another one hundred and seventy-eight dollars into the coffers! Give yourselves a hand."

Kyle's gaze sharpened on someone standing in the center of the field of women. Only five feet in height on her tiptoes, the silver-haired, thin-framed octogenarian slumped, like she hoped to hide within the crowd. What was Vera up to?

While the women clapped, Sutton stepped down from the stage and stopped beside Lane. "Man, that was brutal. Thanks for getting me into this situation, *friend.*"

"Not bad for a curmudgeon." Lane laughed. "I haven't seen so much smiling from you since you caught that touchdown in the championship game our senior year. Your jaw must ache something fierce."

Sutton tugged his bottom jaw back and forth. "Yeah, well, your turn is coming." He groaned. "Marnie Houseman. The woman's at least fifty and married. What do I do on a date with her?"

"You know John won't let you take her out, don't you? It's just her way of having a good time while donating her money." Lane elbowed his friend. "You're off the hook."

"I'd better be. As it is, you owe me . . . big time."

Kyle shut out the banter between the friends long enough to pray he'd also get a middle-aged bidder with a jealous husband. He rubbed his hands and shifted his feet. Compared to this, debuting a new song in front of a loud, beer-soaked audience was a breeze.

Sutton slapped a hand on each hip. "Trey should stand here with us."

"Who's Trey?"

Lane turned to Kyle. "The local veterinarian . . . also single. He claimed he had to work."

"The only smart one among us." Sutton's hand swept toward the other men of varying ages who stood around like cattle waiting to be sold.

"Our next bachelor . . ."

The mayor went through the spiel two more times before introducing Lane Becker. The horseman inhaled a deep breath, then planted a smile on his face. He ran up the steps to the stage. Sutton stuck two fingers in his mouth and let loose with a whistle, and Kyle's ears rang from the shrill sound.

Within minutes, Lane rejoined them, sold to the blonde in the feed store for one hundred and ninety-five dollars.

"She must have robbed her piggy bank." Sutton laughed. "Where do you plan to take her? Carowinds? They have kiddie rides."

"Don't start." Lane ran a hand down his face. "I don't think I've gone out with a twenty-year-old since I was . . . twenty."

The mayor called Kyle's name. He jumped. His companions each shoved a shoulder, pushing him forward. His heart beat in triple time as he climbed onto the stage.

Looking out over the pond of women, he told himself his apprehension was ridiculous. He'd performed in front of hundreds—maybe thousands—of people over the years. Somehow, though, concentrating on the music and getting lost in it in front of an enthralled audience was different from standing up here looking pretty while women shouted numbers low enough to humiliate him. Why would anyone bid on a stranger?

The crowd applauded. *Please, God, don't let me go to the perky blonde from the feed store.* How rich was her piggy bank?

The mayor held an index card with the pertinent facts about him. "Kyle Callahan is new to our community, and he's chosen to start his residence in a way that endears him to us, right, ladies?"

Kyle opened his mouth to correct Mayor Hildenburg regarding his future in Hidden Veil, but the mayor gasped. "Oh my, y'all, this is one generous man. He is offering you *two* chances to spend time with him!" The audience shared the mayor's gasp—as if the news surprised her—and clapped with even more vigor. "You'll purchase these dates with our bighearted bachelor as a set. Now, one is an actual date." She paused for effect. "And one is a private concert. That's right. Kyle is a professional musician, a successful singer and songwriter and former member of the popular Nashville band BC's Posse. As his second date, he's offered to perform a backyard concert for the lucky lady and twenty of her friends."

Kyle's face burned, and moisture broke out around his hairline. He'd used his official biography when filling out the form, one that Toni Atkins, the band's manager, wrote for him. Today, he didn't feel like a success.

As their voices hummed, women tapped their phone screens—presumably to look him up.

The owner of both the Red Dog Diner and Ricardo's Mexican Restaurant had donated gift certificates for the bachelors' dates, so now that they knew his profession, at least the women wouldn't expect a night out at a pricey five-star restaurant. After all, *popular and professional* musicians bathed in money, right? He suffocated the urge to roll his eyes. Even if he bathed that way, where around here would he find a five-star restaurant?

"Kyle has agreed to perform a song for you to encourage your bid." The mayor grinned at him. "Are you ready?"

"Yes, ma'am." He gave the women standing before him a bright smile and enthusiastic wave. "Howdy, ladies!"

He swung the guitar around and planted his callused fingers on the strings. During the introduction by the mayor, standing on stage had been akin to standing in the snow naked. Now, he strummed the opening notes to his favorite composition, "Leaving Love," and his audience grew silent.

The hardest thing I could ever do

Is to leave a love so deep, so true.
Where would I find another
To love me like you do?

He closed his eyes, lost in the words, the gentle melody, the hope of one day finding someone to evoke the emotions he'd poured into the song when he wrote it. Man, it felt good to perform again.

Once the song ended, he dipped his head in acknowledgment of the thunderous applause.

The mayor hurried onto the stage, mic in hand. "That was amazing, wasn't it, ladies? Let's start the bid at fifty dollars for both dates, and you know, that's a bargain!"

Yeah, it was.

At least two dozen hands shot up, and the bidding war began.

Sixty. Seventy.

"Do I hear eighty?" More hands went up at the mayor's question.

This is for charity. This is for charity. Kyle repeated the words over and over. Somehow, he would turn this experience into a song.

When the bidding shot up to two hundred-twenty-five dollars with two bidders left, a voice rose from the center of the crowd of women. "Two hundred and fifty U. S. dollars!"

Kyle gaped at Vera. She'd raised a fist at the declaration.

Another woman, who had taken part in the bidding from the beginning—young and with dark blonde hair—yelled, "Two-sixty!"

Jo's grandmother didn't miss a beat. "Two-sixty-five!"

With each upped bid of five and ten dollars, the two

women skewered one another with glares. He might find the competition funny if Vera wasn't involved. What was the woman doing? Jo was going to explode.

Phones rose above the crowd with women snapping photographs of Kyle and his deer-in-the-headlights look.

"But you won't do it . . . for Jo E's sake?"

This had to be part of Vera's plan. How it would help Jo, he couldn't guess. He only knew he'd cheer for Vera any day against a woman who eyed him like a wolf seeing a defenseless sheep and imagining lamb chops.

A willowy brunette pushed through the crowd. He released a soft whistle between his teeth. Things were about to get more interesting.

* * * *

Jo darted through the festival attendees, her pulse setting speed records as she ran toward the crowd of frenzied women.

Please don't let it be true.

While serving customers at the trailer, she'd listened to the bachelor auction being broadcast throughout the park. She told herself to ignore it. Then Kyle's name was called. She couldn't concentrate on anything but that beautiful voice and the music, the women applauding and cheering, the bids that grew ever higher until . . .

Even after she'd heard Gran's voice, Jo couldn't wrap her mind around her grandmother being embroiled in a bidding war for Kyle. She'd excused herself to the people at the counter, locked the trailer, and rushed across the park to the stage, hoping to prevent whatever her grandmother had in mind.

"Sold to Mrs. Vera Bevins for three hundred dollars." The mayor laughed, her voice enhanced by the microphone she held.

Jo skidded to a stop in the center of the crowd of hooting women. *Three hundred dollars!*

Her glance hit the stage where Kyle stood grinning like *he'd* won the bid. Her lips parted in disbelief, then pinched together. The oaf. Didn't he realize her grandmother hadn't the money to toss down the drain? What was he thinking? What were either of them thinking?

Gran shot Sophie Carpenter, her remaining competition, a smirk of triumph, while a group of yammering friends and neighbors congratulated her. Jo clasped her grandmother's arm and, with as much dignity as she could summon, dragged the woman outside the half-circle of auction-goers.

"What are you doing, Jo Ella? Let me go."

"What are *you* doing, Gran?" She thrust her arm toward the stage. "You can't go out with Kyle."

Her grandmother pulled free and stood straighter. "Why not?"

"Because you're almost three times his age."

"Perhaps I like my men young."

Jo crossed her arms and counted to ten to calm her nerves. "What is this about?"

"Ladies, your attention, please." The mayor stood on the stage and clapped her hands, seeking to be noticed. She'd done the same as Jo's fourth-grade teacher. And, as then, she received the silence she sought. "I must correct something. While we can and should congratulate our dear friend Vera for the winning bid, she will not accompany Mr. Callahan. Vera bid in someone else's stead. The name on the bidding form is Jo Ella Ledbetter."

Her grandmother bid for her? Jo's mouth opened. Closed. Opened.

The mayor's brow wrinkled when she caught sight of Jo. "Well, I see she couldn't stay away from the excitement. Congratulations, Jo Ella, dear."

Not daring to look at Gran or Kyle, she bobbed her head.

"I was about to mention that, honey." Gran had the nerve to smile at her. "You'll go out with him."

Her? Go out with Kyle? "No, Gran. I'm not sure you understand how unfair this situation is to me and to Kyle. And I can't afford three hundred dollars."

"You aren't paying. I am."

"You can't afford it, either."

"Don't tell me where I can and can't spend my money, young lady."

Jo attempted to grasp her temper before it flew off the handle. She tried a different angle. "What is Kyle supposed to think? I don't want him to get the idea I'm interested in him."

Gran's attention snagged on something behind Jo. "Honey, I think—"

"I would never believe you were interested in me, Jo. You've made that clear."

She hung her head and shut her eyes, chastened over the words that offended Kyle. Or maybe it was the embarrassment of getting caught expressing them.

When she opened her eyes and turned around, he stood there, his lips drawn in a tight line and his cool blue gaze zeroed in on her. "I didn't mean to imply you're not . . . I mean . . ." Wait. Why should she apologize when he probably put Gran up to this? "Did you know?"

"Not exactly."

Not exactly? That sounded like a yes to her.

"He had nothing to do with it," said Gran. "It was my idea."

Kyle shifted his attention to her grandmother. "Don't worry, Vera, I'll pay for the bid."

At his offer, Jo felt ten times smaller than her five-eight height.

Gran marched around her and stood toe-to-toe with Kyle. "You will do no such thing. I am responsible for my own debts."

They were drawing a crowd away from the next bachelor's turn on the block. Could Jo give her grandmother's "prize" to someone else—Sophie, who Gran bid against?

That would cause no end of trouble.

"Hold on." Jo threw up her hands in a show of surrender. She stepped toward Kyle. "I didn't mean to offend you."

His facial muscles relaxed. "You've been honest with me. I can't ask for anything more."

With everyone watching and seemingly no choice but to accept, she said, "If you agree, I'm willing to . . . go out with you . . . as a friend."

She raised an eyebrow, waiting for his answer, while he studied her as if searching her face for the fine print in the offer. The longer he took to respond, the more her stomach clenched.

"I think that's the idea." His narrow-eyed gaze shifted to Gran. "Right, Vera?"

Gran had the audacity to look defiant, but she agreed.

When Kyle held out his hand to seal the deal, Jo grasped it, her fingers brushing calluses built over years of playing the guitar. His palm, like hers, was slightly damp. Somehow, it comforted her to know that unease was an emotion they shared. But did he feel the same type of flush that exploded through her body?

"Thank goodness that's settled." Gran's smile could light the park at night. "Now, when's y'all's first . . . friendly get together?"

Jo focused on Kyle. "I'll call you sometime to talk about it."

"I'll be leaving at the end of next month, so . . . ."

Oh, she remembered having heard that news. The end of May couldn't come soon enough.

Nine

Jo rushed into The Rock Community Church—a place she'd always remember as a feed store—file folders filled with sheet music and her notes in hand. Within minutes, students, parents, and other family members would fill the small sanctuary for the piano recital.

She arrived at the first row of chairs closest to the instrument and placed the file folders on one of the cushioned seats. Closing her eyes in the sanctuary's stillness, she prayed for an enjoyable evening for her students, and that they would not be nervous, even if they made a mistake or two.

During their last lessons, she'd stressed the importance of trying their best, while reminding them they still had much to learn. As she prayed, she asked for the grace to take her own advice.

Voices in the entryway told Jo the first of the families had arrived. She greeted the students and their parents as they entered the sanctuary, then arranged for the kids to sit in the front row in the order in which they would play.

When the door opened and closed again. She looked up, expecting to see a stray family member. Instead, Kyle stood at the back of the church, watching her. What was he doing here?

"I can't believe he came." Isaac's mother all but squealed. She jumped into the aisle and landed at Jo's side.

"You invited him? Why?"

Lisa's excitement faltered at the blunt questions. "I wanted him to see how much Isaac's attitude had improved since the night he gave my son his lesson."

Jo bit down on her tongue to prevent her mouth from saying she had given Isaac the lesson. Sort of. Kyle had sat on the piano bench, making sure the boy placed his fingers on the proper keys.

"Did I do something wrong?"

"No, of course not. It surprised me to see him here." She forced a smile to ease Lisa's mind. "It's fine."

Lisa cocked her head, the coy expression on her face a warning. "Maybe afterward you two can arrange a time for your date."

Really? Did everyone in Hidden Veil know she'd put off setting a time for her date with Kyle?

Almost a week had passed since the auction. She still hadn't called him, figuring if she dallied long enough, he may leave town and forget about her. Even if it worked, which she doubted, her grandmother would be out three hundred dollars.

Her chest heaved with a sigh. No matter what, Gran would lose, because Jo would not allow anything to come of that "friendly get together."

Lisa was right, though. She shouldn't put it off, but this night belonged to her students.

Kyle settled into a middle seat, alone in a row behind the families. Jo acknowledged him with a quick nod of her head, her heartbeat pulsing like a jackhammer in her chest as the room grew quiet.

"Good evening, everyone. Thank you for coming tonight to support your children's progress. They've worked hard this year and . . . and . . ." Jo's gaze slipped to Kyle. Big mistake, because the rest of her words flew from her mind.

She'd been nervous enough over the parents judging her teaching skill by the way their children played. Now she feared Kyle, a professional, would judge her, too, and she'd come out lacking.

She jerked her gaze away from him, pretending he wasn't there as she addressed the families. "They've worked hard and are eager to get this over with." The parents chuckled along with her, knowing their children.

One by one, each child performed the song they had studied and practiced for weeks. By the end of the recital, Jo walked on air. Her students had done her proud, even Isaac. The smiles of triumph on their faces matched her own.

Sure, almost every child played a few sour notes, mostly minor and unnoticeable—except to her and, probably, Kyle.

Jo had to admit that, perhaps, Kyle's influence on Isaac had motivated the boy to take more interest in his performance. She had never heard him play with such dedication. It brought tears to her eyes—tears she batted away with several quick blinks.

After chatting with parents and children, everyone left the

church, everyone but Kyle. Jo gathered her paperwork as he walked up the aisle toward her. Each nerve ending stood at attention while she awaited his verdict regarding the children's abilities.

"Those kids were amazing, Jo."

Her heart rate slowed with relief. "It was my first recital as a teacher. The families seemed satisfied."

"From the comments I heard, they were elated, especially Lisa." He eyed the piano. "This was my first recital in years. After talking to the families, I understand how my parents felt—a little pride, a little anxiety."

"Do you have brothers or sisters who play?"

"Three sisters and a brother. I'm the only one who endured years of piano lessons."

"And look how well you've done."

His humor slipped. "Yeah."

Although puzzled by his lackluster response, she reached under a seat for her purse. "You come from a large family."

He nodded. "A wonderful family. My sister, Kelsey, is getting married this summer."

"That's nice." Jo wished she could think of something to say that was more meaningful than those two words. After a draining day at the coffee shop and with the tension over the recital, she was thankful not to have collapsed.

Kyle pointed to the stack of folders in her hand. "Would you like me to carry those to the car for you?"

Again, his gentlemanly manner struck her as unusual, and brought another unwanted comparison to Taylor. Her ex-husband had been courteous . . . at first. That ended before they celebrated their six-month anniversary. Then his true nature took over. Where did Kyle's true nature begin and end?

"It's okay. I have them." Jo slipped around him and into the aisle, headed for the front door. Though she didn't attend the church, the pastor allowed her to hold the recital here.

Kyle followed her down the aisle, his boots tapping on the vinyl plank flooring. She paused at the door and waited while he stepped outside before cutting off the lights and locking the door. First thing in the morning, she'd return the key.

Kyle walked with her to her car. "Do you have time for a cup of coffee?"

"Coffee?"

His mouth twisted. "I guess that's a little like asking a plumber if he wants to work on your sink on his day off."

Despite herself, she laughed. "A little."

"Maybe ice cream somewhere?"

With the mention of ice cream, Jo could taste the Red Dog Diner's homemade salted caramel flavor on her tongue. Would it hurt her to spend a few minutes with him? It wasn't a date or a lifetime commitment.

"It wouldn't count as our platonic date, but it may help you unwind."

The way he looked at her, his gaze lingering on her face, told her he wanted more than to share ice cream in a busy restaurant. Oh, yes. She could read his actual intention as clear as if he'd written it in black and white. He wanted a commitment for their date.

Jo shook her head. "It's tempting, but it's been a long day, and I'm exhausted. I should get home."

Dejection shadowed his face, emphasized by the moonlight. "Sure."

She opened the car door, tossed the folders on the seat,

and climbed in behind the wheel. "Good night, Kyle."

"Good night, Jo."

By the time she turned onto the road in front of the church, he had climbed into his car. The dusk-to-dawn light reflecting off the asphalt surface of the parking lot showed him behind the wheel, sitting in a dark, lonely vehicle.

∗　∗　∗　∗

"No way am I falling for that again." With one finger, Kyle slid Bobby's checker back to the space from where he'd moved it.

Ray brayed like a burro and slapped the table. "He got you this time, Bob."

"I reckon he did." Bobby glared at Kyle, but his eyes held a twinkle of amusement.

"Now whatcha gonna do?" Walter leaned over the table to get a better look at the board.

Bobby waved his hand through the air, brushing him away. "Get on back and let me concentrate." After the other man straightened in his chair, Bobby moved his piece in the proper direction. Without a second thought, Kyle jumped it and removed it from the board. Bobby rubbed his pointed chin. "Looks like someone's been practicing."

"The computer is a worthy opponent." Unfortunately, he'd had too much time on his hands, particularly at night, and he'd spent hours playing computer games.

To his right, Jo crossed the coffee shop and stopped beside a middle-aged woman at a table in the front corner. She bent over and spoke in a quiet voice. The despondent-looking customer nodded her head, so Jo pulled out the chair alongside her and sat. Soon, both wore frowns, and Jo covered the woman's hand with her own, speaking to her in a soothing tone. Whatever they discussed, it looked serious.

At the *clap, clap* of the plastic discs on the board, Kyle turned back to the game to see that Bobby had jumped two of his checker pieces.

"A computer might make a passable teacher, but a female is a worthy distraction, don't you think, fellas?" Multiple chuckles from around the table answered Bobby's question.

Within a couple of minutes, they had finished the game with Kyle losing—legitimately this time—to the checkers king. "Well played, Your Majesty."

Bobby pushed the board and game pieces in front of Gerald and Walter. He folded his hands on the table in front of him. "What's bugging you, Kyle?"

"Who said anything's bugging me?"

"You did. It's written all over your face."

What was bugging him? Several things.

First, he had a notepad with disjointed lines and ideas, but still nothing a music publisher or artist would deem worth singing.

Second, he had an online meeting set up with the former manager of BC's Posse in a couple of days to discuss his future. What would he tell Toni? The spiritual conviction he'd experienced over changing his musical path had grown in intensity since his arrival in Hidden Veil. So had the strength of his resolve.

Third, at the fundraiser, Jo had avoided committing to their date by excusing herself to return to the vendor trailer. She'd promised to contact *him* but hadn't. Declining his invitation at the recital thwarted his plan to pin her down over it. At this rate, Vera's hope for them would not end well, and he would return to Nashville never knowing what he'd done wrong. He wasn't sure who deserved his regret more—the sly old woman or himself.

Why couldn't he take the hint and rid himself of the hope that Jo would change her mind?

Kyle sipped his coffee—black and hot this morning—and considered leaving the coffee shop. He should be at home, writing.

Love lost.

Love found

Undeserved love.

His stomach burned at the thought of looking at those sentences that haunted him one more minute. At this rate, he might never find the right additional lyrics to give the words their greatest significance.

Somehow, they told a story. He just had to put everything together in a way that made sense. Deep down, though, he suspected he was trying to fit a square peg into a round hole.

"What bugs me?" He grinned to hide the turmoil inside him. "It's knowing I lost to you again."

Bobby's mouth twisted. "God don't look kindly on fibbers, son. But I'll cut you some slack and mind my own business."

"For a change," said Ray.

While the two men poked at one another, Kyle focused on Jo and the woman at the table. The customer covered her face with her hands, and her shoulders shook. Jo scooted her chair even closer and wrapped an arm around her, letting her cry on her shoulder.

Warmth detonated and spread throughout his chest. It wasn't rare to see one woman comfort another, but the compassion on Jo's face, the love and kindness she showed to the people of this town, set off a firecracker of awe inside him. It burned with a desire to share in that same—no, a deeper—love.

And then he knew.

There was nothing wrong with him.

Despite her effort to push him away, he couldn't give up on Jo when his gut told him she might be the one he'd waited years to meet. The one he wrote songs about. The one who had inspired him a year ago through an undisguised passion for the music he created. The only one with the potential to convince him to give up the city for life in a small North Carolina town.

"I hear you're tolerable on that guitar of yours, and some say your voice'll do."

Bobby's statement broke through Kyle's thoughts. He narrowed his eyes at the man. Some said his voice would do? "Well, *some* say I pick a passable tune and belt out lyrics without croaking too much."

The old man laughed. "Now don't get your back up. My sister was in that crowd of women who were bidding on your beautiful talent." He flashed air quotes. "Her words, not mine. She went on and on and my great-niece joined in, saying she'd seen you in that contemporary church down the road. So, I figured you might do my church a small favor."

"What kind of favor?"

"Our music minister will be out on a Sunday next month, so we need a substitute. Also, I think our people will enjoy a short concert while you're there. We can't pay you much, but—"

"I'm not worried about payment." But it would be a worry if he did a career one-eighty.

Bobby studied him. "So, you'll do it?"

"Don't you need to consult with your music minister first?"

"Already did." Bobby shrugged. "He's my son, so I've an in."

Kyle chuckled. "Sure, I'll do it. When?"

"Third Sunday in May, the twenty-first. That fit your schedule?"

"I plan to leave at the end of next month, so it's cutting it close, but that will work."

Bobby drummed a victory tune on the table. "Good. You can get with our pianist if you've a mind to have someone accompany you."

Adding a piano would be good. "Who is your pianist, and how do I get in touch?"

The old man turned his head to the side and pointed toward the front of the room. "That woman over there."

Jo? Kyle released his disbelief with a soft grunt. *You don't mess around, do You?*

Ten

"Quick." Bethany shot across the room, interrupting Jo's conversation with Susan.

"What's wrong?"

Bethany pointed toward the kitchen. "It's the dishwasher. It's leaking."

"Again?" The dishwasher had become a pain in Jo's backside and a health hazard. This time, Bethany could have slipped and hurt herself.

She jumped up. "I'm sorry, Susan. I have to go. Will you be all right? Should I call someone?"

"No, you go on. I'll head home. Thanks for listening."

"Any time." Jo said a silent prayer for Susan as she dealt with her father's Alzheimer's diagnosis. "If you need anything, let me know."

Susan nodded and gathered her purse to leave.

Jo dodged tables as she followed Bethany, hurrying with as much dignity as possible toward the kitchen. "I don't understand. Two weeks ago, Stewart said it was a washer. He's always reliable."

"Honestly, I don't think you can blame him. I expect the old machine is begging for retirement. You might decide it's more trouble than it's worth at this point."

Not wanting to fall again and convince Kyle she was a hopeless klutz, Jo slowed her steps as she entered the kitchen.

Bethany grabbed a mop from the storage closet while Jo pulled her phone from her pocket to bring up Stewart's number, not eager to add another repair bill to her account this month.

"With all I've spent to keep this thing running, it might be better to buy a new one." Better for her nerves, but not for her checking account.

With the sound of heavy footsteps behind her, she swiveled to see Kyle in the doorway, his focus on the machine. "Do you need help?"

"Not unless you're a dishwasher repairman or have several thousand dollars for a new machine."

His grin sent a now-familiar flutter spiraling through her. "I'm not a dishwasher repairman by trade, but I've had my share of side jobs. One was as an appliance technician for my dad's company. Why don't you let me look at it? Maybe it's a simple fix."

"I don't know, Kyle." She focused on the machine. "I'm considering biting the bullet and replacing it."

"Before you do that, if you have a set of tools, let me try. If I can't fix it, you can proceed however you want."

Bethany stopped mopping. "What could it hurt?"

Jo glanced from the machine to the water on the floor, and then to the phone in her hand. Bethany was right. What did she have to lose? "There's a tool kit in the supply closet."

She took the mop from Bethany. "Someone needs to man the counter. You may as well take an armful of second stringers with you. I'll be out in a few minutes."

"On it." Bethany washed her hands, grabbed some of the paper products, and left the kitchen.

Jo finished mopping the water from the floor, while Kyle retrieved the tool box she kept for repairing minor issues in the shop. The leak was not as bad this time, but things could not continue this way. Apart from the safety and nuisance aspects, she wasted time and money.

Her reluctance to let Kyle work on the dishwasher had less to do with trust in his competency than shame over her chicken-hearted response towards him at the recital. Why would he even want to help her when she'd done nothing to warrant it? "What can I do?"

After unplugging the machine, he crouched in front of it. "You can hand me tools when I need them."

She could do that.

He felt around the door, especially along the bottom, and pulled his hand away. Water dampened his skin. "It's leaking here, in the right corner." He opened the door, removed the racks, and inspected the inside, especially the piece on the bottom that spun. "I'll take the rinse arm off, so let's start with the pliers."

"Slip joint or needle-nose?" When he looked at her in surprise, she couldn't help but respond with a grin. "My grandfather loved to tinker. I used to help him occasionally." They'd had such fun together.

"Slip joint will do." He held out his hand, and she placed the tool in it. "Seems like you and your grandparents were close."

"They raised me after my parents died."

He paused in loosening the nut. "I'm sorry."

"I don't remember them." Jo sought a less gloomy subject. "I saw you playing checkers. Did Bobby cheat this time?"

"I learned after our first game that he only cheats those he likes." Kyle worked as he talked.

"You impressed him." When he looked at her with his head cocked, she could hear his unspoken thought. Then why hadn't he impressed her?

After removing the metal arm inside the dishwasher, he held it up for her to view. "See the split seam? You'll need a new rinse arm before you can use the machine again."

That sounded better than she'd expected. "Where do I get one?"

"We can order it. It's a simple fix." His grave expression prepared her for bad news. "We're talking a few hundred dollars, Jo."

Her jaw plummeted. "For that little piece of metal?"

"Afraid so."

She ran a hand over her brow as she thought. "I can't continue to put money into this machine every few weeks. Perhaps my repairman knows of a secondhand dishwasher, one whose owner who will let me make payments."

"I'm sure he has good connections." Kyle pushed up from the floor. "I've done all I can do here."

"I appreciate your help. How much do I owe you?"

He placed the piece on the counter. "You don't owe me anything. Except, I have a request."

"What kind of request?" Suspicion colored her voice, but she couldn't help it.

"Someone asked me to give a short church concert next month, because the music director will be gone. Will you play the piano for me?"

A church concert? Her imagination had taken her somewhere else entirely. She needed to rein in her thoughts.

"What date?"

"May twenty-first."

Why did that date sound familiar? Then she realized. "My church?"

"Bobby said you're the pianist. He told me his son will be gone, and he needs a substitute."

"Did Bobby also tell you we're an older church with a traditional service?" Jo attended a contemporary service until her return to Hidden Veil. Now, she went with Gran on Sundays to the church she had attended growing up.

"I'll keep it appropriate."

"You said next month. I thought you were leaving."

"You won't get rid of me before then."

"I didn't mean to imply . . ." *Yes, you did.*

To accept his request meant rehearsing with him. The two of them . . . alone.

"What do you say, Jo?"

What was she, a fearless tigress or a measly mouse? She could do this for the Lord. Although, she suspected He was trying to teach her something she'd rather not learn. "Yes, I'll do it."

The effervescent smile on Kyle's face lit a spark of panic inside Jo. She could handle his interest in her. Probably. But could she handle her growing interest in him?

* * * *

Kyle's laptop chimed from its perch on the footrest of the recliner. Ten a.m. Toni Atkins believed in promptness.

He pushed Davey away from sniffing the screen, grabbed the laptop, and tapped the button. The band's former manager's face appeared, a grin running from one dangling earring to the other.

"Good morning, Kyle." The woman, in her late fifties, sang the greeting as she always did. At one time in her life, she'd courted an ambition to become a singer. Now, she managed musicians she deemed worthy, even if they never produced a dime for her. As a wealthy widow, she did it for the love of the work.

He settled onto the recliner, placing the laptop on his legs. "Hey, Toni. It's nice to see your smiling face."

That the band never caught the interest of an agent hadn't discouraged Toni from being BC's Posse's greatest cheerleader and friend. After the band split up, he'd hoped she would remain as his manager. One day, he hoped to have gigs for her to manage.

"I'm smiling for a reason."

"Oh?"

She waved a hand in front of her face and pressed back into the leather desk chair in her home office. "We'll get into that later. How's the writing coming?"

He'd known she would attack that subject first thing and was prepared to be honest with her. "It isn't."

"Why not?"

"Writer's block." At some point, Kyle would reveal the

true source of his writer's block. For now, he wanted more time to mull over his options.

"I'm sorry to hear that. We've talked about this before, but as fine a musician as you are, Kyle, I think you could make a name for yourself in writing material for others."

Writing songs often fulfilled him in a way that performing them did not. He'd come to Hidden Veil to see where that side of his career would take him. But when the words didn't come—like lately—his day ended in frustration. He went to bed empty of any creative satisfaction and without a clue about his next move.

"Are you sure you shouldn't return to Nashville? Maybe you're not getting enough inspiration in that little town."

He'd found plenty to inspire him, just no inspiration when trying to pen lyrics. "I have a couple of commitments that will take me into late May." After the church performance, he could leave, especially if Jo never used Vera's auction purchase.

"Okay." Toni leaned forward and crossed her arms over her desk. "Let's talk about why I was smiling. With any luck, it will end your writer's block."

His heart rate kicked up. "Okay."

"I've talked to Brian." Toni had remained Brian's manager after he signed with a top agent. "He's recording an album for Southern Shot Records."

An album. The words punched Kyle in the gut. Brian was recording an album already, and for a leading record label. Maybe he should follow his old friend's example and double his efforts to find an agent.

But not until he settled this inner battle over his future.

She put on her now-I'll-talk-like-your-mama face. "I know

things went sour between you and Brian, but you were friends for a long time. It would be a shame to see that friendship wither."

"I don't hold Brian's ambition against him, Toni, but he should have given us more notice."

"I won't argue with you. Maybe my news will help smooth things over. I encouraged him to use one of your songs."

Kyle frowned. "Brian prefers more superficial, commercial material."

"The record company wants something different to broaden his appeal."

"What did he say?"

"He's considering it."

Kyle ran through a mental list of his songs, searching for one that would work with Brian's voice and style. "Did he hint at the song he might want to use?"

"He'll ask for something new."

New? What if he couldn't write another word?

"If he approaches you, Kyle, be open-minded about it. He's set to take off. This could be your in."

Kyle wouldn't hold his breath, waiting for Brian to approach him. Yet if he did, could Kyle trust Brian? The man had burned him once already. "If he contacts me, of course, I'll hear him out."

"That's all I ask."

After the call, Kyle leaned against the back of the recliner and closed his eyes. Toni was right. If Brian succeeded as everyone expected, any songs Kyle wrote could hit the top one hundred in the charts—maybe the top twenty, leading to the break he'd worked so hard to achieve.

Despite the turn things took a couple of months ago, why not contact Brian? Why wait? At least, he'd know.

He grabbed his phone, but a voice whispered in his ear, as clear as if someone stood at his side. "Don't. I have something better in mind."

The phone dropped from Kyle's hand and bounced on the carpet. Someone else might dismiss the voice as imagination or his own doubt. But Kyle recognized the Source, and it sent a chill through him.

* * * *

Jo returned to work with the mail she'd picked up from the post office, including a nine-by-twelve padded envelope. She paused by a couple sitting at one of the bistro tables on the sidewalk. "It's a nice day for relaxing outside."

Debbie Jackson, a former classmate of Jo's, grinned. "We figured we'd take advantage of the warm temperature today. Pretty soon, the heat and humidity will get downright unbearable."

"I understand. Spring is my favorite season." Jo's gaze slipped to the large envelope in her hand. What did it contain?

"Do you have time to join us?" Debbie's husband rose from his seat. "Let me pull up another chair."

Jo motioned him back down. "Thanks, but I've been gone for almost an hour with errands, so I'd better get back inside and help Bethany." She shifted the mail to her other hand and opened the door. "If you need anything, come on in. Otherwise, I'll see you at church next Sunday." The same church where she'd play piano for Kyle's concert.

Within feet of entering the building, Jo's steps slowed, her gaze attracted to the table at the back of the room. Kyle sat with the older men and Gran. He'd become a regular, frequenting the coffee shop almost every day to meet with "the boys," as he called them. She'd noticed that he and Bobby had formed some type of bond, almost like grandfather and grandson.

Today, the five men played Yahtzee, while Gran watched. The clack and rattle of dice bounced around the room. When Bobby waved her over, it crossed Jo's mind to pretend she hadn't seen, but she never ignored her customers. Besides, she adored all the older men, especially that rascal Bobby.

She stopped at his side and rested a hand on his shoulder. "Good morning, y'all."

Kyle stood and pulled out the remaining empty chair for her, providing her with another example of his manners. She could never imagine Taylor standing for her or any woman. "Thanks, but I don't have time to stay."

He sat back down, and Jo pointed to Bobby's empty cup. "Do any of you want another coffee?"

"No, I've had my fill," said Bobby. "I just wanted to say I'm glad you agreed to play piano for Kyle at his concert."

"I'm looking forward to a great time of worship."

"Yes, indeed." Bobby's attention shifted to Kyle, one eyebrow raised. "You two will make fine music together."

Was it her imagination, or did "the old buzzard," as her grandmother called him, imply something else? Probably, since Gran sent a jab to Bobby's ribs, earning her a scowl from him.

And on that note . . .

Jo glanced at the envelope, tightening her hold on it. "I'll see you boys tomorrow." Ugh! Kyle had her referring to them as boys.

She strode to the kitchen, placed the mail on the counter, and inhaled, finding comfort in the smell of brewed coffee. She pulled the large envelope from the stack. When faced with Taylor's bold handwriting, she'd almost thrown it in the trash can at the post office. What was he up to?

"It won't open itself." Bethany stood in the doorway to the kitchen, holding an empty pastry tray. She passed behind Jo and set the tray in the sink. "Momma always said the best way to tackle something unpleasant is head-on. And seeing your wrinkled nose told me *that*"—she pointed to the envelope—"is something unpleasant."

"Mmm-hmm." But what?

Once Bethany left the kitchen, Jo picked up the envelope and shook it. No rattle. What Taylor had mailed her made only a slight shushing sound from the padding. His texts were easy to ignore. This was different. It wouldn't be so easy to overlook a large envelope like this unless she tossed it in the dumpster outside. Out of sight, out of mind.

But something—Jo preferred to think of it as curiosity, not expectation—wouldn't let her trash it. And why waste the energy? Whatever he wanted, the answer was no.

Turning it over, she grabbed a knife and sliced the envelope open, peered inside, then pulled out the photo. She stared at it, remembering that day when Taylor's mood had shone as bright as the sun. It was a day when her hopes and dreams for their marriage still lived. A peaceful day hinting of family and a future.

Oh, he did not!

The man played games with her, and she would *not* have it.

Eleven

Kyle hadn't the right to trespass behind the counter and enter the kitchen. Not this time. Thanks to Vera, though, he had an excuse.

He expected Jo to scold him for being out of bounds, and then shoo him into the main room. Instead, she stood at the counter, her eyes enormous as she stared at the photograph in her hand, oblivious to his entrance. A second later, her expression softened into a wistfulness reserved for sweet memories before it flashed into a mask of anger.

Kyle cleared his throat. Jo flinched and slammed the photo image side down on the counter, her hand pressing on it, like she thought it would walk away. Or did she only aim to shield it from him?

"Is there something you need?" A slight quiver possessed her voice.

"Vera asked me to tell you she went home and would see you later."

She nodded, her laser stare a silent message for him to go away.

He released a long exhale. "I know it's none of my business, but you look upset. Is there anything I can do?"

"I don't need a superhero, Mr. Callahan."

His jaw tightened to match hers. "Good, because I'm no one's superhero." Nothing he did worked. He'd failed to change her mind about him or discover what about him repulsed her. With a heavy heart, he turned, ready to leave.

"Wait, Kyle." Her cheeks had reddened and her shoulders drooped. "I shouldn't have snapped at you. You just . . . You caught me at a bad time. I'm sorry I took it out on you."

Kyle leaned against the door frame. "My sisters say I'm a good listener."

He should go home and work, but what was the hurry? He hadn't heard from Brian since talking to Toni two days ago.

Jo eyed the back of the photo. "Do you have time for a walk?"

He straightened, and the tension of a moment ago eased with the invitation. "Sure."

She slid the photograph into the envelope, slipped it under the rest of the mail on the counter, and led him out the back door. They crossed the parking lot to a side street and strolled the sidewalk that led into a residential area.

Jo didn't seem ready to talk about what troubled her regarding that photo, so Kyle asked, "What's up with the dishwasher?"

"Stewart might know of a used one. He'll call me after he checks it out."

"Hey, Miss Ledbetter!" A little girl around ten waved

from the front yard across the street. Kyle recognized her as one of Jo's piano students.

Jo waved back. "Hello, Haley. I'll see you tomorrow night for your lesson."

The little girl's nose wrinkled. "Okay."

"Based on Isaac and Haley's lack of enthusiasm, you probably think none of my students want to learn piano."

"I was at the recital, remember? Those kids did their best for you. That says something."

With the slow swivel of her head, her eyes met his. "You were your piano teacher's pet, weren't you?"

The question brought back Mrs. Conway's claim to his parents that if she could rub a lamp and make a wish, she'd wish for ten Kyles to fill her student roster. "I was."

Jo sputtered a laugh. "Shocking."

Kyle grinned, glad to see her more relaxed. "I have a teaching background and know how it feels to have a willing and talented student."

"Piano or guitar?"

"Literature and creative writing in a community college."

"Interesting."

He shrugged. "It paid the bills when gigs were slim."

"You don't teach anymore?"

"Not this semester." If his music career remained stagnant, he might have no choice but to return to teaching in the fall.

The walk was to provide Jo with an opportunity to vent, but Kyle sought an answer to the question uppermost on his mind. "Can I ask you something?"

Her brows dipped. "I suppose."

"You teach piano—"

"That's a statement."

Her eyes twinkled with humor, and he chuckled. "It won't be when I'm finished."

"Then go ahead."

"You teach piano, yet you have a poor opinion of musicians." He paused on the sidewalk. "Or is it just me you don't like?"

"I have nothing against you, personally." Jo continued on, leaving him behind. Then she stopped and turned around. "Have you heard of Taylor Morris?"

Taylor Morris? "The pop musician? I've never met him, but I've listened to a couple of his songs. Why do you ask?"

"I divorced him."

Kyle's jaw slipped at the news. Yet why should it surprise him to learn she had once married? And divorce wasn't a rare occurrence. But she had married and divorced someone in the music business.

He searched his memory for what he knew of the ex-husband, a guy whose songs had hit the charts in recent years, each one climbing higher than the last. "Do you want to talk about it?"

She stared at the sidewalk. Crossed her arms. Planted her feet and stiffened her form. The body language said, "Not in a million years."

And yet . . .

＊   ＊   ＊   ＊

Jo hadn't foreseen the surge of emotion his question stirred, a fear that he would judge her harshly for her role in the failure of her marriage.

Kyle caught up with her. "Forget I asked. What happened between you and your husband is none of my business."

He was right. The details were none of his business. But the spark of awareness between them was unmistakable, something her grandmother had fostered with her silly auction bid. So, she'd suggested this walk and brought up Taylor, because he deserved to know why there could be nothing between them.

"I was a rebellious nineteen when I ran off with Taylor. Gran warned me about him, but he was an exciting guy with dreams that didn't include small towns or grandparents trying to be parents. I got lost in those dreams, too, and encouraged him to succeed . . . until he believed all the hype surrounding his life, including his appeal to his female fans."

Kyle's mouth flattened, no doubt sensing the direction of her story.

Jo mindlessly drew circles on the concrete with the tip of her sneaker, fighting to control an anger she hadn't resolved. "I didn't want to give up my job, and he was always on the road. At first, I ignored the rumors, but when the photos began appearing on social media and my phone calls went unanswered . . ." She shrugged. "I couldn't live with someone I didn't trust. We separated six years ago."

"I'm sorry for what you went through."

"So am I, and I won't have my life turned upside down by another egotistical musician."

"Ouch." His wince brought an apology to the tip of her tongue, but she swallowed it. She couldn't afford to soften her stance. "That's why you turned down my dinner offer last year?"

The question threw her, and she stopped walking again. "You never mentioned that night, so I didn't think you remembered."

"Actually, I remember it well."

"Do you also recall the way your bandmates flirted with my friends?"

"As I recall it, your friends flirted with mine first."

She couldn't deny it. "Point taken. But those ladies were single. How many of your friends were married?"

Kyle hesitated, then released an irritated exhale. "One and one on the verge of becoming engaged. Point taken."

Those were two too many attached men for Jo's comfort. She took no pleasure in his answer or the fact that her friends had tempted his friends. Fortunately, it hadn't gone beyond flirtation for any of them.

They resumed their walk, reached a corner, and turned around, the silence between them almost as nerve-wracking as receiving that photograph.

"Not every musician is untrustworthy, Jo. It's a job like any other. Nurses cheat. Teachers cheat. Plumbers cheat. You can't judge people's morals by their professions." His mouth angled into a grin. "Unless they're thieves."

"Or marriage murderers."

Those amused lips constricted. "There are plenty of musicians who are faithful in their relationships."

She shook her head. "That may be true, but I won't take the risk, not when I've already lost once."

They strolled past a couple of houses in silence, until Kyle said, "I didn't ask you to dinner looking for a hookup that night. You caught my attention because of your love for the music. I noticed it from the stage. Hearing us play wasn't simply a pleasurable way to spend an evening for you. It was a deep emotional experience. During my solo, 'I Claim You,' light reflected off the tears shining in your eyes. That night, I wanted to talk to a woman whose appreciation for the music ran as deep as mine."

Jo wanted to believe Kyle's words. Dare she believe in him? "Did you write that song?"

"Yes. I've written several love songs."

Jo heard no boastfulness in his voice. In fact, the only thing it boasted was an odd sense of sadness.

Given she'd renewed her relationship with the Lord shortly before that trip—another relationship she'd left in the dust during her marriage—she had appreciated the lyrics. "It's beautiful. You're right. It reminded me of a love song to Jesus, the way, when we claim Him as our Savior, He claims us for His own, no matter our past or present mistakes."

Jo sensed, rather than saw, him stiffen beside her.

✳ ✳ ✳ ✳

Kyle's breath stalled. That was how Jo heard his song? "You heard the lyrics as talking about a relationship with Jesus, instead of being a love song between a woman and a man?"

"It could apply to both, I guess. However, that night, the second verse affected me most. 'In Your loving arms I'll hide. When my troubles rain down, You'll stay by my side. On this eternal road, I walk. It's an eternal road I walk.' Beautiful, Kyle."

He couldn't take his eyes off of her. "You remember the words?"

"I've watched the song on YouTube several times since that night."

Wow. Something he hadn't expected, but not something he could take personally. She didn't watch because of him. She watched because of the words he'd written.

"You didn't sing it just now." He couldn't resist teasing her, if for no other reason than to calm the flood of mixed emotions flowing through him. Pleasure that his words moved her. Pain over never having attached the same meaning to them.

"Trust me, that isn't something you want to hear." Jo rubbed her arms. "It gives me goosebumps to be reminded of God's presence through every minute of my life, here and eternally. How could those words pertain to anything less than something as perfect as God's love sent to each of us through His Son?" Jo offered him a shy smile. "Maybe I shouldn't give your words a meaning contrary to your belief, but it's what occurred to me."

"No, it isn't contrary to what I believe. What you said caught me off-guard, though." Kyle ran a hand through the longer strands on top of his head, not missing the hair he'd had cut for the auction. "No one has ever commented that they heard praise for God's love in those lyrics."

"Probably because you performed the song for an audience focused solely on country music. I can't help but think it struck someone else in the same way."

Kyle went over the chorus in his head and recalled his mindset as he penned the words. He'd returned from church and gone into the spare bedroom he used as an office to work on a piece he'd started days earlier. For thirty minutes, he sat at the keyboard near his desk and let his fingers skim the keys, as if he had no control over them, his mind a hole to be filled. Lines had burst into his consciousness, lines he hadn't attributed to the beginning of God's call to change his life. That call resulted in a near-audible voice speaking to him two days ago.

"I'd love to hear similar songs from you."

Her voice wrenched him from his reverie. "I write about relationships between people." He regretted the sharp response, so he moderated his tone. "Will you tell me what upset you? I know it involved that photograph."

As they neared the coffee shop, her steps slowed. "Taylor has been texting me lately. Today, I received an eight-by-ten of us at Gran's house not long after we married. That was a good day. Afterward, things went downhill."

Kyle frowned. That explained the earlier wistfulness, supplanted by her irritation. "Why would he send you that reminder? Is he trying to win you back?" A pinch inside his chest took his breath. Jealousy?

"Why would he want me now when he didn't want me during our marriage?"

"Sometimes people want what they know they can't have." Was Kyle doing the same thing? Jo didn't show an interest in him, so that made her more attractive to him?

His stomach muscles clenched. The same could apply to his career. Was he going after success in country music so hard because he rejected the idea that God was calling him to something else? Had he chosen disobedience, or had he misunderstood the calling and those words from the other day?

They reached the rear of the coffee shop, and Jo opened the door but didn't go inside. "As I told you, I won't risk falling for another musician, especially the older I get. Men put a value on younger women."

"By men, you really mean Taylor Morris." Where did she get off lumping him in with that idiot?

"Male musicians attract young admirers. Someday, I won't be able to compete against them."

"Jo, you're a young, gorgeous woman. You're also considerate. I've witnessed that in your treatment of your grandmother, students, and customers—the crying woman at the coffee shop earlier this week. You're intelligent and have a heart for the Lord." He moved closer, itching to place his hands on her hips, but he kept them at his side and settled for lowering his voice. "Can you imagine how attractive a woman with a strong faith is to me?"

A tiny smile crept onto her face before she whisked it away. "Experience can be a cruel teacher."

"I agree. Some men aren't worth the ink it takes to print the marriage license." Like Morris. "But don't throw us all in a music-related dumpster."

For a moment, Jo's stubbornness appeared to falter as she considered his words. Then she shook her head. "I'm not saying someone sets out to cheat. It's the separation from the family while touring. The constant travel. The opportunity for temptation."

"We all face temptation. The issue is in how we respond to it. I'm not someone who—" Why did skepticism look so cute on her?

She stepped aside to let a customer leave, then moved closer again, her voice low. "It's clear we don't see eye to eye on this. I'm looking for a man who's satisfied with his life."

Contentment? Did she see him as unsettled, a wandering

soul with no purpose? Looking at his messy career prospects these days, she might be right.

"Good bye, Kyle."

Jo took a step to go inside, and he grasped her warm hand. A slight tremble ran through it as her fingers wrapped around his. His mind went blank with the unexpectedness of it. She gazed at their clasped hands, and her eyes grew round.

He swallowed. *Soulmates.* The word popped into his head. Despite the love songs he wrote, he never believed he'd find that intensity of love for himself. Did she feel that soul-deep connection, too?

Kyle shook off the premature fantasizing. That level of love was impossible if she refused to see him as nothing more than a musician. "You owe me a date."

"You mean *you* owe my grandmother a friendly get together."

"I said what I meant. This is between you and me, Jo."

She studied his face, then freed her hand and went inside without responding, shutting the door behind her.

As Kyle drove to the house he'd rented, that brief smile Jo flashed when he'd mentioned his attraction to a woman of faith brought a smile to his own face. And when she tightened her fingers around his, he knew. She wasn't as opposed to him as she let on.

Had he shaken the woman who believed she had all the answers? Time would tell . . . if his time in Hidden Veil didn't run out first.

Twelve

"But don't throw us all in a music-related dumpster."

Jo carried paper plates and cups to the kitchen and tossed them in the trash. Kyle's words and the memory of the way he'd looked at her during their walk echoed through her head. With the clasp of his hand in hers—warm, strong—she wanted to believe he was nothing like Taylor. At least two things set him apart. He had more manners than her ex and was a believer.

"Just because his touch sent tingles skittering up your arm, don't forget what he does for a living."

She dropped an empty plastic tray in the sink. While scrubbing it, Jo scolded herself for allowing her imagination to run wild. Soon, Kyle would leave Hidden Veil and that would be the end. Until then, he was a customer. Nothing more.

Gran entered the kitchen, beaming with undisguised pleasure.

Jo wiped her hands. "Kyle said you'd left."

"I'm back. How was your walk?"

"Which of my customers tattled?" Jo leaned a hip against the counter and crossed her arms. "Or was it Bethany?"

"No one tattled on you, and I never said I was leaving for the day. You haven't answered me."

"The walk was fine. I told him he's wasting his time hanging around the two of us."

Her grandmother's laughter sputtered. "It isn't me he's hanging around."

"Gran, I can't, and you know why."

Her grandmother's humor evaporated. "Do you think you're the only one who's ever suffered through infidelity?"

"Of course not, but—"

"Then stop the 'woe is me' prattle." Granny grasped Jo's arm. "Honey, Taylor ruined your marriage. Don't let him ruin the rest of your life. Don't give him that power over you. Show him you aren't afraid to take a chance on the right man."

"Kyle? He's another musician."

"I'm not claiming Kyle is the right man for you. I am saying you'll miss finding your Mr. Right if you don't screw up the courage I know you possess and stop using Hidden Veil as a hideout."

"It isn't as though I haven't dated since my marriage ended." She'd gone out a few times before moving back to her hometown. Was it her fault the opportunities here were few?

Jo thought of her friend, Reagan Hartwell, who never seemed to have trouble finding a date. "All right. I'll try to be more open to someone new."

Gran's hand tightened in a squeeze on Jo's arm. "That's all I'm asking."

Jo pointed a finger at her. "But not Kyle."

Her grandmother mumbled, "Hopeless." She disappeared into the main room of the coffee shop.

The day's mail remained where Jo had left it, the photo still inside the large, yellow envelope that glared at her. She snatched it from the pile and gripped it with both hands, ready to tear it and its contents in two. Haunted by memories of the photograph, she paused. That weekend spent with her grandparents had been ideal. Taylor was attentive, loving, and generous. He treated her like a queen.

Jo swallowed against the tightness in her throat. What if she had quit work and traveled with him? Would he have remained faithful? Or would she have thrown away a good job only to be thrown away herself in the end?

Gran might be wrong about Kyle, but she was right about Taylor. Jo couldn't let him continue to ruin her life. From now on, she'd give him no space in her mind or memory.

The rip of the paper was like a cooling ointment coating her charred confidence.

* * * *

What a morning! It seemed everyone in town—maybe the county—had stopped in for coffee.

Jo ran out of cheese Danishes within the first two hours, prompting gripes from Bobby and the boys. She'd gone through her books over the weekend and discovered profits were up during April, so she made a mental note to provide them with a free pastry tomorrow.

The one regular she hadn't seen today was Kyle, and for some irrational reason, she missed him. She hadn't heard from him since their walk last week. He hadn't even mentioned getting together to plan the church concert.

Had Kyle accepted her reason for not becoming involved with him? One minute, that thought pleased her. The next, she . . . well, she missed seeing him.

"Is rush hour over yet?" Bethany leaned against the counter, her laughter over the whispered question lifting Jo's mood.

"It's a good problem to have, isn't it?" Especially after paying for the secondhand dishwasher Stewart had installed first thing this morning.

"Keeps me employed."

Jo grinned, once more convinced she'd made the right decision to hire Bethany. A competent go-getter, she displayed a sunny disposition, and customers liked her. "We're getting low on paper cups and napkins. If you need me, I'll be in the kitchen, ordering supplies."

She was in the middle of placing the order when Bethany popped into the kitchen, bouncing on her toes. "There's a guy here to see you, Jo."

"Who?"

"Says his name is Taylor." She squealed the name, proving she'd recognized him.

Jo knew only one Taylor who would prompt that reaction. Her hands froze on the laptop keyboard, and she swallowed the lump in her throat. While they were married, he had mocked her hometown, calling it Podunkville. For him to make the trip here, whatever he wanted must be important.

Rather than wait for her to decide whether she would see him, he pushed past Bethany and strolled into the kitchen. *Typical.*

Taylor winked at Bethany, who nearly swooned. Confidence was the man's middle name. "Hey, Jo." His green gaze caught hers and held.

"Taylor." She forced herself to stand. He wasn't a tall man—not as tall as Kyle—but she didn't like the idea of him looking down on her. "What are you doing here?"

"When you didn't answer my texts, I got worried and figured I'd check to see if you were all right."

She was perfect until the day he first contacted her. "I'm fine."

"Good."

Jo looked beyond him to see they had an audience. "You should check on our customers, Bethany."

"Oh, sure." The woman backed away, her curious attention on Taylor. She jerked a thumb over her shoulder. "I'll be out there if you need me."

Once she was gone, Jo said nothing. Taylor had started this game, so she waited for him to make the first move.

He stepped closer, tucking a long lock of straight dark hair behind his ear. "Nice place."

"Thanks."

"You always were a fan of great coffee, so it doesn't surprise me to see you opened your own shop." He leaned back and peeked into the front room. "I saw the crowd earlier. This place was hopping."

"It does well enough."

"I'm sure it does better than 'well enough.'"

Maybe Gran was onto something when she thought Taylor wanted money. He'd never shied away from spending it. In the early days of their marriage, they relied on her demanding but well-paying job to make ends meet.

Tired of her nerves being stabbed by pins and needles, she crossed her arms. "Do you intend to tap dance all afternoon?"

He frowned. "What do you mean?"

"Spit it out, Taylor. Why are you here?"

"I wish we could be friends, Jo."

"I wish for things, too, but that isn't on the list." She shut her mouth before saying more that she'd regret. He always brought out the worst in her.

Taylor ran a hand through his hair, a nervous tic. Jo restrained the urge to smile at having gained the upper hand. Then her grandmother's admonition about forgiveness swept away the urge. When had she become so merciless? "I hear you're doing well."

The nervousness disappeared. "I'm getting the recognition I sought."

"Congratulations." That came out more sarcastic than she'd intended. "You came here for a reason?"

"Like I told you in my first text, I'd like you to attend my concert next Saturday night." He pulled out his phone and swiped his finger along the screen. "Maybe I have the wrong number for you."

"No, I got your message . . . and the others."

"You didn't respond."

"No."

He stared at her as though amazed she hadn't jumped at the invitation. Then he nodded. "I understand we had our problems."

Problems? "You cheated on me, Taylor. Multiple times."

"I know." His fingers parted his hair again, and he paced across the kitchen floor. "I got caught up in the whole fan thing. But I'm not that person anymore."

Oddly enough, he sounded sincere. Was this her moment of truth? Her time of decision? "Why did you send me that photograph?"

"I cleaned out an old box and found it. You were always close to your grandparents, so I thought you might like to have it."

His explanation sounded considerate, but she couldn't help looking for the catch.

"What do you say, Jo? Attend the concert. Afterward, we'll go somewhere and talk."

The texts. The photograph. This personal visit. Surely, he wasn't about to suggest a second chance with her. His words stoked a fire of panic inside her. "I can't."

"Why not?"

Why not? Conversation and laughter, the clattering of dishes, and the *whoosh*, *whir*, and *grind* of the espresso machine intruded on the silence while she scrambled for an excuse.

A handsome face filled her vision. Blond hair. Blue eyes. A smile to light a room and a voice that matched. "Sorry, but I have plans for that night." The words—the lie—gushed from her mouth like Old Faithful.

But why should it be a lie? Kyle owed her a date. He'd reminded her of it after their walk on Friday.

Taylor's brow crinkled. "You're dating someone?"

Oh, now he was insulting. "You find that hard to

believe?"

"No, of course not. Someone around here, I guess. So, who is he?"

Jo had no intention of telling Taylor about Kyle and less intention of mentioning that Kyle was a musician. She could imagine how her ex would relate that fact to himself. *Poor Jo. She's trying to replace me with another music maker.* "No one you know."

"Bring him along. You can introduce us."

She crossed her arms, and her toe tapped the vinyl floor. He was buttering her up for something. "Who do you think you are, my father?" As soon as the words left her mouth, she regretted them, but not enough to apologize.

"I only meant it would be nice to meet him."

"It's a new relationship, and I'm not starting it off by introducing him to my ex." She reined in her temper in an attempt at displaying that mercy she'd lacked so far. "Thanks, anyway. I'm sure it will go well for you." There. That wasn't so hard.

"Look—"

"Jo, I can use your help."

At Bethany's call, Jo crossed to the doorway and peered into the main room. "It's getting busy out there." She waited for him to take the hint.

After a slight pause, he nodded. "I'll talk to you soon."

Once he'd walked outside and out of her line of sight, Jo sank against the kitchen doorjamb. The encounter with Taylor had sapped her energy. Or maybe it was the guilt that weighed her down, the proof of Gran's claim.

"Are you okay?" Bethany laid a hand on her arm.

She drew in a breath and straightened. "Yes."

"Was that really Taylor Morris?"

Jo nodded, but had no desire to explain how she knew him or the reason for his visit. "Let's get those drink orders filled."

The long morning promised to be a longer afternoon. On the other hand, time would probably fly by as it always did when she dreaded doing something unpleasant.

Like asking Kyle to take her out on Saturday night.

Thirteen

Kyle placed his dinner plate in the dishwasher. He'd become more adept at cooking over the years, preferring simple recipes of less than four or five ingredients—two of which were salt and pepper—but he didn't enjoy it. On second thought, it was cooking for one that he didn't enjoy.

Wanting to give her space, he hadn't seen Jo since the two of them talked about her marriage.

He shut the dishwasher door. *Why not face it, Callahan? You wanted to give her time to miss you.*

Not that it would mean much. She would never leave this town, her business, or her grandmother, and he wouldn't ask that of her.

Whoa! He kept trotting miles ahead of himself.

Kyle grabbed his phone, ready to settle down on the couch in the den and watch a movie. The phone played a tune in his hand. He checked the screen for the name of the caller, but it only gave a number. He almost ignored the call, but something told him to answer. "Hello?"

"Hey, Kyle."

"Jo." Determined to control the ridiculous ping-pong balls banging off the insides of his gut, he leaned against the kitchen bar. He practiced patience while waiting for her to speak, to tell him the reason for the out-of-the-blue phone call.

"I haven't seen you at the coffee shop in a while."

She *was* missing him. Every muscle in his arm begged him to punch the air in victory. Part of him gloated over the success of his plan, another part distrusted that success. "I've been writing and . . . things. How did you get my number?"

"That isn't hard when you know where to look."

Ah, the good, old internet.

"How is your writing coming?"

"It's a work in progress." A lot of work and little progress. Good thing he wasn't a staff writer for a music publisher. He'd be jobless by now.

"Small steps can bring larger opportunities."

She was a philosopher now?

After another pause, Jo cleared her throat. "I should have brought this up during our talk last week. Actually, it never should have happened."

Kyle straightened. What shouldn't have happened? Their talk?

"I apologize if I seemed . . . abrupt in leaving the evening of the recital. On those occasions, it's as if I'm performing myself, which makes the night stressful and exhausting."

"You don't owe me an apology, Jo. I understand the stress of performing." Kyle had grown accustomed to playing before audiences over the years, but it had taken months of draining performances every weekend before he felt as though he wouldn't toss his last meal on the stage. While he still suffered from minor stage fright, he'd learned to channel that fear into his music, funneling the emotion into the notes. "Most people don't realize the difficulty of laying their creativity—a vulnerable part of themselves—out there to be judged. To them, it's entertainment, or in your case, proof of your ability to teach those kids to play the piano."

"I'd never thought of it that way, but you're right."

Kyle moved to the couch and sank onto the cushion, once again wondering the reason for Jo's call. Davey flopped onto the carpet in front of him. Kyle imagined more going on than her desire to apologize for something that had happened days earlier.

"I was so proud of Isaac." Her voice lost its tentative quality, and he heard a smile in the words.

"One day, that kid will look back, amazed by how far he's come."

"Thanks to your encouragement the night I hurt my ankle."

"I might have played a minor role in inspiring him, but I didn't teach him execution, Jo. That's on you."

"Thanks. I just wanted you to know that I'm not. . ." She'd stopped as if unsure how to end that statement.

"When you're not face to face with a reminder of your past, you're a happy and gracious woman."

Seconds ticked by without a response from her. Then she said, "I'm sure you're wondering why I called."

"It crossed my mind." Several times.

"Are you busy Saturday?"

"Saturday? What did you have in mind?"

"I thought I'd collect on that . . . get together."

Kyle jumped up and caught himself before stomping on Davey's tail. *For Pete's sake, play it cool. Remember, she's only collecting on what's hers. It's only a business deal.* For her, anyway. "Okay."

His mind raced to come up with ideas for things to do. He had assumed Jo would never take advantage of the date with him, so he had planned nothing in advance. Big mistake. He should have already done his research, already had a plan. When nothing special came to mind—he wanted the day to be special—he gave up. "I'm not as familiar with the area as you. What would you like to do?"

"There's the gift certificate for dinner."

He'd forgotten the piece of paper that sat on the dresser in the bedroom. "I'd hoped for something more, something different."

Again, that pause. "Let me think about it, and I'll call you tomorrow night. Is that all right?"

"Or I can call you." *Back down, boy.* So much for playing it cool.

"I have a piano lesson. I'll call you afterward."

"Sounds good."

"Good night, Kyle."

"Hey, Jo."

"Yes?"

"We'll have a good time."

Once the call ended, he flopped on the couch, hands clasped behind his head and ankles crossed. Saturday couldn't come fast enough. Where would he take her?

Dinner at a restaurant was nothing extraordinary. A movie, too? No theater in Hidden Veil, and while he preferred action or fantasy films, he wasn't sure what she liked.

A romance flick during their "get together" might give her the impression he determined to rush her into something.

A concert was out. Too much of a reminder of the profession he shared with her ex.

Wherever they went, his prime job was to convince her that success as a musician wouldn't turn him into some Nashville—or Hidden Veil—Casanova like Taylor.

By ten o'clock, he'd decided his lack of knowledge about the area wasn't the only thing getting in his way. He didn't know Jo well enough, either. What did she like to do? Where did her interests lie—other than in coffee, playing the piano, and living in a small town?

He had twenty-four hours to plan a date so amazing she couldn't say no to a second one.

With the lack of his creativity, it seemed an impossible task.

✳   ✳   ✳   ✳

Snip. Snip.

Jo sat in the salon chair at Shear Delight with her eyes closed, while Naomi Griffith took the scissors to her straight, fine hair. Every six weeks, like clockwork, she sat in this chair and listened to the *snip, snip* of the scissors.

The stylist took ownership of her clients' hair and had tried for months to talk Jo into a bob. Today, Jo gave in, agreeing to let the woman style her hair into a bob that sat on her shoulders.

Watching in the mirror, her eyes narrowed as Naomi pulled up a few strands at the top of Jo's head, studied them, then frowned. "What's wrong?"

"Sweetheart, you have gray hairs."

Gray hair? Already? "Let me see." She bent forward, grabbed the mirror from the counter, and positioned it to see the top of her head.

"Now don't go frettin' about it. It's only about five strands. No one will even notice them."

"You did."

Naomi snatched the mirror from Jo's hand. "Think of it as a rite of passage."

"Passage to where? Old age?"

Naomi rolled her eyes. "I shouldn't have said anything. Now, you'll go from here to a medical store for a walker."

She wasn't that paranoid about her age, was she? But maybe she should color her hair.

"I heard you're balking at going out with that fella from the auction."

Who started that rumor? Gran? Bethany? Was there no confidentiality in this town? "I'm not balking."

Okay, she had before last night.

Naomi set her scissors on the counter and turned the chair until Jo faced her. "If you want my opinion—"

Not really.

"—you'd be a fool to not give the guy a chance. Why, I hear he's nice, talented, and stuck on you."

Naomi operated out of her home with one customer at a time, so no one else saw the way Jo's eyes glistened. So what if people thought her lack of enthusiasm over a date with Kyle—a nice, talented, and stuck-on-her musician—was silly?

They hadn't lived through the betrayal and humiliation she had faced. The media never dragged them through the muck that they called reporting.

What if Kyle's career took off as Taylor's had done? What about the fawning young women who threw themselves at him while she remained at home, running her coffee shop?

That question triggered another problem. Should things progress the way her grandmother hoped, Kyle could insist they lived somewhere other than Hidden Veil, somewhere like Nashville. Jo couldn't leave again. Gran may not believe it now, but she would need Jo one day.

Naomi picked up the scissors and began clipping the layers. "When you two finally go out, where do you think he'll take you?"

The question shook Jo from her brooding. "I don't know."

She would find out when she called Kyle tonight. If it were up to her, they would use that certificate at Red Dog Diner or Ricardo's, and then he would take her home. From their conversation last night, it was clear Kyle expected more.

In all honesty, she hadn't given the issue much thought beyond the guilt that plagued her. Not liking the idea of using Kyle or anyone else to avoid Taylor, she had picked up the phone three times this morning, prepared to call him and cancel. Each time, she thought of her grandmother's disappointment and changed her mind.

"That man has it bad for you," Naomi sighed, "so I'm guessing it'll be somewhere romantic."

Jo stared at the woman in the mirror. "Where did you hear that news, and how do you know so much about Kyle and me?"

"I was at the fundraiser auction. I saw how he looked at you when he found out you were the winner." Naomi paused, her scissors in the air, and caught Jo's gaze in the mirror. "Besides, you know how people talk. I listen."

True. Naomi rarely shared anyone else's business with Jo, but she had a way of getting people to talk and a good ear for listening.

As much as Jo loved her hometown and its citizens, she found it disconcerting to realize the extent to which people other than Gran knew her business. "You sound like a psychologist."

Naomi laughed. "You didn't know stylists were head doctors? All we lack is a degree and them fancy letters behind our names."

"I'm glad you don't charge me like one." Not that the woman's words had changed Jo's mind about becoming involved with Kyle.

She stared in the mirror at the spot where Naomi found the gray hairs. Nope. No color for her. She'd gone far enough by agreeing to the new style, something she already worried Kyle might misinterpret as a wish to appeal to him. The gray would help to turn off his interest.

Jo expected that to bring her satisfaction, but walked out of the salon without it.

Fourteen

Jo eyed the phone she'd held in a tight grip for the past several minutes. She paced around her bed, to the closet, over to the window, and back to the bed with its wedding ring-patterned quilt . . . of all things.

Why had she promised to call Kyle tonight? Better yet, why had she thought of him as an excuse in the first place? She didn't owe Taylor an explanation for refusing his invitation. A curt decline would have saved her angst over going out with Kyle, and the guilt of knowing she had lied to both men.

Kyle wanted a fun place to go on Saturday. If it were up to her, they would eat at the Red Dog Diner—the Saturday special of meatloaf—and he would take her home afterwards. It would validate her excuse to Taylor and stop Gran's three hundred dollars from going to waste. But that wasn't fair to Kyle.

Her piano student left thirty minutes ago, leaving her no

reason to put off the call. She punched Kyle's name on her contact list, a name and phone number she would delete after he returned to Nashville.

The phone rang and rang. Her shoulders relaxed, and she prepared to end the call.

"Hey, Jo."

"Kyle?" Well, who else would it be? She glanced at the ceiling and grimaced. "Did I catch you at a bad time?"

"No, I'd forgotten my phone in the kitchen and didn't hear it at first." After a rustling on his end, he said, "How did the lesson go?"

Thinking of it, she chuckled. "A tone-deaf alien replaced Charlotte after the recital. She performed well that night, but tonight was a different story. She either missed notes completely or played the wrong ones."

"We all have off nights. I remember one show the band did a couple of years ago."

As he talked, Jo settled into the floral chair in the corner of her room, imagining the frustration and confusion on the faces of the members of BC's Posse when Kyle forgot the lyrics to one of their songs—his song. When he talked of covering the blunder by breaking out into the chorus of "Mary Had a Little Lamb," then followed it up with the words to "How Much is That Doggy in the Window," she laughed harder than she had in weeks.

"The crowd loved it, especially the second song. Each time I sang a line, they followed it up with '*Arf, arf.*'" Jo swiped at a tear under her eye when he howled the animal sound rather than saying the words. "The guys didn't talk to me for two days."

She fought to control her laughter. "That was hardly fair.

I'm sure they've forgotten lyrics occasionally." She couldn't imagine having to memorize the words to so many songs. Although, memorizing notes probably wasn't much different.

"Brian had big dreams and worried that I'd ruined the band's reputation. They finally came around. Now we laugh about it." He paused. "We did."

Jo sensed a story there, too, but didn't press after his voice had gone soft. Was that the underlying cause for him being in Hidden Veil? Perhaps the band members had a falling out.

"Did you find a new dishwasher?"

His question brought her back to the conversation. "Yes, and if I babied it any more, I'd burp it. At least this one doesn't spit up all over my floor." His deep chuckle did weird things to her insides—unexpected and not unpleasant, while being unsettling and unwelcome at the same time.

"I'm glad the coffee shop does well for you, Jo."

"Me, too. Business has steadily picked up each month, which will allow me to remain in the place I never want to leave again." There. Now he knew in no uncertain terms her intention to make her home in Hidden Veil for as long as she lived.

Neither of them said anything for several moments, so she broke the silence by addressing the reason for the call. "Have you chosen a place for our—" She wished to avoid the word "date" as much as she wished to avoid the event itself. "For Saturday?"

"I have."

Jo traced a yellow flower on the material covering the chair as she waited for him to elaborate. When he didn't, she asked, "And?"

"And I'll surprise you."

Being a planner, someone who liked to know the details, his insistence on keeping them a secret left her scrambling for possibilities. "How will I know what to wear?"

"Wear casual clothes and comfortable shoes. I'll pick you up at ten on Saturday morning."

So early? Was this to be an all-day event? "Why don't I meet you there?"

"Trying to wheedle the plan out of me? No way. Besides, my mother thinks she raised a gentleman who picks a lady up at her door. I'm not about to disappoint her." The smile in his voice came across loud and clear when he said, "Relax, Jo. I have it on good authority that you'll love this place."

What authority? She glanced toward the closed bedroom door and the room across the hallway. As if she couldn't guess the identity of his advisor. "All right. I'll trust you."

"That's what I want to hear."

With the softness of his voice, Jo suspected he didn't mean he wanted her trust only in this situation. "One more thing."

"What?"

"We should agree that this isn't a date, so let's not refer to it that way."

She waited for him to respond. "So you want to call it a non-date?"

"That sounds appropriate. We're getting together for a non-date of fun."

"Whatever you say, Ms. Ledbetter." After a bout of rustling on Kyle's end, she heard, "Hey, give it back."

Obviously, he wasn't talking to her. "What's going on?"

He sighed. "I laid a pen on the table next to the sofa. Davey took it."

"Davey?"

"My dog."

"Oh, that's right. I remember you mentioning your dog."

"My sister bought a bullmastiff puppy a couple of years ago and named him Goliath. A few days later, she talked me into getting a brother from the litter, so—"

Ah. She couldn't stop the spurt of humor. "So, you named him Davey? Like David and Goliath?"

"What else?"

The grandfather clock in the foyer downstairs chimed nine o'clock. The quick phone call she had intended had lasted almost forty-five minutes. "I didn't realize we'd talked for so long. I'll let you chase down your pen."

"Yeah, I'm already picturing the slobber on it."

"I've always had a soft spot for animals, so I'm sure Davey and I would get along well." She grinned. "Tell him I said goodnight."

"Hmm. I don't know if I should pass on your message to him, Jo." Kyle sounded forlorn.

"Why not?"

"Because he'll want to meet the kind lady who wished him goodnight. Then he'll start whining. Have you ever seen a sad bullmastiff? It's pathetic. I'll be paying you a midnight visit just to shut him up."

Her lips twitched. "Did anyone ever tell you that you're ridiculous?"

"My mother. And my sisters. And—"

Jo laughed. "Okay, I get it. Everyone thinks you're ridiculous."

"Hey," his voice changed to a low rumble that sped up her heartbeat, "I'm looking forward to Saturday."

"Me, too."

The truth of those two words struck her like a physical blow. She did look forward to their time together on Saturday. And that was sure to cause her a few sleepless nights between now and then.

Before she ended the call, she should tell him the truth behind the timing of the . . . non-date. She owed Taylor nothing, but owed Kyle her honesty. Despite enjoying tonight's lengthy call, she couldn't let him think she expected anything more than his fulfillment of an obligation.

"Good night, Jo."

"Kyle—"

Silence after the chirp proved he'd already disconnected.

*   *   *   *

"I don't know whether to be content with the opportunity or call and cancel." Kyle took his gaze off the bathroom mirror to glance down at Davey. "Any ideas?"

The dog cocked his head and looked at him as if confused. Well, why not? So was Kyle.

After his online research on Tuesday morning, he had dialed Vera's number. She'd confirmed his plan, saying her granddaughter would love it. It took minutes to work out the details, now it was showtime.

He still didn't understand why Jo had chosen today as the perfect day for him to fulfill his auction responsibility. Had Vera pushed her? If so, it didn't boost his ego, but he wasn't so insecure as to let it deter him from enjoying their time together—their *non-date*. For the past three days, he'd reminded himself that he'd be okay if their relationship went no further than friendship. What a crock.

Kyle shook his head. He had agreed to call it a non-date for two reasons. One, to make Vera happy and provide her some satisfaction for the money she'd insisted on bidding. And, two, even a non-date gave him a chance to change Jo's mind about him and, hopefully, about professional musicians as a whole. His one non-negotiable was in picking her up at her house. No meeting somewhere, as she'd suggested.

He ran a hand over the smooth skin of his freshly shaved face. After inspecting the green polo shirt, jeans, and combed hair, he looked down at Davey. "Well, what do you think?"

The dog cocked his head and stared at him as though he'd spoken a foreign language.

Kyle grabbed his keys, told Davey to be a good dog, and left the house.

A few minutes later, he crossed Main Street, turned onto First Avenue, and then onto Vera's street. He parked at the curb in front of her house. Her two-decade-old Ford sat in the drive, in front of Jo's blue Mini Cooper.

Sixty seconds later, he stood at the front door, facing his date—his non-date, who smiled as though she greeted an old friend. Her eyes hadn't gotten the memo about the smile, though, and he suspected the cheerful expression hid nervousness—hopefully, not regret. His desire to make the day special increased times ten.

"Good morning, Jo."

"Hi." She stood aside. "Come on in. I'm almost ready."

What more could she do to prepare? "You look great to me. New haircut?"

She ran a hand over her hair. "It was time for a trim."

His gaze dropped to those hip-hugging jeans and a form-fitting, cranberry t-shirt. She might be in her early thirties, but she looked a decade younger. The sight showered him under a warm waterfall of longing. Make that a steam bath.

At catching his perusal, her brows drew together, and she looked down at her clothing. That tentative expression knocked his socks off with its fragile uncertainty. "You said casual."

"It's perfect." Aw, man, his goose was cooked and on the table.

Jo showed him into the front room, then excused herself and disappeared up the stairs. A heartbeat later, Vera appeared and peeked toward the stairs in the foyer. She turned back to him. "I can't wait to see how your plans turn out."

"Thanks for confirming my idea. I hope she enjoys our time together. I'll try to put my best foot forward."

"It's admirable for you to think of Jo's enjoyment, but be yourself, honey. I wouldn't want you to do anything else to win over Jo E." The wrinkles deepened around her mouth and softened her opinion. "My granddaughter is no longer impressed by what a person does or says or where he takes her. She's learned the hard way to be impressed by who that person is in here." She tapped her chest. "Show her the real Kyle Callahan and let her decide if she's interested."

He laughed. "Yeah, well, I don't think it's wise to introduce the real me on a first date." Non-date.

Kyle pictured the dirty clothes he'd left on the bathroom floor, pondered the fact he hadn't called his parents in about three weeks, saw himself picking the deplorable cooked tomatoes out of his spaghetti sauce. In seconds, an entire list of imperfections presented themselves to him, culminating in his turmoil over his career future. "I'm not perfect and—"

"You hope she'll see perfection."

He hadn't thought of it that way, but with his reaction to her a few minutes ago, maybe he did. "Please don't suggest I lay all my faults before her today." Not that it would matter once he returned to Nashville. In their conversation the other night, Jo spelled out her intention to never leave Hidden Veil.

"Oh goodness, no. Neither of us is that crazy. I'm saying to show her your heart."

It shouldn't be too hard to show Jo his heart. He practically wore it on his sleeve. "Vera, I don't think you should get your hopes up. This isn't—"

Footsteps on the stairs stopped his warning, and a moment later Jo stood at the doorway to the room. "I'm ready if you are."

"Great."

Once they were in the car and headed out of town, she shifted in her seat. "Are you going to tell me where we're going?"

"Nope." Kyle glanced at her. She'd turned to the window, fidgeting on the seat again. "Are you having second thoughts about our non-date?"

She gazed at him, her eyes like quarters, before real and pleasurable laughter rang out. "That does sound silly, doesn't it? We're on our non-date date."

He grinned, enjoying her light-hearted mood, and for several minutes, their conversation revolved around small talk and safe subjects.

"Have all the band members taken a two-month

vacation?"

Before they even reached their destination, Jo had broached the one topic he hoped to avoid. She had unwittingly broken through his safety net, and Kyle felt himself falling into undesirable territory.

Kyle hedged. "Just me."

"So you're missing performances while you're here?

Clearly, she didn't aim to let the topic go. He may as well lay it out there. "BC's Posse no longer exists, Jo."

"But . . . I'm sorry."

He shrugged. "Bands come and go." *So did friendships, apparently.*

"What will you do next?"

Kyle's fingers tightened around the steering wheel as he focused on the road. Was he ready to lay the whole sad tale on the table?

She asked about the band. Okay, he could tell her what happened. It wasn't his fault, but to talk about his future would deny any hope of her seeing perfection in him.

Fifteen

Her question about the band elicited a strong, negative response from Kyle. Why? It seemed simple to Jo. No more performances with BC's Posse, but years until retirement. Surely, he had a plan to move forward.

With the crease of his brow, his mouth formed a hard, straight line. The hand on the steering wheel tightened like a bull rider holding onto the bull rope.

When he didn't answer her, she said, "Have I pried into something you don't want to discuss?"

He released a slow breath, and his knuckles returned to a somewhat normal flesh color. "You asked a logical question."

But?

"Confession?"

Jo stilled. Hers or his? She wasn't ready yet to ruin their day with hers. "You have something to confess?"

She waited as he seemed to gather his thoughts, maybe debating with himself whether to tell her whatever upset him about her query.

"My future is uncertain."

She frowned. As confessions went, it wasn't much of one, not like hers. On second thought, was he considering leaving the music business? A flicker attempted to spark into a flame inside her, never a raging fire, but enough to feel the warmth. "You're not interested in being part of a band anymore?"

"I haven't decided yet."

Jo tossed a wet blanket over that spark. Hadn't he already admitted his indecision? Why should she get excited about the possibility of him leaving the music business?

She'd said she was looking for someone settled . . . content. Obviously, Kyle hadn't found that contentment yet.

"Brian—BC—received a solo contract. He'll be recording an album soon. With his defection, the rest of us discussed forming a new band. In the end, Scotty moved back to his hometown in Arkansas to help his aging parents, and Pete is trying for his own solo career. Like me, our drummer, Eric, is keeping his options open."

"What does that mean? What options?"

"For now, I'll concentrate on songwriting. It's why I came to Hidden Veil—new surroundings, new inspiration. At least, that's what I'd hoped to find."

"Things haven't turned out as you'd expected?" She kept pressing, but for a reason she chose not to examine, his answers were important to her.

"Not yet. Even before I arrived, I faced writer's block." Kyle stopped at a light in Asheboro and glanced her way before turning his attention back to the road. "Full disclosure?"

There was more? "Sure."

"I have a bigger problem." The light changed, and he eased down on the gas pedal, driving a couple of blocks before he continued. "Have you ever had to choose between something you wanted and something God nudged you towards?" He frowned. "Nudged isn't the right word. Shoved is better—right off a cliff."

Several instances came to mind, starting in her youth and working up to Gran's admonishment to forgive Taylor. That last wasn't solely her grandmother's wish. In her spirit, Jo recognized that, for years, God had also urged—shoved—her to show her ex-husband grace and forgive him for his behavior during their marriage. She'd refused to even discuss it with God. "What is He shoving you toward?"

"Contemporary Christian music."

"Oh." Jo fought against the smile that struggled to break free. Hadn't she told him his song spoke to her of loving God?

His glance darted in her direction and back to the road. "You're thinking of our discussion during our walk."

"It occurred to me." She also remembered his curt response to her suggestion that he consider changing his musical direction.

"I can't do it, Jo."

"Because?"

"I've spent years building my career in country music. If I give it up now, I will have failed."

"Changing your career path isn't an admission of failure, Kyle. Did I fail when I left a management job in the city to open a coffeehouse in a small town?"

He shook his head. "Not at all. But you have the support of your grandmother and lifelong friends."

"You don't have the support of your family?"

He paused, his index finger tapping the wheel. "I do."

When he didn't finish, she said, "Opening Jo E's Java was the best decision I'd made in years, but it wasn't something I'd planned to do all along. It hasn't been easy. My bank account proves that."

"And you've proved my point. My folks weren't enthusiastic about my career choice. My dad owns a successful business. It was hard for him to accept that I would probably struggle. Besides, it feels strange to take money for writing or performing Christian songs."

"Why?"

He shrugged. "It should be an offering."

"Are you saying Christian music artists should never earn a living for their creativity and the work they put into it? What about pastors and missionaries and music ministers? They're not entitled to be paid for their labor because they tell others about Jesus? If God is calling you to create music for Him, Kyle, don't you think He'll provide for you?"

"I guess that is a bogus argument that keeps me from having to make a decision. Truthfully, I don't want to start over trying to make a name for myself."

"I wonder if the better question to ask is if it's really *your* name you should worry about." Jo settled back in the seat. Who was she to preach to someone else?

When he said nothing, Jo peered through the windshield. A familiar turnoff approached and her mind eagerly traced its destination. She leaned forward in the seat. "Are we almost there?" Ugh! She sounded like a child on a road trip.

His rich chuckle vibrated through her. "We're almost there."

When he took that turn, she suppressed the urge to bounce on the seat. "We're going to the zoo, aren't we?"

"Yep." The way he drew out that one word said he was pleased and proud of himself for surprising her with the destination.

In all honesty, she was pleased with him, too. She winced and corrected herself. She was pleased with his choice.

* * * *

Jo nearly pinged around the inside of his vehicle. Her excitement told Kyle he'd picked the right place for their date. Their non-date.

With a sigh, she eased back in the seat. She looked relaxed for what might have been the first time since he'd picked her up. "Did Gran tell you how much I've always loved coming to the zoo?"

"Vera confirmed it as a good choice. What is it you love most about it?"

"Everything. The animals, of course—the more exotic, the better. The natural habitat setup. The wonder on the faces of little kids."

"Like the look on your face right now?"

Her lips twitched. "Maybe."

A few minutes later, Kyle parked his SUV in the lot nearest the Africa section and opened the passenger door for Jo. "We can take the shuttle to the North America side or start with Africa. Which sounds good to you?"

"Africa. I want to see the lions and giraffes and hippos and—"

"Bears. Oh, my!" He laughed. "Okay, I've got it. You demand to see all the animals at the zoo."

She cut her eyes toward him and flaunted a cocky grin. "Of course."

They strolled the paved trail side-by-side, following the wooded path to the Watani Grasslands Reserve. All the while, he couldn't get her comment off his mind. *"I wonder if the better question to ask is if it's really your name you should worry about."* She'd dropped that question on him like a piano. He'd fought to respond, but nothing brilliant or even reasonable occurred to him—then or now.

"Look over there!" Jo grabbed his arm, bouncing up and down on her toes as she ensured he paid attention to the spot she pointed to in the grassy area surrounded by trees. "Elephants."

Kyle had never seen someone so excited about a trip to the zoo. He leaned forward and pretended to search the area. "Where?"

Her eyes grew large with disbelief. "There." She jabbed a finger toward the three elephants gathered near the waterhole. "How could you miss—"

His laughter gave him away.

"Oh, you." She slapped his arm with one hand while still clinging to his biceps with the other, a hold that made him want to tighten the muscle until it bulged like Superman's. "I was ready to set up an appointment for you with an optometrist."

There was nothing wrong with his eyes, but if she kept hanging on, he might need his blood pressure monitored. A brief nod of encouragement from her and he'd sweep her off her feet and into his arms, claiming her for his own. After all, that was what he *meant* to convey with the song, "I Claim You." Right?

She must have realized she'd grasped his arm, because she let go. Her cheeks glowed with a rosy color that had nothing to do with the sun shining on them. So much for his romantic fantasy.

They paused at the overlook, watching the elephants, then moved on to the rhinos and antelopes. A few minutes later, they wandered back onto the main path that led to the giraffe deck.

As fascinating as the animals were, Kyle had a hard time focusing on them. He preferred watching the joy on Jo's face, especially while she crouched at the side of a preschooler and called his attention to a lion. The boy gave a mighty roar that had them all laughing. Jo Ella Ledbetter's warmth will make her a fantastic mother.

Kyle slammed the brakes on that thought. She had been honest in giving him her opinion of them as a couple. "Are you having fun?" Stupid question. Anyone watching could see her joy. And he'd done little more than watch her.

She smiled up at him. "Absolutely. This was a good idea. Fresh air. Exercise. Animals. Good company."

She considered him good company? That was a start.

After seeing as many animals as possible—some shaded themselves under trees and out of sight—they reached the end of the Africa section and entered a small plaza. They'd walked for over three hours and he'd eaten a light, early breakfast. "It's going on two. Hungry, Jo?"

"Starved."

They ordered lunch at the café and carried their food to one of the outdoor tables. Kyle couldn't wait to dig into the hamburger that smelled like a steak meal with all the fixings.

Jo unwrapped her paper napkin and plastic utensils. "Would you mind praying over the meal?"

He learned at a young age to say grace before meals, whether he was at home or in a restaurant. The guys in the band used to tease him about it, calling him Moses. After a while, they got used to his "religious quirk" and remained quiet while he said a silent blessing. Under those circumstances, it often involved a simple thank you. Although not one to preach to them, he had hoped his faith would rub off on his friends. Not yet.

Kyle and Jo barely touched fingers, but the connection seemed right . . . natural. Not like earlier, when his pulse raced with the impulse to kiss her. "Father, we thank You for allowing us to share this time, for the opportunity to witness the amazing animals You created and the beautiful world in which we live. Thank You for the food You've provided for our nourishment. Amen."

"Amen."

He enfolded her hand in his and squeezed, because . . . well, it was there, so why not?

"Hey, thanks for listening on the drive here. Other than my sister, you're the only one I've told about the battle I'm having with—" With the God he'd just prayed to?

"I wonder if the better question to ask is if it's really your name you should worry about."

"I know how hard it is to change our plans to accept something different, and you can trust that I won't mention it to anyone else." Her brow crinkled, and she pushed aside her hamburger. "I also have a confession to make, Kyle."

He tried to lighten the sudden plummet in her mood.

"Please don't tell me you're on the FBI's most wanted list." He peered around. "I don't see any cops, but let's try to get out of here alive."

A swift, slight grin slid across Jo's face. "Your life is safe with me." The grin fell into a frown. "Your friendship might be a different matter."

His friendship? Just what was she about to confess?

"I had an ulterior motive for requesting this date for today. Non-date, I mean." She tried to smile, but it looked plastic.

Kyle froze with the hamburger halfway to his mouth, and his own mood plummeted with her words. "Go on."

"Taylor came to see me on Monday morning."

"He doesn't give up, does he?" The words burst from his mouth, and Kyle regretted the way jealousy covered him like slime. "What does he want?"

"To be friends. At least, that's what he said."

"You didn't believe him?"

She shook her head. "Not for a moment. Something else is going on." Bitterness coated her statement.

"So, what's your confession?"

"He wanted me to attend his concert in Greensboro. Tonight. I told him I couldn't because I was going out with someone."

Kyle set down his burger. She had called him Monday night . . . after she'd talked to Taylor Morris. After she'd lied to her ex-husband. "I became your excuse for getting out of seeing him again."

"Yes, and I'm sorry." She hung her head. "If it helps, I've had a wonderful time today."

It helped. But it didn't ease his disappointment in finding

out she'd used him.

He picked up his hamburger, his appetite gone. "Let's finish our lunch and get back on the trail. We still have the North America section to see."

*   *   *   *

She had admitted her lie, cleared her conscience, and should feel better. Why didn't she?

Jo ate half her lunch, dumped the rest in a nearby trash can, and joined Kyle on a hurried trek through the rest of the zoo, unlike the ambling pace of earlier. They spoke, but it wasn't the same. Bits of laughter and no light-hearted banter.

She should have waited until he took her home to tell him what prompted her to call Monday night. Now, the day was ruined for them both. She sighed. Probably for the best. His Nashville ambition and her fear of musicians made them incompatible.

Once they had seen the bison, alligators, and polar bears, among the other animals common to North America, they rode the shuttle back to the Africa parking lot. The trudge across the pavement felt like a trek across a desert.

Once they reached his SUV, Kyle opened the passenger door for her, then walked to the driver's side, climbed behind the wheel and . . . did nothing. He sat, staring at the dashboard. Jo twisted in the seat, but before she could ask if something was wrong, he said, "I blew it, didn't I?"

She swallowed and shook her head. "Not you. Me."

"I worked to make this day extra special for you, Jo . . . for both of us. I wanted you to see me as settled—content." He huffed. "I blew it on both counts. First, I told you my future was up in the air and revealed my ego. Then I pouted, because you preferred to spend the day with me, not Taylor. That's pretty twisted."

"Kyle—"

"I guess I'm not that content guy, after all."

A laugh burst from Jo, surprising her as much as it appeared to surprise Kyle. For the first time since he'd gotten in the car, he looked at her—gawked, actually. She couldn't blame him after all her bluster about non-dates and egotistical musicians.

She tried to control the laughter, but the effort was hopeless. The worst part? She wasn't sure what she found funny. "I'm sorry. We're quite a pair, aren't we?"

His brow furrowed. "I'm not following."

Jo compressed her lips and breathed in and out until she brought the misplaced humor to a halt with a soft hiccup. "We're both upset that we're not perfect."

One side of his mouth lifted, as though he experimented with a smile, before his lips spread into a full-fledged grin. "Speak for yourself, Ms. Ledbetter. I'll have you know I received a 'Perfect Behavior' ribbon in kindergarten."

"Ooh, my mistake." She held out her hand. "Friends?"

Kyle gazed at her hand, and his warm fingers clasped hers. "Be careful what you ask for, Jo."

He leaned over and touched his lips to hers, a feather-light kiss that sent a tingle all the way to her toes. Somehow, that trace of contact—as startling as it was—set off an inferno of confusion and euphoria inside her. The kiss lasted less time than it took her to wrap her mind around it, before he moved those smooth, warm lips to the back of her hand.

The next thing Jo knew, he was pulling out of the parking lot. She released a slow and soothing breath, an effort to get her pulse back under control.

Out of the corner of her eye, she studied Kyle's relaxed posture. The corner of his mouth rose slightly in a smirk. Finding her unprepared for that kiss delighted him. Why didn't his smug attitude upset her?

Lord, help me. I can't fall for Kyle.

Sixteen

Kyle blocked out the noise surrounding him—coffee shop customers, the old men at the table with him. He couldn't get that kiss on Saturday out of his mind. He hadn't planned it, especially after Jo admitted she only called him to escape Morris' invitation.

Although it upset him at first, the more he thought about it, the more optimism filled him. She could have called anyone, made plans with other friends or Vera. Instead, she'd called him. That meant something, didn't it?

Then that kiss . . .

It had taken all he had in him to keep it brief and chaste. He hadn't wanted to scare her or give her one more reason to avoid him. After pulling away, he'd spotted that wide-eyed wonder on her face, a look that said he'd touched more than her lips. He'd touched her heart. And she didn't mind one bit.

She hadn't been at the coffee shop when he arrived this

morning. A good thing, really. He'd struggled the rest of the weekend, trying to decide if he'd made a mistake, if he had led them both down a path neither should go. They expected different things and lived different lifestyles.

But the sweetness of that kiss . . .

His practical side said he couldn't base a lifetime with someone on a kiss. The dreamer in him called it a start.

The drive from the zoo had threatened to send him over the brink with the desire to hold her hand all the way back to Hidden Veil, to—

"Are you gonna move, Smiley, or what?"

At Bobby's question, Kyle snapped out of his reminiscing. He glanced around the table. Had he smiled like an idiot in front of these guys while his mind wandered?

"Sure." He slid the first checker piece his finger landed on.

Bobby snorted. "That's the best you can do?" He jumped Kyle's piece to the chortles of the other men, then pushed his chair back and hefted himself up from the coffee shop table. "Let's take us a walk."

"Why?"

"Because only one thing puts that look on a man's face, and I wanna hear about it."

"I don't have a—" With the set of the man's chin and the one gray eyebrow arching upward, it would do no good to argue the point.

Kyle followed Bobby out the front door. Fortunately, the others remained in the coffee shop, not tagging along behind them like some little old ladies sopping up juicy gossip.

"How'd your date go?"

The news had spread? He might have known. "It wasn't a date."

"Then what was it? And if you tell me an obligation, I'm gonna box your ears for lying."

Kyle breathed a chuckle. "To be honest, Bobby, I'm not sure what to call it. We had a good time, but I'll leave soon, and Jo's life is in this town." He gave the simplest answer, not mentioning her objections to his career. "Nothing can come of it."

They lumbered past a store selling homemade soaps and candles. The fragrances of various herbs and spices drifted out the open door and mixed with the warm spring air to tickle Kyle's nose.

"That didn't stop you from grinning over a memory."

Bobby could read minds now?

The old man pointed to the hardware store across the street. "Did I ever mention I own that place?"

"No." Kyle hadn't really given Bobby's working life much consideration. "I thought you were retired."

"I am. Several years ago, my son bought into the store. He runs the business now. I get updates and a check once a month. When I'm gone, he'll get full ownership."

"I thought your son was the music minister at your church."

"I can have more than one, you know."

True. But what did Kyle have in common with the hardware business?

"I'll get to my point. Don't worry." The man *was* a mind reader. "Never play poker, son. You don't have the face for it."

Kyle laughed. "Something I discovered in college."

At the intersection, they crossed over Main to continue their walk on the other side. "How do you like our town?"

"I like it."

"You gotta admit, there's something about this place that burrows under your skin."

Kyle let Bobby talk uninterrupted. The man seemed to have a lot to get off his mind today.

"I wasn't born here, you know. Once I got out of the army, I had my heart set on opening a hardware store in a suburb of a big city. I even had the location picked out. Had my life all planned. Then one day, fifty-six years ago, my car broke down on the highway outside of Hidden Veil. A beat up, old Plymouth pulled to the side of the road behind me and out stepped a red-headed angel with a mess of freckles across her nose." Bobby chuckled. "She was one feisty woman, insisting she could fix my car and send me on my way."

"Did she?"

"Oh, she fixed the car, all right. Only I didn't leave."

"You stayed and married her."

Bobby stopped and scowled. "Don't go getting ahead of me."

Kyle couldn't help himself. "I've been inside the hardware store. Your son has red hair."

"Takes after his momma." Bobby walked with hands clasped behind his back, his gaze on the sidewalk as they passed the pharmacy and the soon-to-be-open soda fountain. "The point is, I found a reason to stay in town for a few days. Those days turned into a few weeks, and I was torn. I fretted between getting back home to open that store and leaving someone who meant so much to me."

Rather than Bobby and his red-headed angel, Kyle saw himself and Jo in his mind—Bobby's point, of course.

"I asked her to come with me. Do you know the blamed woman said no? She couldn't see herself ever living nowhere other than the town where she grew up." Bobby cocked his head and glared at Kyle with a look of "Get my drift, boy?"

He got it. "So you stayed, opened your hardware store here, and lived happily ever after."

He nodded. "Until she passed seven years ago."

"I'm sorry."

Bobby waved off the condolence. "The thing I'm trying to tell you is that God knows better than us what kind of life we should lead and where we should do it. Opening a hardware store in this little town—even smaller back then— was an act of faith. Frankly, I resented it for a while." He nudged Kyle's shoulder with his own. "You know what? Two years later, that place I had my eye on blew up in a gas explosion. Fortunately, no one got hurt, but that news woke me up. It helped me see God was at least ten steps ahead of me."

Kyle glanced at Bobby. "Why are you sure this is the place for me?"

"I never said that. I said we need to operate from faith."

"Jo has a business here and won't leave her grandmother. My career,"—whatever remained of it—"is in Nashville. Being apart isn't beneficial to maintaining a relationship." Hadn't Jo found that out with her marriage? No wonder she was gun-shy.

"I also never said you were the right man for Jo E." Bobby shrugged. "It's obvious you like her. She's a woman well worth getting to know. But I've watched you, Kyle, and I sense you're dealing with indecision. The type of indecision that comes with a clashing of wills."

He sensed that?

Bobby grinned. "Not that hard to see."

"Please stop doing that."

"What?"

"Reading my mind."

"It's easy to tell what you're feeling, Smiley. You don't hide it well."

Evidently.

Bobby stopped in front of the hardware store and peeked in the window, waving to someone inside. He straightened. "This store has been here fifty-five years and I reckon it'll remain a few more."

"Our lives aren't the same."

"That's a fact. But we have one thing in common. God led me here, and despite what I thought I wanted, He provided what I needed. Before you decide anything pertaining to your future, ask yourself if you have the faith to go where He's leading you."

Kyle couldn't forget the voice that told him something better than a country music career awaited him. Yet he still couldn't see God's call on his life working out. Then again, wasn't that a large part of what faith was all about?

Since coming to Hidden Veil a month ago, he had found himself less satisfied with his old way of living. For years, his life had remained the same day in and day out, year on end—same people, same places, same job. In Nashville, he'd been a routine guy. Was it possible he hadn't wanted country music success as much as he'd thought, because if that was his goal, why hadn't he fought harder to attain it?

Now, something else called to him, something to give his life more meaning, and he hesitated to grab on to it. Lack of faith or obstinacy? Or maybe God would call it something else, like flat out disobedience.

They crossed the street again and arrived back at Jo E's Java. Kyle stopped outside. "I think I'll head on home."

Home? How easily that word slipped off his tongue, and it didn't refer to Nashville. Yet he couldn't stay here, couldn't turn his life topsy-turvy. Could he?

But there was that kiss.

* * * *

Jo carried the leftover pork chops and mashed potatoes to the refrigerator while Gran placed their supper dishes in the dishwasher. Since Saturday, sleep had come and gone in fits and starts. Exhaustion had overtaken Jo, and she planned to call it an early night.

Gran began scrubbing a greasy pan in the soapy water. "I think I've been patient long enough, Jo E. You never told me how your date went on Saturday."

Because Jo had hoped to avoid the subject. But she had to congratulate her grandmother on holding back this long. "We agreed to call it a non-date, Gran, and it went well." Most of it.

Some of it went too well. So well that thoughts of that kiss—as innocent as it was—messed with her head.

At church on Sunday morning, she'd begun playing the wrong hymn, catching herself only after Greg cleared his throat in the microphone and narrowed his eyes at her. Her cheeks had flamed like the candles on the communion table.

At work yesterday, she'd put ten thousand paper cups in

her order cart, rather than one thousand. Fortunately, she'd realized her mistake before finalizing the order. Aside from the unnecessary cost, where would she have stored them all?

Then, she could barely remember her piano lesson last night. The most memorable moment came with Haley's giggles when Jo instructed her to play a song she'd just finished.

How could one tiny peck on the lips, a flash of a touch, distract her so?

"Are you saying it went well enough for a second date?" Her grandmother's eyebrows drew together. "Or would it be a first?"

"Gran . . ." Jo drew out the "a" for emphasis.

Her grandmother threw her wet hands up in the air, sending soapy droplets raining down. "I'm only asking that you not throw out the baby with the bath water."

Jo glanced at the water-filled sink, then at her grandmother. They both burst into laughter.

"I guess that was an odd cliché to choose right now." Gran shook her head. "Honey, I know your fears and I'd be the last to make light of them, but you cannot live your life afraid of making another mistake. If you've prayed about a future relationship, whether with Kyle or someone else, and God has said no, then you have your answer. Don't let anyone change your mind, not even me."

As Gran washed the dishes, Jo stared into the refrigerator, seeing nothing but a bright light. Her grandmother's words were freeing, especially when Gran worried about Jo being left alone should the worst happen.

Yet Jo couldn't recall ever seeking God's relationship guidance. Then, she'd assumed the role of martyr after her marriage disaster, vowing to never place herself in a position of emotional risk again. A safe relationship was all she wanted.

But how rewarding was emotional safety?

"Unless you plan to use that appliance as an air-conditioner, I'd suggest you shut the door."

Gran's words jolted her, and she shut the refrigerator. "Sorry."

When Jo grabbed a towel to dry the dishes in the drainer, Gran took it from her hands. "You're in la-la land, girlie. Go on. I'll finish up here."

Jo's phone went off, preventing her from arguing. Seeing Kyle's name, she grabbed the cell phone from the kitchen counter and walked toward the front room, swiping the screen as she went. "Hello?"

"Hey, I hope I'm not interrupting a lesson or anything."

Her heart beat kicked up at that soothing melody that was his voice. "No. It's fine."

"I've chosen the songs I'd like to do for the concert at your church and wondered if we could get together this week to rehearse."

"I have Thursday night free. Isaac's mom had to cancel his lesson."

"If you and Vera don't mind, could we do it at your house? There's no piano at my place, and I think we'll be more comfortable than at the church."

"I'm sure Gran wouldn't mind. Seven-thirty?"

"Perfect."

They'd taken care of business, and Jo expected him to end the call. *She* could end it herself, but neither of them suggested it. Silence stood between them until Kyle said, "I keep thinking about that chimpanzee we saw Saturday. You know, the one that laughed at the kid making faces at him."

A four-year-old and a chimpanzee? That's what he recalled most about Saturday? For three days, she'd nearly drowned in a different memory.

"I remember." She had to admit, it was funny. "I'm not sure which one of them had the most fun."

Jo curled into the chair by the fireplace as they talked about that day and all they had seen without mentioning her confession or his kiss. That led to other subjects, and by the time they'd finished talking and reminiscing, over thirty minutes had passed.

How did he do that? How did he get her to relax and enjoy the conversation? How did he leave her feeling like a teenager again?

Seventeen

Kyle reached for the car keys on the kitchen counter, then pulled back. Nope. He would not drive into town for coffee. He'd made himself enough of a pest to Jo lately. Other sources in town sold coffee—a couple of fast-food places, the Red Dog Diner, even the soda fountain next to the drugstore. He could even make it himself at the house.

It wouldn't be the same, though. Where would he find the company he craved?

He'd loved every bit of that phone call with Jo last night, especially her sense of humor. Except for the day at the zoo, she normally bottled up her lighter side and stuck a cork in, like it was a rare concoction to be used only when necessary. She didn't uncork it around him, anyway.

Yes, his attraction to her surpassed any feelings he'd had for a woman this early in their acquaintance, probably ever. No matter how hard she tried to dissuade him, being near Jo Ella Ledbetter, even if it was on the other end of a phone, brightened his day.

But he might never be ready to take that attraction to a higher level. What good would it do when they wanted something different in life?

Tired of staring at the white walls of the house, he grabbed the keys, his leather portfolio, and the dog leash. "Come on, Davey."

During the drive to the park, Kyle used Davey as a sounding board for his thoughts about Jo, Hidden Veil, his lack of creativity. He received no response other than a sympathetic lick on the ear, a wet tickle he hadn't felt before cutting his hair for the auction. While he would have preferred a simple paw-shake, at least Davey cared.

After parking the SUV, Kyle attached the leash to the dog's collar. "Let's go."

Davey jumped to the pavement and trotted toward the grass, pulling Kyle along behind him. The canopies and vendor trucks were gone, and the crowds had dispersed. But he wasn't alone. A mother pushed her preschooler on a swing several decades old. A matching-era slide and teeter-totter completed the sad excuse for a playground. An older couple strolled the area, hand in hand.

Kyle's imagination kicked into high gear and replaced the couple with him and Jo. He imagined walking the pebbled trails with her well into their years, still holding hands, still lost in a love for one another.

He jerked to a stop. Davey stared at him as if asking why he had yanked on the leash.

"Because I'm losing my mind."

He had to jump off this merry-go-round. He'd fulfilled his one date-not-a-date obligation with Jo, which left two small concerts—one church, one private—in which to interact with her. Then he was done. Out of here.

Davey led Kyle through the grass, sniffing everything. While his dog had needed the exercise, Kyle had needed the change of scenery to jump start his stalled creativity. He carried the portfolio with his pen and a legal pad to a picnic table, hoping the clean scent of the outdoors, the warmth of the springtime sun, and desperation might lead him to come up with acceptable song lyrics.

Love lost.

Love found.

Undeserved love.

Those three topics spun inside his head and, somehow, ended up on the paper almost every time he sat down to write. But what about them? The first of the three was fairly simple, but that third one, though . . .

He couldn't help but think of how undeserving he was to be blessed with Jesus' love. It wasn't an acceptable subject of a country song.

He picked up the pen and tapped the end on the paper as he prayed for words worthy of the talent God had given him

Love lost. Love lost . . .

Help me out here, God. Please.

After a few minutes of pondering, his pen slid across the paper.

Why can't you see it?
Why can't you accept it?
No one loved you more
Than I did. Than I do.

The words poured out and had nothing to do with the three sentences that wouldn't go away. Not yet.

There is no greater love than my love for you.
Why can't you see it? Why can't you accept it?

While Kyle wrote, Davey laid on his side in the grass, content to soak up the sun.

When will you see it?
When will you accept it?
No one gave you more
Than I did. Than I can.

He was in the zone.

There is no greater—

His hand halted at the movement in his peripheral vision. A man dressed in jeans and a button-down shirt, a lab coat thrown over his arm, and a Jo E's Java paper cup in one hand sauntered up to Davey, stopping a few feet away. "Mind if I pet him?"

"I don't, but he'll let you know if he does."

With the tip of his finger, the stranger pushed up the tortoiseshell glasses perched on his nose, crouched, and held out his free hand to let Davey get a sniff. The dog pushed his nose against the outstretched palm. "I guess he approves. Nice looking bullmastiff. I can see you take good care of him."

"I try."

After stroking Davey and whispering to him, the man rose. "I hope I didn't interrupt whatever you're working on."

Yeah, you kinda did.

As easily as the lyrics flowed—in a draft form—Kyle hoped he'd slip back into the writing mode later. "It's okay."

"I'm Trey Abbott."

Trey Abbott? Kyle had heard the name. Where? Oh, yeah. "You're the veterinarian whose work helped him skip the fundraiser last month." That explained why Kyle's dog attracted Trey's attention. "Smart plan."

Trey grinned. "I've had a few good ideas in my life, but none that ingenious. I really did work." He removed his glasses. "You must be Kyle Callahan, the singing bachelor. You put Lane and Sutton to shame."

Speaking of those two reminded Kyle he should drive out to Becker's place and see the equine center.

"Nice to have another newbie in town. I've only lived here three years."

Trey Abbott didn't strike Kyle as the country boy type. "If you don't mind my asking, why Hidden Veil?"

"The family of a college friend owned a house on the lake. He invited me for the weekend. I took the long way home and wound up here. I'd been trying to decide where to open my clinic. Something about the town called to me."

Bobby's advice to ask God to direct his future had played over and over in Kyle's mind since Monday. To be honest, he didn't want to ask, because he feared he'd ignore the answer . . . as he'd done for months.

"As for why I stay, there's my business, of course, but I like the town, the people." Kyle couldn't let go of the subject. "Don't you find it . . . small? For instance, cities give people more choices for entertainment."

"I guess that depends on the type of entertainment you enjoy. If you like the outdoors, there's a nearby lake with fishing, hiking trails, and kayaking. A group of us get together and kayak. If you're still here, you're welcome to join us next time."

He enjoyed all those things. "Thanks."

"No place is perfect, not even Hidden Veil, but I've formed lasting friendships here." Trey stared at his cup. "A town this size isn't for everyone, Kyle. I guess it depends on what you're looking for, where you're most at peace."

That was the question, wasn't it? What was he looking for? And peace. He thrived on it. He used to, anyway. Now, he hardly knew the meaning.

Trey eyed his watch. "I was killing a little time between appointments, but I'd better head out. I have an afternoon of equine exams ahead of me. Nice to meet you, Kyle."

"You, too."

Trey Abbott gave Davey a last pat and headed off toward the parking lot.

Kyle thought of Bobby and the boys, their hours of companionship at the coffee shop. He thought of the kids playing outside in the neighborhood where he was staying. How long since he'd experienced that kind of connection in the city? He thought of Jo and Vera and Lane and Sutton, of all the people he'd met since his arrival. Nice people. People he'd miss when he returned to his life in Nashville.

He glanced at the paper on the picnic table in front of him. One line stuck out.

Why can't you see it? Why can't you accept it?

He'd written the words as a plea from a man to a woman.

Now, it was as though the words spoke to him, personally, a message not unlike the near audible one he'd received after speaking with his manager. See and accept a new life here? A new career?

His life was in Tennessee, and his career was in the country music business. Why couldn't he see or accept anything other than that?

The answer came with a sharp pain in his soul. Because he didn't want to.

* * * *

He was good. better than good. Better than Taylor.

Jo had recognized as much when she heard Kyle perform in Nashville. But there was something special about his voice, his playing, his entire demeanor while singing songs of praise and worship. He became one with the music.

Kyle had been magnetic a year ago. Tonight, he was electrifying. Determined to prove her worthiness to accompany him, she'd played with more energy than normal, more heart, and glowed with his smile of approval.

Now, her body swayed on the piano bench in Gran's front room as he strummed his guitar and practically prayed the words to "What a Beautiful Name." Her throat tightened and goosebumps broke out along her arms while listening to his mellow voice hit just the right strains. This was only a rehearsal, but his worship was undeniable. And, once more, his talent overwhelmed her.

Truthfully, it was more than talent, more than seeing Kyle in a state of worship. It was the effect it had on her.

When he slipped into "Graves into Gardens," she pressed her eyes closed to keep the tears at bay. Yes, God could do anything. He could turn the worst of any situation into something beautiful. Then why couldn't she hand Him her disappointments and the death of her marriage? Why couldn't she let Him turn her future into something beautiful? Instead, she protected the hurt like a faithful dog refusing to leave its owner's grave.

The music ended, and Kyle rested the guitar against the sofa where he sat.

Jo swiped at the dampness clinging to her eyelashes. "Wow." Her voice cracked, and she cleared her throat before adding, "That was incredible."

"Thanks. I really got into it."

I'll say.

His voice had risen barely above a whisper, reiterating how much the songs had affected him, too. That made his adamant refusal to pen Christian music even more perplexing. "You know . . ." Should she broach the subject? What business was it of hers? She might do nothing but anger him.

Kyle cocked his head. "What?"

"You left off one piece from your list of perfect songs to perform."

"I've cleared everything with the music director, but which one did you have in mind?"

"'I Claim You.'"

His eyes widened before they narrowed to match his pursed lips. "I've already filled the time allotted." His mouth closed, sealing off any further discussion about it, like placing a boulder across a tomb.

Still, she couldn't let it go. "Did you write the song about a particular romantic relationship?" A bolt of envy—or was it jealousy?—streaked through Jo. "She must have been special."

"There wasn't anyone special."

Had there ever been someone?

Jo brushed aside the ridiculous hope that clung to her like mud. She had already told him she could never be romantically interested in him. Of course, that was before Saturday, that sweet kiss, and her inability to accept it at face value—as a friendly peck of forgiveness.

She was ready to move to a safer subject when he said, "I won't disrespect God by singing a song not meant for Him."

She nodded, able to see his reasoning. Would God consider it like re-gifting a song to Him? Like giving a wife a bracelet originally intended for a husband's girlfriend. That still hurt.

Jo vanquished the memory, so tired of giving the thoughtless Taylor space in her head. At least, he hadn't called, texted, or shown up in her store lately.

She couldn't vanquish that song, though. "I understand your point, but what if God gave you that song, intending for you to sing it as praise to Him?" She had no business arguing with Kyle over the meaning of a song she didn't create. "You know, never mind. I'm only telling you what the lyrics said to me."

"You're entitled to your opinion." Kyle stood and placed his guitar in its case. "I think we've done all we can for tonight. How about another session this weekend?"

"Sure. Sunday afternoon?"

"Great."

At the front door, he turned to face her, his intent gaze sweeping her up in a whirlwind of speculation. A goodbye kiss, perhaps?

"I'm thinking it's time to write another romantic ballad . . . for someone special."

Jo's face betrayed her when it broke out in a wide, pleased smile. He walked out of the house, chuckling, and she beat a fist against her thigh, but her smile remained. "Oh, that jerk."

"What did he do?"

Jo whipped around to find her grandmother standing at the top of the stairs. "I thought you were in your room."

"The music stopped, so I figured I'd come down and chaperone." Gran's gray eyebrows waggled. "What did Kyle do that earned him a name-calling?"

"Nothing, really."

Nothing but see right through her.

Eighteen

Davey lumbered alongside Kyle as they wandered the main street of downtown Hidden Veil. The dog sniffed the air, sniffed the light posts, sniffed the legs of passing pedestrians who ventured too close. Once they noticed Davey—how could they miss him?—they shied away.

He reached down and patted the dog's head. "It isn't personal, bud."

Maybe he should have taken Davey home after their playtime in the park, but the hour spent rehearsing with Jo last night prompted the bright idea to stop by Jo E's Java and introduce her to his dog. Now, it seemed like a single dad introducing his kid to a woman who might become the child's stepmother. Was he getting ahead of himself?

A lightness filled his chest at the recollection of the bright look on Jo's face when he mentioned writing a love song for someone special.

Not wanting to take Davey inside the coffee shop, Kyle

stopped and peeked through the window. Before he could locate Jo, a woman walked outside. Ears perked and nose in the air, Davey sniffed at the smell of coffee drifting behind her out the door.

"Oh, hello." The woman, her blonde hair verging on brown, smiled at Kyle as if he were a slice of strawberry cheesecake and she'd just abandoned her diet. A laugh tickled his throat when she ran her tongue over her lips, completing the image. While he labored to recall where he'd seen that pretty face before, she held out her hand. "We never officially met. I'm Sophie Carpenter."

He took her hand, and she wrapped her fingers around his in a grip that led him to wonder if he'd ever get them back. "Kyle Callahan. Nice to meet you, Sophie."

She cocked her head and studied him, still gripping his hand. "You don't remember me, do you?" Her bottom lip drooped into a flirty pout.

He studied her. Had he seen her at a gig somewhere? "I've met so many new people since I arrived in town, but you look familiar." How old was she? Twenty-two? *Maybe.*

"That's because you saw me at the auction. I fought Vera Bevins for the right to have you take me to dinner and sing to me."

He nodded as it finally clicked. "I remember now. To be honest, I'd never done the auction thing before. The process rattled me."

"Bless your heart." She stepped closer and squeezed the hand she still hadn't returned. "I forgive you."

Gracious of you.

Kyle took a step back, seeking air not tainted by the strong floral scent she wore. He bumped into a metal chair, knocking it into the bistro table as the legs screeched across the concrete. Davey shuffled out of the way.

"Those women looked at you like you were a piece of meat in a display case. It's easy to understand why you'd want to forget that day."

Kyle kept to himself how he'd hoped Vera would win the bid. "Well, it was good to see you." Maybe the hint would free his hand without him needing to offend her by tugging on it.

The coffee shop door opened, and Jo walked outside. Her gaze slipped to the joined hands belonging to him and Sophie. Her eyes narrowed and her lips pinched. He almost grinned. Almost. Still, warmth torpedoed through his veins.

He had been right. She could no longer pretend an indifference to him.

* * * *

What on earth did Sophie Carpenter think she was doing?

Like Taylor, Kyle Callahan attracted women like a magnet, proving the rationality of Jo's caution. Still . . .

Knowing the flirtatious young woman, it was easy to assume she had initiated the touch. But Kyle didn't seem to mind, because so far, he'd done nothing to free himself from her hold.

Jo urged her expression to relax, but her facial muscles remained tight, like forcing a smile with a shoe stretcher. "Sophie, Bethany is preparing your order. She said you were in a hurry, so it should be ready soon."

Sophie frowned and released Kyle's hand, but her gaze

absorbed every inch of his face. "When will I see you again, Kyle?"

His glance bounced off Jo and landed back on Sophie. "We might bump into one another again. I'm in town off and on."

I'm in town off and on. Was that an invitation?

"Let me know next time, and we'll grab coffee." Sophie's hand found its way back to Kyle's arm, fingers crawling up it like a spider. "Or something."

Jo's jaw tightened. "You'd better hurry before your order gets cold." The words slipped between her clenched teeth.

"It'll keep." Sophie gasped as though a sudden memory hit her. "Did you hear the news, Jo?"

"What news?"

"Someone donated *ten thousand dollars* to help with Ryan's medical bills."

Ten thousand? That equaled a large portion of what they'd raised on the Saturday of the fundraiser. "Who was it?"

Sophie glanced at Kyle and shrugged. "Evidently, the person was anonymous, but I've heard it was someone in Hidden Veil. Whoever gave the money is certainly generous." The woman squeezed Kyle's biceps and strutted into the coffee shop.

It was all Jo could do to keep from sticking her foot in the woman's path over that sly squeeze of Kyle's arm. Honestly, what was wrong with her? She hated this feeling. Not only did it bring back horrible memories, but it amplified a fear she'd thought she'd gotten a handle on . . . until Kyle showed up in town.

Jo glanced at him. Did Sophie believe he donated that

money? Had he? The day of their non-date, he talked about avoiding starting over so he wouldn't struggle with his finances again. It was possible Kyle had done better with his music than he'd let on. It didn't matter to Jo, but she couldn't say the same for Sophie. The woman wasn't above chasing a dollar . . . or a bank account filled with them.

Kyle rubbed his palm down the leg of his jeans. "She has quite a grip. My hand almost went to sleep."

Bless his heart. She stopped herself from adding an eye-roll.

He lowered his gaze. "And you were no help."

For the first time, Jo noticed the dog sprawled at his feet, his stout body halfway beneath the table. The other half took up part of the sidewalk in front of her business. "That's Davey?" The dog sat up at hearing his name, knocking over a chair, which Kyle set right.

"That's him. Always alert and ready to protect me from all threats, be they man, beast,"—Kyle leaned forward and spoke, his voice soft and conspiratory—"or predatory woman."

Then Davey needs more training. "Good thing I pose no danger." Jo crouched in front of Davey and held out her hand for the dog to sniff. When he showed no sign of fear or aggression, she rubbed his tan head and black muzzle. "I was wondering when I'd meet you, Davey."

"I'm glad you aren't afraid of him. Some people are."

Not Sophie Carpenter. But the dog's presence had likely gone unnoticed by her. Her laser focus had beamed a hole through Kyle.

Jo pushed to her feet. "Can I get you anything?"

"An Americano." Kyle held up the leash. "I'd come in,

but I don't want to leave Davey out here alone."

"Have a seat and I'll bring you a cup."

"Yes, ma'am."

Oh, how she tried to guard herself against the gaping smile that brightened Kyle's face, but the sight of it kicked her heart into high gear. To combat it, she repeated two words to herself over and over. *Sophie Carpenter. Sophie Carpenter. Sophie Carpenter.*

✳   ✳   ✳   ✳

Inside the coffee shop, Jo diverted her course after someone called her name, drawing her attention to three women at a table near the center of the room. "It's good to see y'all."

The youngest Hartwell sister, Brianna, pulled out a chair from under the table. "Have a seat, Jo. We want to know if something is true." She was a perky, caramel macchiato-drinking college student who often came in to study.

Jo glanced out the window at Kyle sitting at the table outside—the perfect excuse to avoid whatever gossip they wanted to discuss. "I have a customer waiting for a coffee."

"This won't take long." Shaina Weber was as equally perky as her friend, a couple of years older than Brianna, and a newcomer to Hidden Veil. She adored Viennas—sweet and strong.

Harmoni Basinger, Shaina's shy, yet free-spirited aunt, sat in the third seat at the table. She owned In Harmoni, a soap and candle shop a couple of doors down from Jo E's. People around town knew Harmoni for her soft heart for non-human species, especially those that grossed out others—

snakes, lizards, rats. Jo shuddered just thinking about having such *pets* occupy the same space where she slept. Not much older than Shaina, Harmoni preferred an organic green tea.

Jo eyed Shaina. "Shouldn't you be at work?"

"I worked last Saturday, so Trey gave me the afternoon off."

"Nice of him."

Sophie scooted behind Brianna, a paper tray with three cups in hand. "If you learn who donated all that money, Jo, I'm dying to know. I heard it came from a Richmond lawyer's office."

The three women at the table glanced at one another. They'd probably already heard Sophie's story about the anonymous donor. Sophie couldn't keep a secret, and when she spread it, it was at full volume.

"I'm sure you'll be the first I tell."

Jo monitored Sophie as she left through the front door, making sure the woman kept moving, crossing the street to return to the insurance office without stopping for another handsy talk with Kyle.

And what would you do if she decided to stop, Jo Elia Ledbetter?

She forced her attention back to the others without searching for an answer. "What did you want to ask me?"

Brianna leaned across the table. "We've heard Taylor Morris was here. Is that true?"

Jo froze. Several people were aware of her marriage and divorce, but she hadn't used Morris as her last name since she was twenty-seven. By now, most had probably forgotten her ex-husband's name and didn't connect her to the man whose songs climbed the music charts.

She could deny Taylor's visit, but she'd lied before and suffered the guilt. "It's true."

Brianna and Shaina gazed at one another, two examples of the young and impressionable types that had broken up her marriage.

No, that wasn't fair. She knew these women. They may be young, but they had good heads on their shoulders and weren't marriage breakers.

Harmoni merely drank her tea and scrolled through the screen on her phone, showing no interest in the conversation. She was a lovely but different personality, the kind to blaze her own trail, not caring where it led or how she'd get back.

"So you met him? What was he like?" Shaina asked her questions in a calm, casual manner. Still, interest buzzed below the surface.

"I met Taylor years ago. He's . . ." Jo struggled with the answer to the second question and gave up. "Taylor came. He left. That's all I can say. I'm sorry, I need to get back to work. Enjoy your drinks." She hurried to the kitchen to wash Davey's scent off her hands and prepare Kyle's coffee.

How long would it take before people connected her to her ex-husband and began feeling sorry for her?

Nineteen

Kyle's gaze tracked Jo as she entered the coffee shop. The look on her face at seeing Sophie holding his hand roamed fresh in his mind. The air had crackled with female animosity. At first, he'd assumed it was Jo's jealousy, and his optimism swelled. Now, doubt set in. Jealousy could be wishful thinking. Maybe she simply didn't like Sophie.

He pulled out a chair at the bistro table for himself, then pointed to the concrete. "Down, Davey." The dog plopped onto the sidewalk, resuming his previous sprawl. Since ample room remained for people to pass without inconvenience, he didn't make Davey move.

Even though it was a weekday, the warm spring weather had brought shoppers to downtown Hidden Veil. People walked through the doors of a realtor, lawyer, accountant, and the bank at the corner. But the two places seeming to do the most business were Locke's Drug Store across the street and Jo E's Java.

A man in a suit and dress shirt, top button undone, passed Jo E's. He greeted Kyle with a smile and a "Nice day."

After a month in town, the friendliness of the people here hadn't ceased to amaze him. Not that people weren't friendly in Nashville, but most he met were tourists, college students, or other musicians. Of course, he'd made friends with a few people from church and the community college in which he'd taught. No one he missed enough to rush back to Nashville to see.

The phone in his pocket played a lively tune, and he pulled it out. His stomach twisted at reading the name of the caller. Evidently, Toni had her way. "Hey, Brian."

"Kyle, dude, what's going on?"

"Saving the world, one song at a time." Instead of the world, Kyle needed to save himself from the massive wall that blocked him from reaching his creativity and stalled his ability to be that crusading songwriter. But he wouldn't cry on Brian's shoulder.

"Good."

"What's up with you?" Like Kyle hadn't heard already.

"Busy days. I'm prepping for some studio work coming up."

Kyle tried to tame the envy crawling over that wall like a kudzu vine. He reached for just the right note of enthusiasm in his response. "That's great."

The muffled sound of a guitar played in the background on Brian's end. "It's why I'm calling."

He was calling at Toni's suggestion.

Sophie Carpenter walked outside carrying her drink order. Seeing him on the phone, she smiled and walked on. Brian's call was good for something.

"I'm supposed to include a love song—a romantic ballad." Brian's voice called his attention back to the phone conversation. "Your specialty, Kyle."

"You want to include one of my songs on an album?" But Brian didn't want him to record that song with him. Maybe he should have suggested *that* to Toni on their video call last week.

Kyle supposed he should feel grateful for the offer. If Brian's album did well, national exposure could get this change in Kyle's career going in the right direction. But it felt like the upper crust threw bread crumbs to the peasant. Then again, maybe crumbs were better than nothing at this point.

"Not just any song, man. A new one. Would you be willing to write a new song for me?"

Once more, that nudge to take his music in a whole different direction pressed on his conscience, urging him to decline.

"I have another . . . invitation." *Invitation? Get real, Callahan.* "When do you need an answer?"

"As soon as you decide. You'll need time to write, then there'll be rehearsals. No later than a week."

Despite his vacation frame of mind, Kyle's bank account would soon push him to return to Nashville, or at the least, come up with a solid plan for moving forward. "I'll get back to you then or earlier."

"Great. Take care."

Before Kyle could respond, Brian had disconnected the call, leaving him to shake his head at the phone.

The door to the coffee shop opened, and Jo stepped outside. She eyed him, then the phone. "Is something wrong?"

He set the cell phone on the table. "What makes you think that?"

"You looked like you were about to squeeze the circuits out of that thing."

"No, all's good." He pointed to the cup in her hand. "Mine?"

"I'm sorry it took so long. I got waylaid."

"Not a problem." He'd seen her talking to a group of women at a table, one being the young brunette studying the day Vera pressed him to enter the bachelor auction.

A paper bag rustled as Jo placed the cup of steaming black coffee on the bistro table. She handed him the bag. "Here you go."

"What's this?" Kyle peered inside. "Cookies?"

"Dog treats. I keep them for my customers who walk their dogs downtown."

"They look good." Kyle pulled out the treat and sniffed it.

"I'll bring you your own, if you'd like." She pointed to the bag. "Those are for Davey."

"I'll pass, thanks. She brought you something, bud." The dog bounced up into a sitting position. Kyle tossed the treat into the air and Davey caught it, making quick work of chewing and swallowing it. Then he waited for more. "What do you say to Jo?" Kyle tipped his head toward her and, like a ventriloquist, said, "Thank you."

"You're welcome, Davey." Jo's lips twitched. "I'd better go back inside before Bethany comes looking for me."

He wanted to ask her to stay, wanted to pull her onto his lap and run his hands through that perfectly arranged head of dark hair. He wanted to kiss her again—a proper kiss this time—and tell her how he loved just looking at her. Man, that woman was burrowing into every crevice in him that needed filling with affection.

Leaving Hidden Veil might be one of the hardest things he'd ever do.

✳ ✳ ✳ ✳

Jo opened the door to let Kyle into the house. A month ago, he'd had his hair cut, nearly shaved on the sides and back, to make a good impression on auction bidders. While the short hair brought out the strength of his beard-stubbled jaw and the blue in his eyes, she hoped he'd let it grow a little longer. A neat style that crept past a man's ears and to his collar in the back had always quivered her stomach.

On second thought, Taylor wore that style, and that quiver ended badly.

Kyle carried the guitar case, ready for their second rehearsal. "I didn't see Vera's car. Is she gone?"

"She's spending the afternoon with a friend." Gran had been cagey about the identity of that friend. "Would you like some iced tea before we start?"

"Just water. It's better for my throat." He set the case against the sofa and followed Jo to the kitchen.

"Gran left those for you." She pointed to a plate of chocolate chip cookies. "She said you can only have them if you don't hit any wrong notes during our rehearsal."

Kyle laughed. "That sounds like her. She's a feisty woman. I like feisty women." He reached for the water she'd poured him, and for a moment, they both held the glass. His gaze caught hers as he added, "No matter the age."

Heat rushed through Jo at the suggestion in his words, the intensity of his stare. She let go of the cold glass and turned to the counter by the sink to pour her own water, drinking half of it before facing him again. The icy drink had helped to cool her insides, and gave her time to get a hold of herself and overcome the light-headed feeling that had hit her.

This infatuation, or whatever she felt, was getting absurd.

He set the glass on the counter. "Are you ready to get to work?"

Please. How could he look at her in that wolfish way one minute and the next act as if he hadn't sent her head spinning?

Maybe she'd blown his interest in her out of proportion. Maybe it had been so long since she'd dated that she couldn't distinguish a man's interest from her own imagination. This wasn't a date. "Let's do it."

From his place on the sofa and hers at the piano, they played through the list of songs. The notes blended in flawless harmony.

"That was terrific, Jo." Kyle put aside his guitar. "You sure you've never considered playing professionally?"

"I'll leave that to people like you and Taylor."

At the mention of her ex-husband, or maybe the reminder of her opinion of professional musicians, they both grew quiet. She had meant nothing negative in her comment, and that caught her by surprise. Until recently, had she said those words, it would have been uncomplimentary.

Kyle stood and grabbed the glass from the end table. "I could use more water and a few of Vera's cookies."

"Sure." Jo led him into the kitchen and set the snack on the breakfast table. "Instead of water, would you rather have coffee or tea?"

"Tea sounds good."

"I hope you like it sweet. Gran has a sixty-forty recipe—sixty percent tea, forty percent sugar."

His eyes lit up. "I am a Georgia boy, you know. Sweet tea runs through my veins."

"And right through the root of a sweet tooth."

"Guilty." He pulled out a chair at the table and sat while she poured them both glasses of iced tea and set two luncheon plates out. "What about you?"

"I prefer salty and can demolish a bag of potato chips in no time."

Kyle feigned shock, then turned a cookie in his hand, his brow crimped in deep concentration. He studied it as though counting the visible chocolate chips. "Sweet and salty . . . the best combination."

How was she to respond to that . . . that obvious line of flirtation?

* * * *

It was all Kyle could do to keep from bursting into laughter. Jo's expression was priceless, as if she couldn't decide whether to come back with a flirty statement to match his or bolt from the kitchen.

Either way, he promised himself to knock her off center once in a while. It might be good for her. At times, she was wound tighter than the strings on his guitar.

His good mood turned with the thought. He wouldn't be here much longer to keep that promise. Two weeks from now, he'd return to Nashville and his old life. Living alone. Scrabbling for his place in the country music business. Jo would remain here with her business, her grandmother, the people she'd known since childhood.

Two weeks.

Her hesitant response to his sweet and salty comment turned into a slight smile, but he hung his hopes on the glimmer shining in those brown eyes. "You don't make things easy."

"It's only as hard as we both make it, Jo."

She looked out the window facing the backyard, but he figured she saw little of the grass or the maple tree or the neighbor's back porch. "And what if it were easier?"

The quiet question came out of the blue, and he caught his breath before asking for more detail. He needed to be sure his brain had formed a proper translation. "You're saying . . .?"

"I'm saying that despite my protests earlier and, admittedly, my fear . . . I-I like you, Kyle Callahan." She turned away from the window, her gaze meeting his stare. "That's all I'm saying."

That was enough. For now.

Movement in the yard alerted Kyle of a visitor. "I didn't know you had a dog."

"We don't."

"Then you have a visitor." He pointed to the small, multi-colored mutt sniffing around the yard, part terrier and part . . . whatever.

"That's Corky. He belongs to Mrs. Mulden next door and has no sense of boundaries."

Kyle could relate. Jo had stretched the boundaries of his

emotions and desires.

Mitch and his family would be gone through June. Maybe he could stay in town for another month . . . just to see where things went. But that might amount to playing with fire. What if he found he didn't want to leave Jo? Maybe she wouldn't want him to stay.

Jo opened the back door and stepped outside. The dog ran to her, jumping on her legs, reaching only as high as her knees. She bent and rubbed his head, as she'd done with Davey.

Kyle followed her out the door. "Davey would have this little guy for breakfast." At her soft gasp, he realized his stupid joke had fallen flat. "Not that I would let him hurt another dog or any animal."

She tucked in her lips to restrain a grin, and he chuckled. She'd suckered him into believing she took offense at his statement. Not wound as tight as he'd thought.

"He is cute." Kyle crouched and scratched Corky between his ears. The dog changed allegiance in an instant, panting in excitement and sharing his canine breath.

When Jo turned to go back inside, she tripped over Corky. The dog yelped, and Kyle's arms shot out to catch Jo. She fell into him, knocking him against the wood siding of the house.

His mind registered a slight throb at the back of his head. He blocked out the pain, concentrating on the pressure of her hands gripping his shoulders. Her chest rose and fell with her labored breathing, and she smelled of roasted coffee and lavender perfume. Her eyes widened with shock, then fluttered closed as she leaned in.

Kyle's arms tightened their hold, not settling for a quick brush of his lips against hers. This time he lingered, lost in a kiss he'd imagined for weeks. A year, if he were honest with himself.

His fingers threaded through her hair as he drew her closer. She came willingly, unyielding in her pursuit of his mouth. He drank in the sweetness remaining on her lips from her grandmother's iced tea.

"Why are you in my house, Corky?"

Kyle and Jo jerked apart at the sound of Vera's voice coming from the kitchen. Their hands dropped to their sides.

Vera approached the door, and her mouth quirked with humor. "I can't leave you two alone for a moment." She shooed the dog from her kitchen and into the yard. With a flick of her wrist, she closed the back door, shutting out Corky, Kyle, and Jo.

From inside the house, Vera shouted, "Carry on!"

Kyle gazed at Jo. She gazed at him. Their incredible moment had vanished. They both inhaled a deep, calming breath before the humor of the situation caught up to them. They laughed like fools while the dog jumped up and down at their feet.

When he gained control of himself, Kyle wrapped his arms around her and tugged her closer. "You heard what she said."

Jo's eyes smoldered. "Oh, I heard."

Twenty

Jo stared at her reflection in the bathroom mirror. She had a dinner date. She had . . . a dinner date . . . with Kyle.

Doubt and anticipation carried on a battle inside her stomach. Hair arranged. Makeup applied. Casual pants and blouse—nothing too tight or too low.

They were going to Ricardo's for Mexican food. Great. She could already feel the indigestion brought on by nerves. She should call and cancel.

But she didn't want to.

Grabbing the lipstick tube, Jo opened it and studied the color. Deep red. A color that said "Come get me. I'm yours." A color that described her behavior Sunday afternoon.

She could have prevented herself from falling into Kyle's arms, could have stopped herself from initiating that kiss. She could have pretended he was the pharmacist, Gene Locke—older, paunchier, and in love with his business, instead of a younger, more handsome musician whose songs spoke of his heart.

Supporting herself with her palms pressed to the bathroom counter, Jo hung her head. *Lord, what am I doing?* She breathed the prayer for at least the hundredth time since Sunday, once more getting no answer.

She snapped the cover back on the tube. The red was too much. Just too much.

At the squeak of a floorboard, she looked into the mirror to find Gran standing in the bathroom doorway.

"You had no reservations on Sunday, Jo E."

Her grandmother knew her so well. "What was I thinking to kiss him, then agree to this date? We'll only disappoint one another."

Her grandmother stepped into the room, talking to Jo's reflection. "Don't overthink it, Jo E. You're not marrying him. You're only going out for a nice meal."

"I don't know, Gran. Kyle is . . . I don't think he's . . ." She struggled for the words that expressed the impression he left on her.

"He isn't like Taylor?"

Jo put the lipstick in the drawer. "I was a fool once and can't let it happen a second time. I don't think I could take the disappointment."

"Honey, joy and disappointment walk hand-in-hand. No relationship is perfect. In love, you learn to cherish the good times and accept that you might never change the bad."

"I never saw disappointment in you or Grandpa. Yours was a wonderful marriage. You both wanted the same things and had the same outlook on life. I don't remember more than a couple of occasions when you spent time apart."

"Maybe we erred in hiding some of those hard times from

you—the squabbles and the worries. When you came to us, you were so young. We tried to ensure you were happy after all you'd gone through with your parents' accident. We wanted to provide you with a loving family and help you experience brighter days. Perhaps, over the years, we made our marriage seem so bright that it blinded you to the darker side."

Surely, her grandparents' hard times were nothing compared to what she went through with Taylor. "What happened during your worst time?"

Gran looked away. "We almost divorced."

At the quiet admission, Jo froze, watching her grandmother in the mirror. She had no memory of her grandparents separating or even arguing. Minor disagreements, yes. But marriage-killing arguments? No.

"It happened before you came along, after your momma married your daddy and they moved away." Gran sighed. "I was bored and feeling put-upon by a man who worked long hours. He didn't want me working outside of the house. But in his off hours, he often went fishing with his buddies. So one day I left. Ran away."

Jo whipped around. "Where did you go?"

"I went to stay with my sister in the mountains."

But she came back. They worked things out. "What happened?"

"After a couple of weeks, your grandfather came after me. He said, 'Vera, I've had enough of the nonsense. I want you to come home.'"

"He didn't!" She couldn't imagine her sweet grandfather being domineering.

Gran held up a finger. "He wasn't talking about *my*

nonsense, exactly. He was talking about *ours*. See, we were both at fault. I should have talked to him much sooner, but I kept my unhappiness to myself, thinking it would go away. He should have realized by my distance that something was wrong, but he dealt with his own hurt by adding more distance between us.

"We carried on one slam-bang argument, but once we got our issues out in the open, we worked through them. Our marriage wasn't perfect from then on, but we loved each other in a deeper, more lasting way."

"You found your happily ever after?"

She chortled. "Oh, my stars. Sometimes, I'd like to bury that term six feet under. It gives a couple the wrong impression. We still experienced frustration and downright hostility toward one another. But we learned not to give it a foothold. We learned to talk it out. And we protected you from our arguments."

She wrapped an arm around Jo. "Honey, that happily ever after exists when you understand that every relationship has trials, but you're willing to work at it, anyway. No person is perfect, but you accept their flaws as they accept yours. You'll encounter ups and downs in your romance as with anything else in life. But how can the ups come if you're busy worrying about the downs?"

"You're saying I should take a chance that Kyle won't treat me as Taylor did?"

"I'm saying to look beyond the trifling things and see the man's heart. Find out what's important to him. Let him know what's important to you. Then, if he's the right one, find a way to meet in the middle."

Look at his heart? Wasn't that what God had tried to tell

her? Hadn't she convinced herself that Kyle's songs spoke of his heart? And they were beautiful.

Jo hugged her grandmother. "I love you, Gran."

"The feeling's mutual, girlie."

The doorbell rang, and the two women pulled apart. Gran looked at her watch. "He's right on time."

Taylor was always at least fifteen minutes late. "Plus one for Kyle?"

Gran winked. "A definite plus one."

∗　∗　∗　∗

Kyle opened the door to Ricardo's and followed Jo inside the restaurant. He'd heard the owner, Rick Burns, didn't have a Latino bone in his body, but the food was as close to authentic as a customer could find without leaving the country. Based on the full tables, the rumor was true.

Rick also owned the Red Dog Diner across the street, where Kyle had eaten a few times, including the evening after he and Jo returned from the zoo. He'd give the food there two thumbs up, so he had high hopes for his dinner tonight.

Then, there was the company.

The hostess led them past walls painted an earthy orange and covered with various colorful artwork—half-jugs of clay, bright paintings, even images on black velvet—to a four-person table at the back of the restaurant. The place brimmed with comfort and a honky-tonk-on-Saturday night noise level.

He pushed in Jo's chair and took the one next to her. "Maybe I should have suggested somewhere quieter, where we can talk without shouting."

She leaned toward him, her shoulder brushing his. "The nice thing is we can talk without being overheard." She lowered her voice, but moved closer. "It's cozier that way, don't you think?"

He'd take this kind of cozy any day. "I like the way you think, Jo E."

She tossed him a saucy grin and opened her menu. "I don't really need this. I order the same meal every time."

"You come here a lot?"

"Not much. I go out with Reagan Hartwell and her sister Brianna once in a while." She closed the menu. "If given a choice, Reagan won't go anywhere else."

"Not that there's much choice." As soon as the words left his mouth, he realized his mistake, confirmed by the loss of her smile. He attempted to dig himself out of the hole he'd dug. "Hidden Veil is growing on me, though."

Her shoulders relaxed. "It has a way about it."

They ordered and munched on tortilla chips and salsa between easy, sometimes humorous, bits of conversation. Despite the busyness, their meals arrived in quick order—her chicken enchiladas and his flautas. The food was as excellent as he'd heard.

Kyle had finished three of his four flautas when his phone rang. He pulled it from his pocket and eyed the screen. *Brian.* He'd ignore it, let it go to voice mail. After all, it hadn't been a week since the guy's first call.

"Do you need to answer that?"

"It's just Brian."

"BC?"

"Yeah. I'll handle it later."

Her focus dropped to her food, and conversation became sparse.

The call from Brian probably reminded her of the big issue that stood between them—his career.

They hadn't gone another fifteen minutes when his phone went off. *Come on, Brian. You're killing my night.*

Jo put down her fork. "Again?"

Kyle nodded.

"Maybe you should answer. It could be important."

"I doubt it." What if Brian changed his mind about wanting songs from Kyle? In that case, it would be best to know before he wasted more time pondering what to do.

The phone's incessant noise continued to aggravate him.

"Kyle, answer it or he'll just keep calling."

"I'm sure you're right." He swiped the screen. "Brian, what's up? I told you I'd let you know my decision."

Jo's shoulder tensed against his. He hadn't told her about Brian asking for a new song.

"This couldn't wait," said Brian. "The record label has moved up the recording date. You need to tell me now whether I can count on you."

Why couldn't Brian have understood one person counting on another when he split from the band, taking his name and solo talent with him, and leaving the rest of them with their jaws on the floor and holding the pieces of a shredded venue contract?

"How far up?"

"A spot came open in early July. I'll need time to learn the music and rehearse."

Kyle released a low whistle, and Jo's curious gaze leveled on him. "If we work something out, that puts us both in a bind."

"Can't help it."

With the way things had gone these last weeks, could he write lyrics and music to a new song under such pressure—a song worthy of recording on *anyone's* album?

"Come back to Nashville, Kyle. Let me lay out the plan and brainstorm with you. Two days. That's all I'm asking for."

Surely God wouldn't have provided this chance without sanctioning it.

Kyle glanced toward Jo, who had returned to eating. No. She nibbled, her face a study of worry. Just when they were getting started on something deeper than friendship.

When he boiled down his career choices, this opportunity to get his work on an album was too good to pass up, even if it meant a quick trip to Nashville and sharing co-writing credits with Brian. "I'll head there in the morning but need to be here on Sunday. I have a concert."

"A concert, huh? Oh, wait. Is this one of those church things you do?"

Stripped down meaning: Is that all you can get these days?

Because of his beliefs and refusal to take part in some of their fun outside of work, Kyle's bandmates had called him boring. They meant it in a good-natured way, but it stung sometimes. What they saw as boredom brought him comfort and a guilt-free lifestyle. And he'd found the time here far from boring, especially since Jo had become the highlight of his stay.

"Yeah, it's a church thing, and I can't miss it."

"Fine. We'll have you back on Saturday." Brian paused. "It'll be like the old days."

The old days weren't so long ago. "I'll call you when I get to my apartment tomorrow." Kyle stuffed the phone in his pocket and took his seat, his food probably cold. "I'm sorry."

"That's okay. Nothing serious, I hope."

"Not serious." Not unless his songwriting well had truly run dry. "He wants me to write a song for his new album, and they've moved up the timeline. I'll return to Nashville tomorrow for a couple of days and be back here on Saturday." When her gaze dropped to her plate, he took her hand in his. "I will be back, Jo."

She studied his face and nodded, but he figured their enjoyable evening out had taken a nosedive.

Twenty-one

Gran stood in the church's vestibule, searching the sanctuary. "I haven't seen Kyle this morning."

"He isn't here." *Yet.* Jo had to believe he would arrive soon and not desert her . . . the whole church.

"He was supposed to return from Nashville yesterday."

Her grandmother's wide-eyed gaze turned to her. "You think he didn't come back?"

"It was a temporary trip. He'll arrive in time for the service." Jo hadn't heard from him since he called her from his apartment Wednesday night, not even a peep from him on Saturday. "I tried calling him but got no answer."

"I'm sure he will be here soon." A thread of worry wove through Gran's encouraging words.

"I might have given him more credit for courtesy than he deserves."

Though, his courtesy, or lack of it, wasn't uppermost in Jo's mind. She'd missed seeing him these last days. Missed hearing his laughter while he sat with Bobby, Ray, and the others. Missed the feel of his gaze following her around the coffee shop as she worked. She'd missed their nightly phone conversations and a repeat of her heart nearly bursting with happiness while kissing him.

What she'd like to miss was the foreboding that came with his absence—a sense that she relived the past mistake of expending emotional energy on someone she couldn't trust to keep his word.

"We were supposed to run a soundcheck this morning. Even if he shows up, we've missed that opportunity."

"He'll be here." Gran nodded, clearly trying to convince herself as much as Jo.

People filed into the sanctuary from the front and rear doors. A group entered together, friends who didn't attend her church—Lane Becker, Trey Abbott, even Sutton Vance.

Lane approached first. "Good morning, Jo. Mrs. Bevins."

"Good morning. You came to hear Kyle?"

Kyle had mentioned meeting all the men and the friendships he had formed. He'd even planned to meet them at Crooked Creek this week to help repair the arena for use with Lane's new therapy center. Maybe Kyle would show for that.

"We're always up for praise time." Lane glanced over his shoulder at Sutton, who had stopped to share a laugh with an older couple. "Even Sutton came."

"You all are always welcome." Jo looked past Lane to another group of friends entering the church. "Reagan and Brianna are here." Along with Harmoni and Shaina.

Lane half-turned to see them. "That's our cue to find our seats before Sutton sees them and walks out."

And before Reagan said something offensive to Lane. Jo added those two dramas to a silent prayer that included a plea for Kyle's quick arrival.

The two men retreated to the right side of the sanctuary. Trey waited to speak to Reagan, his vet tech, then followed his friends. When would Reagan see the light about the issues that held her happiness at arm's length? Instead, she held onto bitterness and refused to turn to the person who wanted to give her everything she needed.

Speaking of bitterness . . .

Who was Jo to find fault in someone else's resentment?

After Jo spoke to the women, they settled into pews on the left side of the sanctuary, getting as far from the men as possible. Gran had already left to occupy her normal seat toward the front, leaving Jo alone to deal with her mounting anger toward Kyle.

Look at the heart.

Now wasn't a good time to look at Kyle's heart. She'd only see irresponsibility. Disappointment came with the territory when falling for a musician, and she could no longer deny she had fallen for Kyle Callahan. When would she learn?

"Hey." At his voice, she spun to face the doorway. He rushed inside, carrying his guitar case. "I'm sorry I'm late."

"We were supposed to practice." Jo winced at the condemnation in her tone.

* * * *

His work in Nashville, topped by the rushed drive back, had

exhausted Kyle, but he couldn't blame Jo for worrying that he wouldn't make it to the church on time this morning.

With a second glance, Jo looked more angry than worried. Had she believed he stood her up, as well as standing up her congregation and the Lord? It showed how little faith she had in him.

He second-guessed his decision not to call her when he arrived late last night, choosing to not wake her. Within minutes of his getting home, he'd fallen into bed to toss and turn most of the night as lyrics and melodies ran through his head. He had decisions to make and emotions to sort through. At some point, the past few days caught up with him and he'd fallen into a deep sleep. Not even the alarm on his phone had roused him.

While he felt guilt over his tardiness, that emotion flipped to irritation. "Yesterday was a rough day. I got a late start back and didn't get in until after eleven last night. I overslept this morning."

Was that a momentary look of compassion that crossed her face?

"It's done and you're here now. The service starts soon, and I'm expected at the piano."

Probably not compassion. She turned toward the front of the sanctuary.

"I'm sorry you had a bad day, Kyle, and hope you're feeling rested. How did your time in Nashville go?"

"It went so well, Jo, that I'm more confused than ever about my future. Thanks for asking."

The fictional conversation rolled through his mind as he tried to decide if he should feel hurt or anger.

"Kyle." She turned around, a hint of that sparkle in her

eyes. "I'm glad you're here."

That was more like it. He couldn't have held back the grin if he'd tried. He didn't try.

He trailed her down the aisle of the sanctuary, placed his guitar case off to the side, and sat in a chair in front of the choir he'd soon direct.

The first half of the service moved smoothly as the choir and congregation sang the old hymns Kyle grew up on— "Majesty," "Are You Washed in the Blood," and "How Firm a Foundation"—beautiful music that spoke to his heart every bit as much as the songs he'd soon play. The music minister had prepared the choir well. They needed little more from Kyle than the direction to start and stop.

After dismissing them to sit with their families in the pews, he left the altar, grabbed his case, and entered a back room to spend a few minutes fine-tuning his acoustic guitar while others took over the service. He also said a prayer, asking that he be worthy of the time the church had given him. He prayed for those sitting in the congregation that needed to hear the words he would sing.

The fatigue of earlier had left him, replaced by normal pre-performance jitters, which were balanced by a level of excitement and anticipation he hadn't experienced since the band broke up.

After the last note on the piano from Jo ended and the offering plates had been passed, Kyle waited outside the sanctuary for the pastor's introduction.

"We have a special treat for you this morning, and with it, you get a break from hearing me preach, though some of you might fuss over missing your opportunity to nap." Pastor Jim paused to allow for sporadic laughter to run through the congregation. "I want to thank Kyle Callahan for stepping in to fill Greg's shoes this morning. He recently became a part of our community—"

From backstage, Kyle winced at the insinuation that he'd made Hidden Veil his permanent home.

"—but has spent several years performing with a Nashville band. He's a singer, a songwriter, and best of all, a child of God. Now, he and our pianist, Jo Ella, will provide a mini-concert of praise to the Lord." He paused again for their applause, added his own, then glanced over his shoulder and nodded to Kyle before descending the steps to settle in a nearby pew.

Kyle inhaled and walked into the sanctuary. A stool and microphone near the piano awaited him.

He scooted onto the stool, laid his guitar across his lap, and adjusted the microphone. Too bad he hadn't made it in time for a soundcheck.

"It's a splendid morning to praise God, right?" Responses came with a chorus of amens shouted from the congregation. "I believe God speaks to people through music as much as sermons and the written word. Thank you for the invitation to share through song what I believe, and I want to thank Jo for agreeing to accompany me." He gestured to her. She'd replaced the earlier scowl with a smile and a posture of readiness.

With the guitar propped across his legs, he signaled to her to play the opening chords of "Amazing Grace." He joined in with the guitar, closed his eyes, and let the music and lyrics of the hymn, along with his mellow voice, carry him into a state of worship.

Throughout the next songs, he and Jo worked together as

though they had been partners for years. His playlist included a mix of old and new music—the traditional hymn and contemporary praise song. He sat. He stood. He clapped his hands to the music and urged the congregation to clap with him.

Watching the pleasure on the faces of the mostly older people in the pews provided him with an incredible thirty-five minutes of pure adrenaline slathered on a foundation of spiritual bliss. He'd worried that they wouldn't like some of the newer songs. No doubt some didn't, but most received them with pleasure and worship.

At the end, Kyle led the congregation in singing "How Great is Our God," then returned to the stool. "What an amazing time we've had this morning. Let's give God the glory!"

The congregation joined Kyle in clapping. Several people stood, including Vera. He glanced at Jo. Her grin reflected his own joy. She thought they had finished. Not yet.

"I find one of my greatest pleasures in writing a song. A couple of years ago, I left a Sunday service, feeling God's presence more than usual. That afternoon I wrote what I'd convinced myself was a love song between a man and a woman and performed it in the honky-tonks where our band played." He waited for the gasps and shocked looks, seeing a few, but not as many as he'd expected.

"Recently, someone who heard me perform that song pointed out that it had everything a love song needed . . . a love song to God. I rejected the idea and the suggestion to sing it this morning, thinking it would be like offering God leftovers. Then I went over the lyrics, prayed that God would open my eyes to see what she had seen. He did. God redeems lives. Why can't He redeem a song? I'd like to close with 'I Claim You.'"

* * * *

Jo couldn't have moved from the piano bench if someone had shouted, "Fire!" and everyone in the church dashed out the doors. Not while Kyle performed that special song. Why choose it for this morning, and why not tell her in advance?

Goosebumps ran up her bare arms. The first time she'd heard it, she had known it was special. The words spoke of the calling out of a seeking heart to the One who could fill it with more than a finite, earthly relationship. At least, that was how she'd interpreted the words.

Her attraction to Kyle started that night a year ago. Maybe it began with the difference in his demeanor when he sang it, like now. It was as though he sat alone in the sanctuary, eyes closed, voice soft and prayerful. She closed her own eyes and concentrated on the words, but all she really heard was the thump of her heart in her ears. It beat with gratitude that stemmed from more than a personal spiritual experience. A gratitude she wasn't sure how to classify.

Once the song and the service ended—people approached the altar to speak with both her and Kyle, mostly Kyle. Sutton, Trey, and Lane took their turns, though Sutton appeared quiet, not his usual grumpy, wise-cracking self. She prayed that whatever he'd heard in Kyle's songs would be a life-changer for him.

"We're headed to Ricardo's for lunch," said Lane. "You two want to join us?"

"Can we join you, too?" Brianna dragged Shaina and Harmoni forward. Reagan hung back, a scowl aimed at her sister's head.

Jo held her breath and suspected the others held theirs. Except Kyle. He didn't seem to understand why the atmosphere suddenly grew so tense a machete couldn't hack through it. Leave it to the effervescent Brianna Hartwell to ignore the frowns and stone jaws of her sister and Sutton Vance.

Lane turned to his friend with a silent question. Sutton shrugged. "You go on. I have plenty to do around the farm." He spun on the toes of his boots and walked out.

All eyes turned to Reagan, who threw up her arms. "I'm out of here, too."

"Reagan!"

She ignored Trey's call and followed Sutton's path, storming out the front door of the church.

Brianna shook her head and sighed. "I'm sorry. I hoped for an opportunity to bring everyone together."

"It was worth a try." Lane's melancholy gaze followed Reagan. "Sometimes, it takes time."

"Time? It's been years." Brianna crossed her arms. "Those two are the most stubborn people I've ever met."

"Bad break up?" asked Kyle.

Jo placed her hand on his arm. "Not exactly." She gave him a look she hoped he'd interpret as she'd explain later. Evidently, it worked, because he said nothing more and neither did the others.

She liked the gruff and grumbly Sutton but wanted to shake some sense into him. How fair was it for him to hold the entire Hartwell family responsible for honoring the wishes of the oldest sibling, Paige?

As they left the church, Jo couldn't stop thinking of Reagan. She must be seething at missing the chance for a meal at her favorite restaurant. When would she release her anger at Lane and realize he wasn't responsible for her fiancé's death? After ten years, she still held to her condemnation with both hands. As Sutton held to his.

Jo sucked in a breath. As she held to hers.

Why had she never truly understood how unforgiveness affected relationships with others—those who'd had nothing to do with someone's hurt feelings? Friends and family suffered through the consequences of a couple's broken relationship, too.

She saw the pain on Taylor's face when she rejected his invitation to the concert. Yes, if she were honest, her bitterness affected him, too.

Twenty-two

On Monday morning, the door to Jo E's opened and Lane Becker walked inside, his strides quick and purposeful. Dried mud—mostly dry—splattered his shirt and jeans. A few splashes had pelted his face with ochre globs and spotted his light brown hair.

As he approached the counter, Jo glanced behind him to be sure he hadn't tracked that orangey clay across her floor. At least he'd cleaned the bottom of his western boots. "What happened to you?"

Lane looked down at his clothes and grimaced. "I've got an old stud that decided it'd be funny to roll in the mud, shake it on me, then lead me on a trek through the pasture. I didn't have time to change. As it is, the guys will be at the ranch before I get back."

"Kyle mentioned being part of your repair crew this morning. He's looking forward to it and believes in your mission." They were to start work at nine this morning.

"Thanks." Everyone knew the equine therapy center was to honor Lane's late brother, so they understood the note of sadness in his voice when talking about it.

"When is the opening?"

"We're planning our first session for September. That reminds me. Things will get pretty busy around Crooked Creek. Uncle Monte and I are looking for a cook and housekeeper. Do you know of anyone who might be interested?"

After thinking for a moment, Jo shook her head. "Not right now, but if I come up with someone, I'll send her your way."

"Great. Can I get four Americanos and four cinnamon rolls to go? On second thought, you better make one of those coffees a Sutton Vance special."

"Coming up." Not long after opening her shop, Jo had added the Red Eye to her menu after Sutton requested it. He preferred the brewed coffee with a shot of espresso. With a farm and a houseful of siblings to look after, she could understand why he needed the extra boost of caffeine.

Lane dug into his wallet and handed her a plastic card. "I'm a mess and don't want to run off your other customers. Ring it up, please, and I'll wait outside for my order."

She did as he asked and returned the card before getting busy filling his order.

Bethany added more napkins to the basket on the counter and a handful to the bag holding Lane's rolls. "How can I help you with the party?"

Party? After a confused moment, Jo recalled having mentioned to Bethany a plan to celebrate Kyle's birthday on Sunday afternoon at the coffee shop. "It won't be anything elaborate. Just refreshments and conversation."

"How old will he be?"

"Thirty-two."

A year and three months younger than Jo. That had bothered her at first, given her ex's fondness for younger women. Funny how it didn't bother her now. She was coming to accept that Kyle wasn't Taylor. When Kyle told her something, he kept his word. He hadn't looked twice at cute females like Brianna and Shaina. The image of his hand in Sophia's intruded on her thoughts. No. That was on Sophia. Kyle was only being polite, not wanting to hurt her feelings.

She prepared another of Lane's Americanos. What if Kyle couldn't attend the informal get together? She'd already invited their friends. "Maybe throwing him a surprise celebration is a crazy idea. I don't even know if he likes surprises. What if he hates them or thinks I'm pushing our relationship too far, too fast?"

Was she pushing too fast? They'd had an amazing week since the church concert—hiking, a movie, a picnic in the park, a trip to Winston-Salem to tour historic Old Salem. She'd taken two full days off last week and hadn't regretted a moment. He told her he'd extended his stay in Hidden Veil to the end of June. That gave her another month to get to know him and, maybe, change his mind about leaving.

But what if he didn't feel the same way?

"Don't put that worry cap on."

Jo grabbed a third paper cup and stuck it under the espresso machine. "He could up and leave at any time, Beth. He has a life in Nashville, one I know from experience that I'm not suited to share."

Kyle told her about his Nashville trip and the song Brian asked him to write, the doubt over his ability to accomplish the job, and the hard, yet fulfilling, days he'd spent working with Brian. Kyle was a songwriter. It brought him joy and satisfaction. How could she expect him to give up something that was so much a part of him, a talent God gave him?

She shook her head and added brewed coffee to the espresso in the cup, then grabbed a plastic lid from the stack in the holder on the counter. "No. I think I should rethink the plan."

Bethany exhaled like a snorting bull. "I'm going to say something, and you can fire me if you like, but it's for your own good."

Jo stopped, the lid half-covering the to-go cup marked "Red Eye" with a Sharpie. Steam snaked through the uncovered portion and dampened her hand with its hot moisture. She eyed Bethany's stance—stiff and straight as a broom handle, hands on her hips, feet wide, and eyes fiery. Certain she'd probably regret it, Jo said, "Go ahead."

"Girl, you are the only one in Hidden Veil who doubts your relationship with Kyle. Everyone else is waiting to throw the biodegradable confetti when the two of you begin your life together. Do not get cold feet and let us down."

Biodegradable confetti? Jo had always imagined flower petals should she marry again. Oh, now she really was getting ahead of herself. She snapped the lid on the cup before all the heat escaped.

Bethany sighed and softened her voice. "I don't know what happened between you and that Taylor What's-his-name."

The first time Taylor came into the shop, Jo's friend had

nearly swooned. After Jo's conversation with Brianna and the others, she asked Bethany to keep his visit to herself and told her of her connection to Taylor without badmouthing him. Even so, Bethany had formed a less-than-flattering opinion of him as an ex-husband.

"I understand your caution. But Kyle's a good guy. I know it. See him for who he is, Jo, and don't compare him to someone else based on what he does for a living."

With those words ringing in her ears and the order ready, Jo slipped all the cups in corrugated sleeves and placed them in the disposable tray. She carried everything outside to Lane.

"Here you go. Three Americanos, a Red Eye, and four cinnamon rolls." She handed him the tray and sack with the pastries.

"Thanks, Jo. I'll see you Sunday and will tell Kyle you said hi." He grinned and walked to his truck.

". . . you are the only one in Hidden Veil who doubts your relationship with Kyle."

Okay, a party it would be.

✳   ✳   ✳   ✳

Kyle had driven almost five miles from downtown Hidden Veil when the GPS announced his arrival at Crooked Creek Ranch. Jutting hills covered in lofty oaks, hickories, and pines surrounded rolling pastures. A black mailbox stood next to a stone drive. The name Becker in cast iron crowned the top and confirmed he had the right place.

Sitting a couple hundred feet back from the road was a two-story, Cape Cod-style house built by Lane's retired parents in the eighties. These days, the well-kept home of brick and vinyl siding—a family home—housed two bachelors, Lane and his great-uncle, Monte Becker.

Kyle drove past the house and down a trail—part stone and part dirt—that led to the barn. The SUV's tires *thunk-thunked* as he crossed a wood-planked bridge spanning a narrow creek. An old cabin sat among the trees on his left, its large porch and Adirondack chairs inviting company. To his right, horses grazed in a neat pasture.

Ahead sat a few small outbuildings and a large, red metal barn with an attached lean-to on one side. Parked beneath the safety of the lean-to's roof was a two-horse trailer in front and a larger cattle trailer behind. He chuckled over the pickup trucks near the barn. Here he was driving a "Momma" vehicle. Even if he returned to Nashville for good, he might look into trading in his SUV for a man truck.

If he returned? After last week and working with Brian, was there any doubt? Bouncing ideas off each other and getting a sense of what Brian wanted had stoked a songwriting fire inside Kyle. In the past few weeks, he'd feared he'd lost that ability. Probably, he needed the proper motivation. A chance to hit the charts provided it.

After Brian apologized over his role in the break-up of the band, and once they'd gotten past the awkwardness, the two of them worked well together, as they had for several years.

Brian was a gifted performer, more so than Kyle. He knew how to work a raucous, sometimes inebriated, crowd. Kyle found it embarrassing and irritating to deal with drunks who heckled the band and jumped on the stage. Yeah, sticking with writing songs made more sense for him. He didn't need the money or prestige of performing.

And he could write anywhere, couldn't he? Even Hidden Veil. Everything—everyone—else was a quick plane trip away.

Kyle parked next to an old pickup that had seen better days a decade ago. Two men stepped out of the shady barn and into the morning sunlight to meet him. From the pasture behind him, a horse whinnied.

He climbed from the vehicle. "Where's Lane?"

Sutton adjusted the John Deere cap on his head, revealing a thatch of curly brown hair any woman would envy. "He went for coffee. He ought to be back soon. Glad to have your help."

"Happy to be here."

"Good to see you again, Kyle." Trey reached out and shook Kyle's hand.

"You too."

Another truck rumbled down the drive, this one not nearly as old as the beater on the other side of Kyle's car. A minute later, Lane scooted from the cab, holding a tray and paper sack. The cups had Jo E's Java printed on them.

"Thanks for coming, y'all." Lane sauntered forward, dressed in a muddy tee-shirt and jeans, the scuffed boots Kyle had seen on him the day they met in the feed store, and a blue ball cap that read "Healings Springs Equine Therapy Center."

"What happened to you?" Sutton took three giant strides to Lane's side.

"Don't ask."

Sutton grabbed the tray, checked the cups, and removed one for himself. "I need this."

"Hey, man, don't spill those." Lane rolled his eyes.

"No sweat." Sutton handed out the other coffees.

Kyle took his cup and looked around. "Nice place, Lane."

"Thanks, but I couldn't keep up the property without Uncle Monte. The guy works hard around here and still tends his cattle."

Trey sipped his coffee and said to Kyle, "I hope you're better at construction than I am." He wore a polo shirt with "Abbott's Veterinary Clinic" embroidered on the front, glasses, and no hat. Not quite farm and ranch material like the other two. More citified, like Kyle.

"We'll find out. I'm better at appliances and electrical issues."

Lane glanced up to the sky. "God provides." Sutton released a rude huff, which Lane ignored. "As I told you, we'll work inside the cabin today, getting it ready for the psychologist to use as an office. It will also be a gathering spot for breaks and conversation. I need a ceiling fan installed in the front room and an electrical outlet replaced upstairs. Sutton could do it, but you'll leave him free to help me with a construction project, his specialty." He looked at the vet. "Want to help Kyle?"

"Sure." Trey adjusted his glasses on his nose. "Tell me where to put the smoke alarms, and I'll install those first."

Lane eyed the cabin. "I can't believe I lived there for so long without one."

"Never tell my dad. He'll drop from the shock." Trey turned to Kyle. "He's a fire chief."

Ah.

In minutes, they entered the cabin Kyle had passed earlier. It reminded him of his grandparents' cabin in Tennessee— Kelsey's now—only this one was a decade or two older and larger than his sister's, even with Kelsey's addition of a bedroom and bathroom. The outside looked better than Kelsey's place. The inside smelled of must and soot. Dust floated in the few rays of sunlight that penetrated the trees and beamed through grimy windows bare of curtains or blinds.

Lane stood at the door, hands on his hips. "We have some work to do in here, but the bones are good. The place only needs a thorough cleaning out, a little refurbishing, and some TLC. I'll back my pickup to the porch and we can load the bed."

The four of them spent the first hour hauling boxes and old furniture stored in the cabin out to the porch or loading them onto the bed of Lane's truck.

"Most of this stuff belongs to my parents. Some of it is mine." Lane stared at one box in particular. "Some of it belonged to Matt."

Sutton slapped his friend's back as he passed by to enter the cabin again—a sympathetic slap.

After last week's lunch, Kyle and Jo had spent a couple of hours at the park where she explained the odd reaction to Brianna Hartwell's self-invite to lunch.

He learned that Sutton's animosity toward the Hartwell family came when his relationship with the oldest Hartwell sister ended and she moved away. At her request, her family refused to tell him where she'd gone.

Reagan's anger ran as deep as Sutton's, but she aimed it at Lane. She blamed him for his brother Matt's enlistment in the army and eventual death in Afghanistan. Not only had Lane lost a brother, but Reagan had lost a future husband.

Clearly, under the surface, Hidden Veil was not the

Utopia its residents liked to put forth. It was equally clear that the people he'd met here cared for one another. Even if some warred with others, he'd witnessed family-like bonds between people not blood-related. Maybe that was the best a person could ask of a community.

"The furniture will go back inside once we're finished with the repairs." Lane closed the door behind him, and he and Sutton climbed the stairs to the second floor.

As Kyle installed the ceiling fan, Lane and Sutton hammered and sawed, replacing floorboards in the bedrooms upstairs. Trey installed a smoke alarm in the short hallway near a bathroom, explaining how his fireman father had drilled into him the importance of the alarms. "He's right, but obsessed with fire safety."

"You decided not to follow in your dad's footsteps?"

Trey paused while tightening a screw. "No. I left that to my brother. He's a smokejumper with the U. S. Forest Service in Idaho."

"My dad owns a large appliance company in Atlanta. Kevin, my older brother, works for him. Dad wasn't too happy when I went into the music business."

"I hear you."

Kyle removed the overhead light in the middle of the front room. "I thought you'd be at the clinic today."

"If anything important comes up, Shaina will call me, but Reagan is more than competent." He chuckled. "So much so, sometimes I'm not sure I'm needed."

Kyle hadn't talked with the vet tech, but with long dark hair and a curvy figure, she could easily turn a guy's head. Only the sour expression had marred her good looks on Sunday. She may be competent with animals, but was she pleasant with people? Jo seemed to like her, so he'd reserve his opinion for a proper meeting.

Trey, however, spent the next few minutes extolling the woman's good points—excellent points. It didn't take long for Kyle to see the lay of the land.

"Have you asked her out?"

Trey stopped in the middle of placing a battery in the smoke alarm, and Kyle almost laughed when the guy looked as though he would choke on his tongue. "She's my employee. I won't risk that relationship."

Yeah, keep telling yourself that. "I get it. I shouldn't have poked my nose into your business."

Trey set the cover of the smoke alarm on a rung of the small ladder he'd used and stared at it. "It's okay, but I get enough ribbing from the two upstairs."

"It's probably because anyone can see you care about her."

"Almost anyone," mumbled the vet. "She's waiting for another hero, Kyle. That's not me." A miserable, wry laugh crossed the room. "I'm far from it."

Kyle paused in the middle of attaching a fan blade to a bracket. "I figure most of us have at least a little hero inside us. I mean, look at you. You save people's pets every day. Nobody likes to see an animal suffer. That's got to count for something, so don't sell yourself short."

Trey snapped the cover on the new smoke detector. "That's done. What can I do to help you?"

Kyle pointed the screwdriver at him. "See? Heroes always want to help." That reminded him of Jo's comment that she didn't need him to be her superhero. "Maybe Reagan only needs you to walk alongside her, not take over and save the day."

The vet's eyebrows rose above the frames of his glasses.

Kyle shrugged and returned to attaching the blade to the bracket. "Just a thought."

Something for Kyle to keep in mind, too.

Twenty-three

"You're going to Nashville again?" Jo stopped in the middle of dishing up the chicken and rice casserole she'd made after inviting Kyle for supper. The spoon hovered over the dish.

He stepped behind her and rested his hands on her hips. "I won't be gone long. Brian called and wants to go over the song I've written. If everyone likes it, they'll include it on his album and I'll have a better shot at writing more for other artists."

"Or performing them yourself." How would she handle his traveling for concerts? Knowing he'd leave again this week for a meeting was hard enough.

Kyle nuzzled her cheek, his aftershave competing with the aroma of the thyme and sauce from their meal until she couldn't decide which smelled better, him or the casserole.

Him. Definitely him.

"I like your confidence in me, Ms. Ledbetter."

Jo didn't tell him it wasn't confidence or that thinking

about him performing ruined her appetite. She added a heaping spoonful of the casserole to a plate—his plate. "It seems you had a real brainstorm, considering you couldn't—" She clamped her mouth shut.

He let go of her and backed a couple of steps away. "Couldn't finish a song for weeks? It works that way sometimes."

"What about writing Christian music? I thought you felt the Lord leading you in that direction." She had felt it during the church concert, and while it wouldn't completely resolve her anxiety over his career choice as a musician, it might make it more palatable to know he worked for God rather than himself.

"This song came easily, so I guess I was wrong. Evidently, I only needed encouragement in the sense of having something of mine recorded for an album." Kyle shifted to stand beside her. He tossed a piece of lettuce from their salad into his mouth, showing no awareness of her discomfort over the conversation.

She scooped more casserole into the spoon. "Just because they came easily, Kyle, doesn't mean it's the right move for you."

"I could follow the tracks of your thoughts in the dark, Jo." His voice had taken a guarded turn. Not quite angry, but not quite understanding. "You think my working in the Christian music industry will keep me from straying."

"I never said that."

"No need. I see it on your face, hear it in your words." Kyle drew her to his side until she nearly melted with the warmth of the contact and comfort of his solid body. "We haven't been together long," he whispered in her ear, "but if you don't know by now that I'm not Taylor, I'm not sure what I can do to prove it to you."

Don't go to Nashville.

A sigh drifted over her lips. He could make his own decisions. How could she deny him something that made him happy? If only she could convince her more risk-averse side that everything would work out for them, because he reciprocated these feelings she'd developed for him over the past eight weeks. It started with taking him at his word. It started with trust.

She dropped the spoon in the dish and turned in his arms. "I'm sorry. Of course you're not Taylor. When do you leave?"

"My flight leaves tomorrow morning. I'll be back Saturday night." Kyle leaned down and kissed her—long, slow, and oh so sweet. When he'd convinced her she had nothing to worry about, he pulled back, picked up the plates, and carried them to the kitchen table. "Where's Vera?"

"Gone for the third time in two weeks. She won't tell me where, only that she's going out."

"Maybe she has a hot date." He waggled his eyebrows as he pulled out her chair for her.

"I doubt that." Jo laughed at the idea of her eighty-one-year-old grandmother on a date. As she settled into the chair, though, his words rolled around inside her head. "Do you know something I don't?"

Kyle took his seat at the table. "No, not really."

"Oh, that sounds mysterious. Spill."

"No mystery about it, Jo. I'm as much in the dark as you. Maybe she's letting us have some alone time."

That sounded like her grandmother.

He grasped her hand. "I, for one, am grateful."

Jo cast aside her qualms, choosing to enjoy the evening, especially when she wouldn't see Kyle for a couple of days.

But the doubts loomed like a toxic cloud able to suffocate her.

*   *   *   *

The boys—Ray, Gerald, and Walter—hooted at something they found funny. They'd gathered at the large table, once again, without Bobby or Kyle.

Jo took Gerald and Ray another coffee, plain brewed. They refused to drink the "fancy stuff" she sold. "Where's Bobby this morning?"

"Don't know." Gerald took his coffee and set it on the table in front of him.

"Said he had an obligation." Walter elbowed Ray. "If you ask me, I think it was female business."

They all laughed again.

Female business? "Are you saying he's dating someone?"

Walter peered up. "I'm saying he's awful secretive, and secretive often involves a woman."

How well she knew.

Jo shook off the pain of the past and walked away, her mind sifting through the names of unmarried women who might have attracted Bobby's attention. The list of older widows in town was at least a page long.

While she had a quiet moment, she ground fresh coffee beans in the grinder on the counter along the back wall. With the commercial grinder, she could do a pound in about thirty seconds. Even in that short time, the noise grated on her ears. The smell of the roasted Arabica beans and anticipation of the flavor explosion in a cup of plain, black coffee made up for the annoying sound. She could use the caffeine this morning—pumped straight into her veins.

Bethany leaned with her back against the front counter. "How was your supper Monday night?"

A smile bloomed at the memory before her mouth drooped at recalling Kyle's return to Nashville. "It was nice."

"You two have hit it off. I'm happy for you." Her head tilted. "Come to think of it, I haven't seen Kyle today or yesterday."

"He went to Nashville."

"Two trips in a short time. Things must be good with his music business."

"I guess so."

Probably sensing Jo's unwillingness to discuss it, Bethany dropped the subject and stretched across the counter. She craned her neck, looking toward the older men seated at the side of the room. "Bobby isn't here either. It isn't like him to let the boys meet without him. Do you think he's sick?"

"According to Walter, he said he had another obligation." Jo put the last word in air quotes. Obligation? Funny, that was the word Gran used Monday night to explain her absence from supper.

An hour later, Jo took her last bite of the sandwich she'd brought for lunch, a meal she'd forced down after not eating breakfast. She missed Kyle something fierce.

When the phone rang in the coffee shop's kitchen, she grabbed the pencil alongside the landline, ready to scribble an order.

"Jo E's Java."

"Jo?"

Though the man's trembling voice sounded familiar, she couldn't place it. "Yes. Can I help you?"

"Jo, it's Bobby Goodwin."

"Oh hey, Bobby. We were concerned about you earlier, but the guys said you had other plans this morning."

"Yeah, about that . . . Jo, I'm at the hospital."

"The hospital? Were you in an accident?" Why call her and not one of his sons?

"No, it isn't me. It's Vera."

Jo leaned against the countertop for support. "Gran? What happened?"

"The ER doctor is running tests, but she thinks Vera suffered a heart attack."

Heart attack? Jo's own heart fell like a rock to shatter on the linoleum. Her knees threatened to buckle, and all that held her up was a death grip on the counter. "I'm on my way."

"Get someone to bring you. You shouldn't drive upset."

Her first thought was that Kyle could drive her, but he wasn't around. Everyone else was working, including Bethany, who should remain here to serve their customers. "I'll be fine."

Jo hung up, grabbed her purse, and rushed into the front room of the coffee shop to tell Bethany of the emergency.

"Should I call your pastor?"

Whether the pastor knew didn't concern Jo at the moment.

But on second thought, Gran would appreciate all the prayer available, including Jo's. "Please. I'll keep you informed."

She rushed out the back door, then drove as fast as possible without risking an accident or a ticket. Gran didn't need her injured, too, and being pulled over for speeding would only delay her arrival.

She had to be fine, because Gran needed her.

The automatic doors of the emergency department swooshed open. Jo trotted across the tile floor to the front desk, every nerve tingling. "I'm Jo Ella Ledbetter. They brought my grandmother in earlier. Vera Bevins."

The woman consulted the computer screen in front of her. "Yes. She's in ER 5, but you'll need to wait in the next room. Through the double doors—"

Before she finished, Jo was halfway across the room. When she arrived in the waiting room, Bobby paced in front of a group of chairs. He looked up. "Jo." He wrapped his arm around her shoulders, urging her several feet away from the television in the room. "Let's talk over here."

"What happened?" As Bobby had done, Jo whispered, not wanting to disturb others in the room.

"We went for brunch. She seemed fine, but as we left the restaurant, she collapsed, clutching her chest. I called for an ambulance. In the meantime, the owner of the restaurant gave her aspirin." His hand shook as he ran it through his still-ample head of gray hair. "The doc said it likely saved her life."

Jo nodded, swallowing the lump of emotion in her throat.

No one needed her to break down right now, least of all Gran. "The doctor's with her?"

"Yes."

The door opened, and a doctor walked in. The petite woman couldn't be much older than Jo. "Ms. Ledbetter?"

"Here." Jo hurried toward her. *Please, God, I'm asking that you spare Gran.*

"You're Jo Ella?"

"Yes."

"I'm Dr. Phelps. Mrs. Bevins came in conscious and asking for you."

Jo's fingers trembled inside the doctor's firm hand. "How is she?"

"We're transferring her to the cardiac catheterization lab. They'll run tests to determine whether there's a blockage."

"And if so? Will my grandmother need surgery?"

The doctor patted Jo's arm. "Don't worry. She's in expert hands, and we'll keep you in the loop. Does she see a cardiologist?"

Jo rubbed her forehead. "No. She's never had an issue."

Dr. Phelps glanced at Bobby, then her gaze swung back to Jo. "She was fortunate to have someone with her when the attack came on."

Thank you for Bobby's presence, God. That seemed strange, though.

"There's a waiting room on the second floor. It's best if the two of you stay there. It's where they'll look for you."

She had lots of questions, but the ones pertaining to her grandmother's health would wait until the doctors had run their tests. "Thank you."

"Thanks, Doc." Bobby placed a hand on Jo's back.

Her eyes burned with tears begging to be shed, but Jo held them in. Gran's prophetic words, spoken only weeks ago, returned to taunt her. *"I won't be around forever, not on this ol' earth. We both need to face it. Why, I could keel over any minute. What would happen to you? Death is inevitable, and I can't stand the thought of leaving you alone, Jo E."*

Would a heart attack separate Jo from the woman who meant the world to her? Had Gran experienced a problem and not told her?

Days ago, she might have believed she wouldn't be alone if the worst happened. But now she had no one to lean on. No one to hold on to. No one to wipe away the inevitable tears and tell her everything would be fine.

Not true. She had Bobby. But no Kyle.

After pacing in the waiting room for fifteen minutes, which seemed like fifteen hours, she drew in a shaky breath and dropped onto a stain-splotched chair. Bobby sat next to her and handed her one of the two paper cups he'd carried from a machine in the next room. The steaming coffee inside warmed her icy hands. "You were with Gran at brunch? Or were you just in the same place at the same time?"

A flush covered his craggy face. "We weren't ready to talk about it, but we've been seeing one another for a couple of weeks now."

Jo stared at Bobby. "Seeing? As in dating?"

"Yeah, I guess you could call it that."

Now her grandmother's absences made sense, as did Walter's comment about Bobby having female business. "Why keep it a secret?"

He heaved a breath. "Vera wasn't sure you'd approve." He sipped his coffee, made a face, and set the cup on the table next to his chair. "It's not like yours."

Ignoring his comment about the coffee, she asked, "Gran thought I wouldn't approve of you?"

"Not me." He shrugged. "I hope not, anyway. Your grandmother and I have been friends for years, but Vera knows how close you were to your grandpa. She worried you wouldn't approve of her seeing someone else."

The decline in Grandpa's health had been the deciding factor in Jo's decision to return to Hidden Veil. She wanted to help Gran care for him, and it would have broken her heart to think of him passing without her being at his side. So, she'd come home. Oh, how she missed his smiling face, but . . . "He's been gone for two years. Gran is entitled to move on."

"I'm glad you see it that way. That will put her mind at ease."

Maybe, but as she'd spoken the words, an unwelcome thought entered Jo's mind. Had Gran pushed Jo to remarry, so she could be with Bobby Goodwin? Had she held her grandmother back from sharing a life with someone else, someone who wasn't Grandpa?

Worse, had worry over telling Jo about Bobby put stress on Gran, bringing on the heart attack?

Jo sprang to her feet, her stomach churning. She needed a few minutes alone. "I'll be back in a moment."

She headed to the ladies' room and stood inside the quiet space with her back against a wall, trying to catch her breath. She'd thought she wanted to be alone, but she'd lied. Compelled to hear his voice, to hear him tell her she had nothing to worry about, she pulled her phone from her purse to call Kyle.

After tapping the call icon, Jo waited through five rings before it rolled to voicemail. "Hey, it's Kyle. Leave me a message."

Jo ended the call and returned to the waiting room, the weight of grief slumping her shoulders as she took her seat next to Bobby. "Has anyone come to give an update?"

"Not yet."

Jo and Bobby sat for several minutes in silence until he stood and stretched. "I hate this waiting. I think I'll go for a walk myself."

Not long after he left, Pastor Jim entered the room, and Jo met him halfway. Yet the one person she wished was here, holding her hand and providing encouragement, was hundreds of miles away.

Twenty-four

Kyle itched to get back to Hidden Veil. He missed the coffee shop boys and the other new friends he'd made. He missed the ease of getting around without the heavy traffic. Most of all, he missed Jo. He had intended to return to Hidden Veil by Saturday, but this morning's breakfast meeting nixed that plan.

Brian wanted a finished melody, and he wanted it now. His old partner's nerves teetered on the edge with the desire to record only the best for his first album, so Kyle didn't blame the guy. If their roles were reversed, he'd feel the same.

But they weren't reversed.

Sitting at the keyboard in his bedroom office, Kyle closed his eyes while repeating the first line of the lyrics to Brian's song, focusing on the various pitches. Every songwriter wrote in different ways. For Kyle, the lyrics generally came first, then he used them to find the natural melody.

He held a hand against his stomach and winced. Man, that

breakfast hadn't settled well. The upset stemmed from either the sausages he'd eaten or anxiety over his commitment to stay in Nashville until he'd finished the song.

He drew in a breath. No. This pain was more than mental. It was physical.

At an exuberant knock, he strode through his apartment and opened the door. Toni Atkins waited on the other side. Her grin, wide and natural, had him responding in kind. "Welcome home, stranger."

Odd. Kyle now saw himself as a stranger in this place he'd called home for years. He moved aside for her to enter. "Come on in and have a seat. I wasn't expecting you."

Toni made herself comfortable on his couch, crossing her thick legs and grinning at him like she'd won the lottery. "Brian said you were here, so I thought I'd stop by and give you the good news in person."

He eased into his recliner. "Good news?"

"I ran into Cody Weller at a brunch this morning. We spent a few minutes reminiscing about the band. He remembered your performance of 'I Claim You.'" She inserted a dramatic pause that teased him with more to the story, holding him in suspense. Just as the pause stomped on his last nerve, that broad grin reappeared. "Cody wants to talk with you about adding the song to his next album."

Kyle sat up. Cody had struggled in the business, along with BC's Posse, until he caught a skilled agent's attention—a little like Brian's experience. In the past year, he'd recorded two top twenty songs. "Huh."

She straightened, and her brow creased. "You can do better than that."

He tried to imagine how the song might sound being sung

by Cody. If it became a hit, the songwriting royalties could ease some of his future financial uncertainty. So why this subdued attitude? Probably due to not feeling well. "That would be amazing, Toni."

"He said he'd contact you soon."

"I'll look forward to talking to him."

"You're not as excited as I'd imagined, not as excited as I am. This is great news. So what's wrong?"

What was wrong? He'd already pledged the song to Someone else. "I'll need time to think about it." Pray about it.

"What's there to think about? This is a wonderful opportunity for you, Kyle."

He'd performed the song for the church as praise to God and gave a noble speech about God redeeming it for Himself. A heaviness fell over him, like a light being doused by a canvas tarp, leaving him in darkness. How would it look if he allowed 'I Claim You' to be recorded as a secular song?

I wonder if the better question to ask is if it's really your name you should worry about.

Yet the potential was on the table. Like Brian's request for a song for his album, was this God's sign of direction for his career? Had he been wrong in thinking he should switch his focus to Christian music?

"Kyle?" Toni frowned.

"Yeah, I'll talk to Cody and work something out." Cody might accept another song from Kyle. "I appreciate all you do for me, Toni, especially when it doesn't benefit you."

She moved toward the door. "Listen, I take care of my boys and girls, and one thing leads to another. One day, I'll manage your concert tours. Then, I'll reap the monetary benefit. For now, I enjoy the work."

Once he shut the door behind her, Kyle searched for his phone, finding it on the desk beside the keyboard. He checked for messages. Not wanting to be disturbed while he wrote, he'd put it on mute and forgotten to check it. Mom had called, but she could wait a little longer. What couldn't wait was telling Jo he'd stay in Nashville for a few more days.

After listening to the phone ring and ring, Kyle was about to give up.

"Hello." With that one-word greeting, she'd imparted both distress and distance.

"Hey, Jo. I miss you." A tinny noise in the background—like a voice through a sound system—brought him to attention when someone called for a doctor. "There's something wrong. What's up?"

After a few nail-biting seconds, words tumbled out. "G-Gran had a heart attack."

A bowling ball of anxiety dropped into Kyle's stomach, joining the discomfort already there. Vera had a heart attack? "I'm sorry, Jo. How is she?"

"They're prepping her for an angioplasty and a stent."

Surgery. "Is anyone with you?"

"Pastor Jim and Bobby. Reagan and Mrs. Mulden, Gran's neighbor. I have plenty of company."

At least Jo had people with her. She wasn't alone.

A sense of super hearing kicked in to tell him what she didn't say. *You're not with me.* Another bowling ball labeled "Guilt" slammed into the first one.

Kyle glanced at the lyrics on the computer screen, then at the keyboard. He recalled Brian's agitation that morning over the song not being finished on time. And the contract that could ruin him if he let his personal life keep him from following through on his word.

What about Toni's elation over Cody Weller's interest in his song? Man, that was another dilemma to deal with.

"Kyle?"

But something—someone—had become more important to him than his career. How had it happened so quickly? How had she burrowed into his heart to this extent? But he cared for both Jo and Vera. Because of it, he couldn't let them down. "I'll catch a flight back this afternoon."

A sob broke over the phone. "Thank you."

Those two words relieved the weight of the bowling balls, even as his stomach continued to burn.

* * * *

Jo wished she could say she'd never experienced such a shattering time in her life. She couldn't. This ranked up there with the loss of her marriage and the grief of watching her grandfather's life fade away. Thankfully, she was too emotionally exhausted to cry anymore.

And Kyle would return soon.

She occupied a chair in the waiting room with its sterile walls, bland furniture, and a wall-mounted TV. The channel no one had changed played some home renovation program, the old structure reminding her of Gran's house. She left her seat when her mind compared a house renovation with Gran's surgery. Her grandmother was almost forty-five minutes into a heart renovation.

Jo's phone dinged and her empty stomach lurched,

expecting to see Kyle's text with his flight information from Nashville and his arrival time in Hidden Veil.

Was it selfish to want him to drop everything to be by her side? Perhaps. She'd been an independent woman for a long time—a big girl, able to handle an emergency without a man's shoulder to cry on. But the simple thought of having him here eased the burden she carried.

She checked the message. A gray cloud of disappointment hung over her. Bethany texted, asking for an update. She typed a brief response and hit send.

"Are you okay, Jo?"

She jumped at the light touch that landed on her arm, not having heard Reagan approach. "It's the waiting."

"The doctor said the surgery would be at least an hour, then Vera will spend time in recovery. Many people are praying for both of you. She'll be fine." Reagan leaned closer. "Does Kyle know?"

Their friends already associated Jo and Kyle together as a serious couple, and she found the idea . . . appealing. Her attitude toward him had changed in a matter of weeks. Enough to admit the injustice of her prejudice against all musicians?

"He's still in Nashville, but on his way. I had planned that get-together for his birthday on Sunday."

Reagan nodded. "I'll let everyone know it's canceled."

"Thanks."

"How about a soda or something? Have you had anything to eat?"

"I'm not hungry." Jo gave her friend a quick hug. "I appreciate you being here when you should be working." Unlike Kyle, who could write his songs almost anywhere,

Reagan could only accomplish her work at the clinic.

"When Trey heard about Vera, he insisted I come to keep you company." Reagan returned the brief squeeze.

"He's a great guy."

"He's a great boss."

Okay, maybe she had been wrong and there was nothing romantic between her two friends, at least on Reagan's part.

Jo glanced at the clock on the wall. Over an hour had passed since Gran went into surgery. What if the worst happened? What would she do?

"How can the ups come if you're busy worrying about the downs?"

Gran had spoken of the ups and downs of romantic love, but didn't the same apply to any relationship? Joys and disappointments walked hand-in-hand when any definition of love was involved. With God's help, she would learn to accept whatever came—with Gran and with Kyle.

"Isn't that the doctor?"

At Reagan's question, Jo looked up. The cardiologist walked toward them. She studied his facial expression, his body language, to gauge whether the news was good or . . . not so good. He gave nothing away.

He stopped in front of her. "Your grandmother is in recovery, Ms. Ledbetter. The surgery went well, and she'll go to ICU soon."

Jo's chin dropped to her chest. An odd sound, something between a snivel and a giggle, burst out of her. *Thank you, God!*

* * * *

243

Kyle stared at the boarding pass on his phone as his body sprawled across the couch. His bag waited by the apartment door, and the plastic trash can from his bathroom sat on the floor . . . within puking distance.

He should be halfway to the airport. Jo needed him. He needed to be with her and to see for himself how Vera fared. He would, too, but . . .

His gut roiled. How could he travel for over three hours, to include a layover at the airport in Charlotte, feeling like death squeezed his insides?

Ninety-nine percent sure of the culprit—those sausages— Kyle couldn't risk that his sudden illness was a stomach bug. He moved his free hand from his abdomen to his forehead. No fever. No chills. But he couldn't chance passing on something viral to Jo, who might pass it on to Vera.

No. He wasn't leaving his apartment today.

Kyle moaned, not with pain but at the thought of telling Jo. She'd broken down over the phone, grateful for his decision to drop everything to be with her. Now he had to disappoint her.

The sooner he got it over, the better.

The phone went off. According to the screen, he was too late. He tapped to answer. "Hey, Jo."

"I didn't know if you were on your way, but I figured I'd call."

"Yeah, Jo—"

"Gran came through the surgery with no complications. She's in recovery."

A lightness filled Kyle's chest as he thanked God for the way He answered everyone's prayers for Vera. The good news did nothing for his stomach. "That's great, babe."

"Are you okay? You sound funny."

"Yeah, I'm . . ." Why pretend when he had to tell her, anyway? "No, not really. Listen, I won't make it back there tonight."

A few beats passed. "Oh."

"I'm sick and can't get back today. I don't know when I'll feel up to traveling."

A few more beats of silence. "I'm sorry, Kyle. Of course, you can't travel. Have you seen a doctor?"

"I'm sure it's food poisoning. Don't worry about me. Take care of Vera, and I'll get there as soon as I can. Just keep me updated on her condition, okay?"

"Sure. Get some rest."

"I will."

He clicked off in time to grab the trash can.

Twenty-five

Kyle stood inside the vet clinic, waiting for Davey. For his last trip to Nashville, he'd driven and taken the dog with him. This time, he'd flown and boarded Davey at Trey's clinic.

He placed his hand against his stomach. Still queasy. Nothing like the last two days, but it had grown worse in the past couple of hours. He'd never eat another breakfast sausage for the rest of his life. The anti-everything pills he'd downed had helped, and by mid-morning, he chanced a flight.

Between bouts of sickness yesterday, Kyle worked on Brian's song, achieving more than he'd expected. Yet Brian let him know what he thought of him leaving Nashville early. Kyle let it roll off his back, able to finish the song anywhere. Brian simply wanted control over the process.

Reagan brought Kyle his dog and handed him the leash. "Thanks." The bullmastiff's tail wagged, but his gaze remained on Reagan.

"Let's go, bud." He tugged on Davey's leash, trying to get the dog out of the veterinary clinic and into the car. It was like pulling a healthy, fifty-year-old oak from the ground with a lariat of twine.

"Come on, dude. I need to get you home, then I have another stop to make." He should have run his errand first, but he wasn't thinking straight. Did food poisoning make a person inept?

Jo texted a brief message yesterday to say her grandmother was improving and expected to be transferred to a regular room. She'd added she hoped he felt better and ended by saying he shouldn't hurry back.

While he appreciated her consideration, the tone of that last bit bothered him. Why wouldn't she want him to rush to support her during this time, at least, returning as fast as he could under the circumstances?

"Need some help?" Reagan Hartwell's rosy lips twitched at Kyle's fruitless efforts to budge Davey. The dog ought to at least act like he missed Kyle.

"He likes it here and doesn't want his vacation to end."

She caressed Davey as though he were a baby, smooth-talking him until he followed her to the door. Trey was right. She was good.

Reagan's forthright gaze zeroed in on Kyle. "I apologize for Sunday. My sister caught me by surprise."

"Things like that happen." He had no desire to step into the whole Reagan-Lane feud and take sides. "I heard you were at the hospital during Vera's surgery. How was Jo doing?"

"She was a wreck until the doctor told her everything was fine." Reagan opened the door to the Abbott Veterinary

Clinic, propping it open with her body as he walked into the sunshine with Davey trotting at his side. "I came back here soon after. How was she doing when you arrived?"

Evidently, she hadn't spoken to Jo and wasn't aware he hadn't flown in on Wednesday night. He loaded Davey into the SUV and attached the restraint tether to his harness. "I haven't seen her yet. I had food poisoning and didn't make the flight then or yesterday."

"Ugh. Been there. But I'm sure she'll be glad to see you." Reagan winked, then leaned into the vehicle. "Bye, Davey. Come stay with us again soon."

After dropping his dog off at the house, Kyle drove into downtown Hidden Veil. He parked in the lot behind the row of buildings that faced Main Street. Now for the hard part. He needed to enter All That Blooms without Bethany seeing him from the coffee shop across the street. Kyle wasn't worried about Jo since he expected her to be at the hospital. Hopefully.

His stomach rolled. He probably should have called the florist to place his order, but he wanted to examine the quality of their product first. Like he was some expert in floral design.

Kyle stuffed his hands in the front pockets of his jeans and rounded the corner onto Main Street. Keeping his head low and his shoulders hunched, he tried to hide in plain sight.

Until he plowed into a body—a soft and petite body.

He reached out, catching the woman's waist to keep her from falling. "I'm sorry. I wasn't watching where I was going. Are you all right?"

Her arms wrapped around his shoulders. "Oh, I'm more than all right."

At the seductive tone, Kyle dropped his hands and stifled a groan. *Sophia.* He struggled to recall her last name while trying not to grimace. Other than her first name, all he remembered about her was her talent for flirting.

He resisted glancing at Jo E's.

Sophia gazed up at him, beaming, her fingers still clutching his shoulders like ten creepy leeches. Her laughter covered the sound of a passing car. "It's been a while."

Not long enough. Kyle wiped away his annoyance and fumbled for a polite smile.

"How is that sweet dog of yours?"

"Good." He hadn't thought she'd even noticed Davey the day she flirted with him outside Jo's place. He stepped back, forcing her to drop her hold on him. "Well, uh," he rubbed the back of his neck, "I'm in hurry, so I'd better—"

"You promised me coffee the next time we met."

He didn't remember it that way. In fact, he'd been purposely vague in his comment about possibly bumping into her in town sometime. He hadn't meant it literally. And to think he'd almost reached the florist and safety.

Kyle had seen Sophia's kind too often to count. Women like her only responded to bluntness. "Listen, Sophia, I'm flattered by your interest, but I'm seeing someone else, someone I don't want to lose. It isn't a good idea—"

"Jo?"

His patience wavered on the edge. "Yeah, so that coffee won't be possible." *Coffee or anything else.*

Her jaw tightened, then relaxed. Before he could say goodbye, she clamped her hands on either side of his face and drew his mouth down to meet hers, kissing him like they stood in a private place. Alone. Kissing him as though he cared about her. Not a drawn-out kiss, but one packed with power and possession. A kiss he did nothing to stop.

She stepped back, turned, and strutted inside the insurance office. He stood outside All That Blooms, staring in shock.

Kyle flashed a quick glance across the street, blew out a shaky breath, and stepped into the florist shop.

Good thing, for Sophia's sake, his illness really was food poisoning and not a stomach bug. He hoped.

With the way he still felt, maybe he should rethink his plan to visit the hospital this afternoon.

* * * *

Having stopped by the coffee shop before driving back to the hospital, Jo delivered Garnet Clark's coffee order, a service she only offered the nonagenarian—a fancy term for a 90-something person she'd learned from Gran.

She spent a few minutes wandering around Yesteryear Antiques and Collectibles. Mrs. Clark had crammed the store with old things, large and small. The objects gave the store the organized but light-filled appearance of a dusty Victorian attic. Garnet Clark was a treasure in herself, and Jo's mood brightened with the few minutes she'd spent with her.

The previous two days had sapped her—emotionally and physically. First Gran's heart attack, then this nagging concern over Kyle's absence. Sure, he'd sounded sick on Wednesday and promised to return as soon as he felt well again. But she couldn't get out of her head his response when she asked if he was all right. *"Yeah, I'm . . ."* He'd caught himself in mid-sentence and changed his answer to a no. As though he almost told the truth and changed his mind?

Jo hated the suspicion and distrust amped by memories of Taylor lying to her about where he was and what he was doing. By the time yesterday afternoon rolled around, she'd convinced herself it would be best if Kyle didn't hurry back. She had no room for the added stress of pretending his absence didn't matter.

She opened the front door of the antique store and stepped onto the sidewalk. A couple down the street caught her attention. The woman, Sophia, stood in front of the insurance agency, embracing a man.

Jo's eyes widened, and her chest tightened. Not just any man. *Kyle.*

His hands clutched Sophia's waist while hers gripped his shoulders. Did she think she'd fall if she let go? And what was he doing in town? He hadn't called or texted to say he was returning. As far as she knew, he was still in his bed in Nashville, not here in Hidden Veil. With Sophia. Holding her!

After slipping into the shadows of the antique store's doorway, she couldn't stop the compulsion to peer around the front display window. A gasp choked her. Now he was kissing Sophia. Out in public. Across the street from the coffee shop.

She darted into the doorway's shadows and pressed her back against the window glass, fighting to catch her breath. Didn't he realize, if she were at work inside Jo E's, she might see them? Obviously, he only cared about kissing a young, beautiful woman.

If he cheated on her when she could see, what had he done

while she wasn't looking?

On second thought, when had he left Nashville? Yesterday? Wednesday? Jo had no proof he'd ever left Hidden Veil.

Her eyes filled until she couldn't see any clearer than if she looked through the glass bottom of the old Coke bottles she'd examined in the antique store.

Sophia was gorgeous and young and personable. Why shouldn't he want to be with her?

Jo's heart sank into a quagmire of insecurity and bad memories. She couldn't—wouldn't—go through the heartache and humiliation of that type of betrayal again.

Half of her felt vindicated in her belief that another musician was not in her future. The other half wanted to rush home and curl into a ball on her bed.

Either way, she was done with Kyle Callahan and anyone else who strapped on a guitar, skated fingers across piano keys, or crooned a ballad with a voice she could get lost in.

At least she'd learned early on she couldn't trust Kyle or depend on him to be with her in a crisis. She considered herself fortunate to have discovered those things. Really.

If only she'd done so before losing her heart to him.

Heart. Look at the heart. Those words continued to repeat in the depth of her spirit.

She had looked and found little difference in Kyle's and Taylor's hearts.

* * * *

With each lift of Jo's feet, the toes of her shoes skimmed the edge of the porch steps. She trudged to the front door, slipped the key in the lock, and entered the house.

If not for the two children expecting piano lessons from her this evening, somehow, she would summon the strength to drag herself up the steps leading to the second floor and down the hall to her bedroom. But then, she might give in to the urge to sprawl on her bed for a good cry.

How could she have been so stupid?

She tossed her purse onto the living room couch and flopped down next to it, drained—mentally, physically, and, especially, emotionally.

Over and over, Jo saw the image of Kyle and Sophia kissing on the sidewalk on Main Street. They hadn't had the decency to do it in the shadows. Later in the afternoon, the woman had the gall to come into Jo E's and order coffee. Bethany said her step was light and smile as bright as a headlamp. Thankfully, Jo hadn't been there.

But she had received a text from Kyle saying he still wasn't one hundred percent well and wouldn't see her until tomorrow. What a joke. He'd been well enough to kiss someone else.

The doorbell rang. She groaned, slid off the couch, and opened the front door. Mrs. Mulden stood on the porch, an aluminum foil-wrapped dish in her hands.

"There you are." She pushed past Jo and entered the house, the smell of a casserole following her. Sweet as she was, Mrs. Mulden had no more sense of boundaries than her dog. "I made one of your favorites, Jo."

She inhaled and could visualize the steaming beef and gravy. "Stroganoff?"

"Yep."

Now Jo truly wanted to cry. She'd skipped lunch and loved the neighbor's Beef Stroganoff, a dish Mrs. Mulden took to just about any pot luck. But as hungry as Jo was, how could she eat with her stomach tied in knots? "You shouldn't have gone to the trouble."

"Nonsense. You've spent all your time at the hospital. It's the least I could do." The woman moved closer, studying Jo's face. "What is it, Jo? You look done in. Please don't tell me Vera took a turn for the worse."

Jo's throat tightened, but she refused to give in to tears or confess her troubles. "I'm just tired. It's been a long week."

"I'm sorry, honey. You know, something else waited for you to come home." Mrs. Mulden's eyes sparkled and her creased skin dimpled even more with her wink. She shoved the casserole into Jo's hands. "Let me go home and get them."

"Get what?"

"You'll see. They showed up this afternoon and were placed on your porch. I didn't want to see them wilt, so I took them to my house. Be back in a sec."

The woman dashed out the door, her sixty-six-year-old legs moving with gusto. Jo carried the casserole to the kitchen and set it on the counter, tempted to grab a fork and dig in. It smelled amazing.

Less than ninety seconds passed before Mrs. Mulden hurried into the kitchen, her hands full. She placed a vase with an ample bouquet of various flowers on the table—pink roses, white carnations, and pink and white alstroemeria blooms. It covered the center of the table and added a faint sweetness to the smell of the Stroganoff.

Jo walked across the room to get a closer look. "You

bought flowers?"

Mrs. Mulden grinned from ear-to-ear. "Not me. I told you. They arrived this afternoon."

"They must be for Gran. I'll take them to the hospital in the morning."

"No, honey. They aren't for Vera. They're yours."

"Mine?" Who sent them? Ugh. It would be like Taylor to use their beauty in an attempt to win her over. But she hadn't heard from him since she'd turned down his invitation to his concert.

The only other person . . .

She swallowed and pulled the card with her name on it from its clear plastic holder. Had he spotted her watching from down the street? Was this his attempt to gain her forgiveness?

Jo turned the card over and read the message.

I've missed you and look forward to seeing you tomorrow. Love, Kyle

Seriously? What she'd seen this afternoon was him missing her? And why not tonight?

She grabbed the vase and marched to the door leading to the one-car garage.

"What are you doing, Jo?"

Crossing the concrete floor, she opened the lid of the large, plastic trash can and dropped Kyle's example of his love inside, cringing at the sound of shattering glass as it hit bottom.

When she turned, Mrs. Mulden stood in the doorway, her mouth open and eyes wide. "Jo Ella Ledbetter, what is going on?"

"Thank you for the dinner. That was sweet of you and I'll enjoy it. But if you'll excuse me, my first piano student arrives soon."

The poor woman shuffled out the back door, her expression twisted with confusion. Jo had no room in her thoughts for confusion when anger took up the space.

From the start, she knew Kyle could shatter women's hearts. Before the trip to the zoo, though, she had vowed she wouldn't be one of his victims. She had broken her own vow.

Twenty-six

Kyle dropped his phone on the bedspread beside him. He'd stared at the screen countless times. Listened for the special tune that played with a phone call or the *ding* that indicated a text. Nothing. Not one response from Jo to his phone call last night. She hadn't even acknowledged the flowers delivered yesterday afternoon.

He knew little about All That Blooms. Were they a reputable florist? What if Jo hadn't received the arrangement? The owner had seemed friendly and competent, assuring him they would deliver his order as soon as possible. The arrangements he'd seen were fresh and stunning.

Kyle shifted the pillow propped against the headboard and crossed his ankles on the mattress. He'd grown up with three sisters all too eager to school him in the "language" of flowers and their colors.

Language of flowers? Who comes up with these things,

anyway?

For him, the pink he'd chosen represented the way he saw Jo—soft, sweet, and feminine, like his sisters.

He winced. Like his sisters? What was he thinking?

Red roses were fiery. Exciting. Passionate. Jo could be red—fiery and sexy and loving.

Kyle hung his head. Aww, man. He should have picked the red.

But red roses meant love. Was he ready to go down that road? How long before you realized you loved someone? Already, he could admit that what he felt for Jo knocked on the door of intense emotion. And he had signed that card with the word "Love," not something he'd ever done before.

Maybe that was the reason he hadn't heard from her. Had she taken his choice of pink as a representation of bland feelings or friendship? Or what if he'd scared her off with that "Love, Kyle" line?

Or . . .

A shocking thought screeched through Kyle's brain like a bird of prey, the flapping of the words beating inside his head. He snatched his phone and called the one person who would commiserate with him while setting him straight.

"Hello? No one is calling you, Goliath." The last part sounded muffled, like Kelsey had covered the phone.

Davey's brother barked in the background. Ordinarily, Kyle would have laughed, but this wasn't an ordinary call.

"So, what's wrong that you're calling me early in the morning?" His sister changed gears faster than a NASCAR driver.

"I think I did something stupid."

"You? Never."

"Hey, it may be early, but I'm not too sleepy to recognize sarcasm when I hear it."

She laughed. "Sorry. Tell Dr. Callahan your problem."

"I'm serious, Kels."

"Okay. Tell me."

"You know I've been seeing Jo—"

She gasped. "You proposed! Please do not tell me that is your something stupid."

He pinched the bridge of his nose. "I could always call Mom and talk to her."

"Desperation noted. Go on."

She listened without interruption as Kyle explained about his trip to Nashville, Vera's heart attack, the food poisoning, and the flowers he'd sent Jo. He included his choice of color and Jo's lack of response. "She isn't the type to ignore something like that without a thank you. Why haven't I heard from her? I should have sent her red roses, right?"

Here he was, a thirty-two-year-old man—three days from now—caught in a panicked attempt to consult his younger sister for relationship advice. Something was wrong with this picture, but as she'd said, he was desperate and didn't care.

"Calm down, bro. I'm only going by what you've told me of her, but I'm sure it has nothing to do with your relationship or the color of the flowers you sent. Her grandmother had a heart attack. The woman has a lot on her mind. It's possible she spent the night at the hospital and hasn't seen them yet."

Kyle bolted upright on the bed and stopped short of slapping his forehead. "What an idiot I am." And self-absorbed.

"Mmm . . ."

"Don't say it."

The rumble of a chuckle answered for her. "You're back in Hidden Veil?"

"I risked throwing up on the person sitting next to me on the plane and flew home early yesterday afternoon. By the time I finished my order at the florist, I wasn't feeling well enough to see Jo or her grandmother."

"Then Jo doesn't know you're back?"

"I texted yesterday afternoon and called last night. No response. I guess that squashes the theory of her spending the night at the hospital."

"Unless she turned her phone off."

Maybe. But he had a sinking feeling that wasn't the case.

Monday night, when Kyle first told Jo of his trip to Nashville, she had shown no enthusiasm. After a while, she acted as though she accepted it and wished him a productive trip, saying she couldn't wait until he returned. She'd capped the evening off with a series of kisses that had him thinking twice about going.

Something happened between then and now that caused her lack of communication. Time to confess all. "I can guess why I haven't heard from her."

"Is this the something stupid?"

"It depends." Most likely.

"On what?"

"Whether Jo knows." Kyle told Kelsey of yesterday's encounter with Sophia, her kiss, and—the stupid part—the shock that kept him from reacting as he should. "Not only that, but we were across the street from the coffee shop."

"Whoa. She could have seen what happened."

No kidding. "I checked the parking lot behind the coffee

shop before I went to the florist. Her car wasn't there, so I assumed she'd gone to the hospital."

"You were standing on Main Street, Kyle. She didn't need to be there. What if someone else told her?"

Like Bethany? Bobby? No, he couldn't imagine either of them saying anything to Jo before reaming him. But Jo knew many people in town. Any of them might have said something.

He ran a hand through his hair. "I should have pulled away from Sophia, making it clear to anyone watching that the kiss wasn't my idea."

"It's too late for that."

Unfortunately. "How do I manage this problem, Kels? More flowers? Groveling at Jo's feet?"

"You don't manage it, Kyle. You tell her the truth. It's possible she hasn't contacted you for another reason. If people in that town are as familiar with one another as you've said, it isn't a matter of *if* she finds out. It's a matter of *when.* That snake-in-the-grass Sophia seems just the person to tell her."

A definite possibility. "You're right. I need to be the one to tell Jo, or it will cement her belief that there's no difference between me and Taylor Morris."

"You know what you've got to do, brother, and the sooner, the better."

"Yeah. I'm feeling back to normal this morning and headed to the hospital soon."

"Do you realize you called Hidden Veil your home?"

Kyle went back over the conversation. He had, hadn't he?

His cell phone vibrated. "Hold on. I have a text from Jo."

Thank you for the flowers. Jo Ella

That was it? And both the first and middle names? His now-normal stomach clenched, and he rubbed his forehead. "I think it's too late to tell her, Kelsey."

* * * *

Kyle shifted the colorful bouquet of mixed spring blooms to his other hand and pressed the elevator button.

After Jo hadn't answered her phone Friday night, he called the hospital to check on Vera's condition. Of course, they refused to give out any information, something he'd anticipated. He called Bobby and learned that they had transferred her to a regular room. Bobby never asked why he hadn't called Jo for the information. Either he was too worried about Vera to focus on that detail or he already knew something wasn't right.

What if Jo sat with her grandmother this morning? He'd called her twice, finally accepting that she didn't want to talk to him.

Once the elevator doors swished open and he entered the car, Kyle punched the button for the hospital's third floor. Alone in the elevator, he propped his back against the rear wall and prayed for the courage to face Jo.

The elevator doors parted, and Kyle braced himself for whatever awaited him. He followed the sign directing him to the room where they'd transferred Vera. Would Jo refuse to let him in?

He listened for conversation inside, then peeked through

the opened door. Vera, small and fragile-looking, dozed in the bed, the room empty of visitors. He turned to leave.

"Come on in here, Kyle."

He crossed the room in four strides, stopping alongside the bed. "I didn't want to wake you."

"Who can sleep with all the activity?"

He grinned at her quiet but spirited response. "How do you feel?"

"I won't lie. I've felt better. The heart doctor says I'm doing as well as my age will let me."

"I'm glad to hear it."

Her soft laugh sounded more like a puff of air. "If I'm a good girl, I'll leave this place tomorrow or Monday. How do you feel? Jo said you were ill."

"Good as new."

"When'd you get back in town?"

"Yesterday afternoon. I put off seeing you until I was certain I wouldn't bring something with me."

"Pull up a chair." Her words came out hoarse and tired. She pointed to the flowers. "Looks like you brought something, anyhow. Are those for me?"

"No one else." He handed over the mixture of white, pink, and purple flowers. Not a gardener, the only ones he'd recognized were daisies.

"Beautiful, honey. I'll ask the nurse to put them in water." Vera set the bouquet on the bedside table. Other plants and arrangements filled the room, along with a couple of helium "Get Well" balloons. Clearly, people loved this lady. "How was your trip to Nashville?"

"Productive."

If he were honest, the past couple of days, his thoughts

had fluctuated between guilt over considering Cody Weller recording his song and a concern for Vera's health. Yesterday, he'd added to the worry that he'd ruined his relationship with Jo.

"I asked Jo E about you last night. I think something is wrong." Vera reached out and laid a weak, bony hand against his cheek. "I don't know what happened between you and my girl, but don't let her get away. I like you too much, and she needs someone like you."

Like him? Would Vera change her mind if she knew about Sophia?

He winked, avoiding the subject. "Are you expecting Bobby to walk through that door? I hope you aren't using me to make him jealous."

She lowered her hand. "That old buzzard?" But her expression softened. "You heard we were seeing each other?"

"Jo said the two of you went to brunch. I put two and two together."

"He's a good man . . . like you."

Kyle didn't feel like a good man.

He turned at hearing footsteps on the tile floor behind him. Jo walked into the room. She saw him and stuttered to a stop. Her steady gaze rested on him rather than her grandmother. "Hey, Jo."

"Kyle."

He stood to give her his chair, but she moved to the other side of the bed. "How are you this morning, Gran?"

"Ready to go home."

Kyle waited as the two of them discussed the doctor's latest instructions and all the things she couldn't do once she returned home in a day or two.

Vera yawned. "If you don't mind, Jo E, I'm tired. I need some sleep."

A moment of confused indecision flashed across Jo's face before she settled the bedsheet over her grandmother's shoulders. "Sure, Gran. I'll sit here."

"No, honey. You go with Kyle to the cafeteria for some breakfast. I hear the food's good enough. In the meantime, I'll get some winks."

"I'll see you later, Vera." Kyle walked out the door with Jo following. "I don't know about you, but I could eat breakfast."

Jo shook her head. "I've spent little time at the coffee shop these last days. I should check on things there."

Kelsey was right. He needed *everything* on the table and out in the open. The sooner it came from him, the better. "Jo, we need to talk." When she hesitated, he added, "Vera expects us to eat breakfast in the cafeteria. We shouldn't upset her." That last wasn't fair, but he couldn't let Jo leave without hearing him out.

She walked several feet down the hall, and he thought he'd lost her. Then she stopped and turned. "I am a little hungry."

Twenty-seven

A little hungry? Oh, please. You ate breakfast an hour ago and couldn't stuff another thing in your mouth.

Carrying a tray with a serving of toast and a glass of water, Jo weaved through the half-filled hospital cafeteria to a table along a side wall. The location allowed them more privacy than other tables. "Here?"

"Suits me." Kyle placed his tray on the table. He'd loaded it with a pile of scrambled eggs, three bacon strips, two biscuits, and a yogurt/granola parfait.

The idea of eating all that food left Jo nauseous. She settled in a chair across the table and removed her plate and coffee from the tray. "You didn't eat breakfast before coming to the hospital?"

"I haven't eaten much since Wednesday. This morning, I was in a hurry to see Vera. Prayer?"

Jo almost declined, thinking it hypocritical of him. Instead, she nodded, and he reached across the table for her hand. She folded her hands in her lap. He frowned and withdrew his arm.

After the "Amen," she picked up her fork. If only she'd gripped his hand with the same control and confidence as she did the utensil and shown him that his behavior didn't faze her. But she couldn't think of anything other than his kissing Sophia—in public for her and all her friends to see. He'd humiliated her.

What was the difference between Kyle's unfaithfulness yesterday and seeing photos on social media of Taylor in the arms of various women? None.

Jo focused on her eggs, sliding a small amount onto her fork, and the headache she woke up with this morning roared. Kyle had called last night, but she'd let it go to voice mail. Oh, how sweet and caring he'd sounded on the phone—like the serpent in the Garden of Eden.

He picked up his coffee cup and took a sip. "Vera looks good, tired, but good."

"The doctors look at her age and condition, then they smile at how well she's doing." Jo sat amazed by the calm in her voice and her ability to carry on a normal conversation. Inside, temptation pushed her to hurl accusations at him.

"That's great news." He set his cup down. "I'm sorry I couldn't be here earlier. How are you dealing with Vera's attack?"

Distraught. Frightened. Deceived. Betrayed. All the adjectives fit, though the last two involved him and not Gran.

"I'm fine, now that she's healing." Jo didn't want to discuss her state of mind. "How did your time in Nashville go, other than during your illness, of course?" If there was an illness.

Kyle studied her, then shrugged. "Up and down. Brian liked the lyrics, and Toni stopped by my apartment with some good news. She said Cody Weller wants to record a song I wrote."

Jo had heard the name on the radio. He had a couple of country music hits under his belt. It sounded as though Kyle considered Cody Weller's request good news, so the singer must have influence. She couldn't quite bring herself to say she was happy for Kyle. She picked up her coffee cup. "Which song?"

He poked at a piece of egg but didn't put it on his fork . . . or look at her. "'I Claim You.'"

Jo used every ounce of self-control inside her to set her cup down without a clattering thud that would alert everyone around them of her irritation. "When you performed the church concert, you said you realized the true meaning of that song."

He stiffened into a granite statue. "It's a great opportunity, Jo. Cody has already had two hits. His next CD releases soon after Brian's does, which means my name will be out there twice in a short time. Hopefully, that draws interest in my work."

Jo pushed her plate away, her stomach rippling with tension. Not only was he unfaithful to her, he was unfaithful to God. "Then you've decided songwriting for the country music market is the road you'll follow? What about performing?" Her calm had disappeared.

He broke a biscuit and dropped both halves on his plate. "Plenty of songwriters also perform." Two vertical ruts formed between Kyle's eyes. "I won't let what I do for a living affect our relationship."

Her jaw tightened. "Either you're naïve or you think I am. It's already affected us."

Kyle exhaled and sat back in his chair. "I know I wasn't here for you after Vera's heart attack. I wanted to be, but—"

"But you had a good excuse. I know. I've heard them before."

He peered at the people entering and leaving the cafeteria and lowered his voice. "I called you several times. You never answered."

Jo's head pounded. It started last night after her tantrum resulted in tossing Kyle's flowers in the trash. "I responded this morning."

"With a lukewarm text." He pushed his half-finished breakfast aside. "I saw a small, private sitting area outside. There's something else I want to discuss with you. Why don't we go out there?"

Jo swallowed. It was one thing for her to reject him. It was another to realize that he wanted a private talk so he could reject her. Honestly, she understood why he no longer wanted her. She could be a hot mess of insecurity and neediness on a good day. Today was not a good day.

Yet wasn't this why she had agreed to accompany him to breakfast? To end things between them . . . for good?

As soon as they stepped outside, the heat and humidity in the air sapped Jo's breath. Kyle led her to a bench, but she remained standing, so he did, too.

"Something happened yesterday, and I need to tell you about it." He reached for her. "I care a lot for you, Jo, so I—"

"Don't." She raised her hands to fend him off. "I'd rather you not spout some excuse to end our relationship. We . . . I had a good time, but—"

"I'm not ending anything. Why would I when I meant what I said on that flower shop card?"

"About missing me?" *Fat chance.*

"I did, and I signed it with the word love. That word isn't something I casually throw out there."

Oh, how she wanted to believe him, but the evidence proved otherwise. "Yesterday afternoon, I took Garnet Clark a coffee. When I left the antique store . . ." Her voice froze. Why couldn't she spit the words out?

A flush colored his face. "You saw Sophia and me."

Jo nodded.

"I thought as much when you wouldn't respond to my calls." He drew closer, stopping before invading her space. "What you saw wasn't the way things happened."

"Something else I've heard before."

"All I can do is ask you to trust me and believe I didn't initiate that kiss."

Kyle seemed sincere, but so had Taylor. "And you didn't end it."

The flush deepened in color. "That's true. She caught me by surprise. That won't happen again."

"Even if you had kissed her first, Kyle, it doesn't change the fact that other issues stand between us."

He spread his feet and crossed his arms. "My choice of career?"

"You were the one I wanted sitting alongside me in that waiting room, but you were hundreds of miles away when I needed you."

"I explained—"

"Yes, you did." Jo hugged her waist. "But what about next time? Where will you be? Will you want to come home?

Creating music is your life, Kyle. It isn't fair of me to ask you to give it up."

"This isn't a case of either/or. And what if I decide to give it up, at least, as a performer?"

Jo shook her head the same moment his phone went off. After listening to the sound for several seconds, he yanked it from his pocket and eyed the screen. "It's Cody Weller."

Kyle's song—his "Christian" song. Another bone of contention between them.

Jo could see the war within him. Did he answer or let it go to voicemail? "Go ahead."

"No."

This was like the night Brian called during their dinner at Ricardo's. Kyle wouldn't rest until he'd answered. When she gestured toward the obnoxious phone, he bobbed his head. "I'll tell him I'll call him back."

As soon as he clicked the icon and turned away from her, she opened the door and stepped into the hospital building. They had said all that mattered.

When she looked back through the glass wall, he hadn't even realized she'd left. How long did it take to say "I'll call you back" and hang up?

* * * *

Great timing, Cody.

Kyle gritted his teeth, ready to end the call as soon as possible so he could try to salvage his relationship with Jo.

Besides, he needed more time to decide how to handle this situation. His doubt over allowing Cody to record the song screamed in his brain.

"Hey, Cody."

"Hi, Kyle. I'm sorry I missed you while you were in Nashville. Did Toni mention my interest in recording your song for my next album?"

"She did, and that's great news. Listen, I'm in the middle of something right now. I apologize. Can I call you back?"

"Sure. I think you should know that this won't be my standard album."

At any other time, Kyle would have asked what he meant, but it could wait. "I want to talk to you about it." Just not right now.

"I'll be on the road for the next couple of days, so why don't you call me on Monday?"

Relief washed through Kyle at the reprieve. "Thanks."

With the call over, he turned around. "Sorry, Jo, I—"

She was gone. With her went the opportunity to work out their problems.

Kyle shoved the phone in the back pocket of his jeans, surprised he didn't rip the material with the force. He pulled out his car keys and walked in the opposite direction of the hospital building. No sense going back inside and upsetting both Jo and Vera. He'd committed enough misdemeanors this week and didn't want to add to them the greater crime of causing Vera to suffer another heart attack.

Angry-looking indigo clouds rolled in from the southwest. In the distance, a flash of lightning streaked across the sky. He stalked across the parking lot. The rumble of thunder summed up his mood.

✳ ✳ ✳ ✳

Kyle padded into the kitchen on bare feet, yawned, and started a pot of coffee—a full one—to keep himself awake. He stifled another yawn as he glanced at the clock on the microwave. Nine thirty-eight. He hadn't climbed out of bed this late since his college days, not even after a gig that lasted until the early-morning hours.

With his palms planted on the counter, Kyle watched the glass pot of the coffee maker fill, drip by drip by drip. He still had time to dress for church.

How could he focus on worship with his life in such disarray? Wasn't that when he most needed his connection with God? Yet . . . Okay, he was big enough to admit he couldn't face God or his new friends today.

The brewed coffee filled the kitchen with its incredible aroma, reminding Kyle of Jo's coffee shop. The reminder turned into a memory of how they left things yesterday. She was afraid. He got that. After all she'd been through once, he couldn't blame her for not trusting him, especially since she'd seen that disaster with Sophia with her own eyes. Could he trust himself? Maybe not when he'd let Sophia call the shots and froze like a water fountain in February.

His phone buzzed and the word "Mom" popped up on the screen. He loved his mother, but he wasn't sure he could deal with her right now. He'd let it go to voicemail. At the last second, he swiped the icon. "Hey, Mom."

"Happy birthday, Kyle."

He blinked several times, trying to bring her words into focus. Oh, yeah. Sunday. June fourth. His birthday.

"Thanks, Mom. I'd forgotten." *Please don't break out the song.*

"I wanted to catch you before you left for church."

Kyle didn't mention he wouldn't go this morning. That would call for too much explanation. "I'm making coffee." He must be more tired than he'd realized if he thought that information was worth relaying.

"What are your plans for this afternoon? How will you celebrate?"

A nap? "I'm keeping it low key this year."

"Dinner out with that girl you've been seeing?"

He snapped to attention. She knew about Jo? His eyes narrowed. *Kelsey.*

Kyle breathed a long sigh. He couldn't slam his sister when he'd let the cat out of the bag about her Christmas reunion with Justin. "No. As I told you, I'm keeping it low key." He searched for a change of topic, anything to steer his mom away from asking about his chaotic love life. "How's Dad?"

"He's good . . . said to wish you a happy birthday." She paused. "I read on *Country Music Melody* that Brian will release an album later this year. I'm glad he's doing well."

"You read *Country Music Melody*?" It was an online tabloid with all the news and rumors about the industry. Kyle tried to picture his mom scrolling through the site, looking for the latest gossip.

"Where else would I go to keep up with my talented son's profession?"

"You are something else, Mom."

"I hope that's a compliment."

"A big one." She'd always taken a sometimes-excessive

interest in her children's lives, but she meant well.

"What's next for you, Kyle? Your biggest fans want to know."

As he poured himself a cup of coffee, he told her of his agreement to write a song for Brian's album and Cody Weller's interest in recording one of his songs.

"But?"

Kyle stilled with the hot mug halfway to his mouth. "What do you mean?"

"I heard a 'but' in that explanation, not the confidence I would expect to hear. What has you worried?"

What had him worried? He set the coffee down. Everything.

"I'm asking myself questions about the future. With the band's breakup, I've reached a crossroads in my career and feel pulled in two directions, even though I know where I want to go." Did he? He was no longer sure.

At the abnormal silence on the other end, he wondered if the call had dropped. "Mom?"

"What you said reminded me of my teenage dream. Did I ever tell you about becoming an actress?"

"An actress?" Oddly, Kyle could see it. At times, his mother acted like a teenage drama queen.

"Yes. I saw myself as the next Farrah Fawcett." She'd switched to her storytelling voice. "I even had the hair for it."

He chuckled, picturing photos he'd seen of her in her twenties.

"I tried out for a part in a local commercial and got it."

"You've never mentioned your stardom."

"Because after the audition and learning I'd gotten the part, I couldn't imagine acting as the life for me. I enjoyed playing parts in school plays and even trying out for the commercial." He heard her exhale. "When faced with becoming a professional actor, I found no peace with the idea."

No peace. When was the last time his work brought him peace? Months. Without him explaining, somehow, his mother had gotten to the crux of his problem, hadn't she? "How did you find that peace, Mom?"

"By asking myself who I should live for." She mumbled something, then said, "Dad is motioning to me to get off the phone. He's ready to leave for church."

"Hey, Mom?" He caught her before she hung up.

"Yes, honey?"

"Thanks."

"Have a lovely day, sweetheart."

As Kyle fixed his breakfast—a bowl of granola and strawberries—he asked himself who he wanted to live for. The quick and easy answer was himself, but so far, it hadn't brought him that peace he sought. Besides, it ran counter to his belief in the correct answer.

Davey sat at his feet, staring up at him with anticipation and wearing that hangdog face. "Sorry, guy. I forgot to feed you, didn't I?"

Kyle had been so engrossed in his problems since rolling out of bed, he'd forgotten about his dog's needs. Not the only thing he'd forgotten recently.

What about his commitment to give his life to the Lord, to follow Him, obey Him, and build a relationship with Him? To live for Him? To put Him first in all he did? His heart pounded. He'd forgotten to take to heart the day he'd promised to claim Jesus as Lord of His life.

He poured the food into Davey's dish and supplied the dog with fresh water, then reheated his coffee. Afterward, he let the dog out into the fenced back yard.

No wonder peace had dehydrated like a snowflake in August. Over time, he'd abandoned that commitment in favor of making the decisions that satisfied him. As long as he kept within the boundaries of what God considered right, moral, and just, he was obedient. He was living for God.

Hollow, wrong-headed, and deceptive, legalistic thinking.

Even though he knew the answer, he grabbed his Bible and searched through Proverbs for words of wisdom. Over and over, he returned to two verses in the third chapter.

Let love and faithfulness never leave you; bind them around your neck, write them on the tablet of your heart. Then you will win favor and a good name in the sight of God and man.

Kyle sat the kitchen table for over an hour, trying and failing to recall one time when God had let him down. But in seeking to follow his own path, all he had accomplished was to prove that God couldn't trust in *his* faithfulness. Like his sister said, if he wanted to live his best life, he would choose to live it God's way.

He slipped into a time of soul-dredging prayer—a time to ask forgiveness, to rehydrate his sense of peace, and to recommit to obedience. Because, yes, his good name concerned him. Not so much in the sight of man, but in the sight of God.

Twenty-eight

Sunday night, Kyle slept the sleep of a man at peace after remembering Whose he was. Now, he needed to prove it—to himself, to God, to Jo. The first step came with a phone call.

He tapped his fingers on the kitchen counter until a hoarse, sleepy voice mumbled, "Hello."

"Hey, Cody, it's Kyle Callahan. Sorry for the early-morning call."

The man cleared his throat. "No problem. I was hoping to hear some good news from you today."

"I wish I could give it to you." Kyle took a breath. "I'm flattered that you want to record 'I Claim You' for your album, but I can't let you use the song."

"That's disappointing. Will you tell me why?"

"It isn't a love song. Well, it is, but not involving a romance." He was making a mess of this. "It's a song of praise to God." At Cody's laughter, Kyle tightened his grip on the phone. What was so funny?

"I can't tell you how glad I am to hear you say that."

What? "Why?"

"It proves I understood the song's meaning and made the right choice."

"I'm not sure we're on the same page, Cody. I won't let you include it on a mainstream country album."

"Then let me tell you what I'd intended to say on Saturday."

When Kyle was more interested in fixing things with Jo than in listening to Cody. "Okay."

"For a while, I'd felt God urging me to record an album of Christian music. I kept brushing it off. Then I hit the country charts, so I figured I was wrong, but that compulsion didn't go away. In fact, it grew stronger."

Kyle had known Cody was a good guy, but wished he'd realized they shared a common faith . . . and a common struggle.

"A few months ago, I heard you sing 'I Claim You.' I stood in the corner of that bar with my eyes closed, pouring my worship out to the Lord. I imagine God granted me success last year, so when I finally followed His call, people would be more apt to pay attention. It was an eye-opener for me, and I gave in. I believe in the power of that song and believe it should be on my album, Kyle."

It took Kyle several moments to absorb all Cody said and to ask God for direction. Confirmation came with a calm assurance and a new sense of excitement. "I can't wait to hear you sing that song."

"Great. We'll officially request a license to record it."

They talked a few minutes more, ironed out some details. When the phone call ended, Kyle sank into a chair at the kitchen table before his knees gave way. Davey sat at his side with his head on Kyle's leg. "It's crazy how God works, bud." Crazy good.

Yesterday, he'd received a clearer picture of his career future. It didn't include stardom as a country music artist. God said no to that desire, as He'd said no to his mother's desire to become an actress. It should bring him sadness. Instead, it brought freedom and empowerment. With his desire to obey the call to minister through creating Christian music, confidence that God would provide for his needs left him seeing a brighter future.

His prayers hadn't stopped with his career. He'd sought God's direction for life in a small town with a dark-haired coffee shop owner, which led to the second call on today's to-do list.

＊　＊　＊　＊

When the car in front of her stopped suddenly, Jo slammed on the brake pedal. Her arm swung out to protect her grandmother. Placing her hand back on the steering wheel, she held tight to hide the quiver of her fingers. "I'm sorry, Gran."

"I am fine, Jo Ella, but you had plenty of space in which to stop." Her grandmother wrapped her hand around Jo's forearm and squeezed. "Don't worry so much. I won't break."

She'd already broken. Her heart had broken. Next time, it might not be repairable.

Once more this morning, Jo left her livelihood in the

capable hands of Bethany. After she'd waited for the hospital to prepare the discharge paperwork, the nurse wheeled Gran to Jo's car around eleven. During the drive home, she maneuvered along the roads with care. She avoided potholes while being extra vigilant at intersections, conscious of her speed, and alert in the presence of on-coming traffic.

In the past, Jo had paid little heed to protecting Gran when they rode in the car together, the thought of an accident on the fringes of her mind. She'd just received a lesson in the amount of stress involved in protecting a loved one fresh out of the hospital, someone who had already undergone physical pain. Gran had endured enough these last days. No way would Jo risk her grandmother's return to the hospital.

She had spent most of Sunday sitting by her grandmother's bedside, unwilling to leave until Gran threw her out of the room, telling her to not return until she'd gotten a good rest.

"The last thing I need is them wheeling a bed into my room for you to join me."

Seeing some of her grandmother's normal spunk had convinced Jo to leave yesterday.

Once they reached home, she hovered as they approached the front porch. "Let me help you up the stairs."

Gran shook off her hold and grasped the rail. "I can do it myself."

Jo backed off, accepting her grandmother's gruffness as a reaction to all she'd been through in recent days. That didn't mean she wouldn't stay by Gran's side, ready to help when necessary. It meant the next few weeks might prove trying and call for massive amounts of patience.

"Bobby said he'd stop by to see you this afternoon."

Bobby had put in almost as many hours at the hospital as Jo. Seeing him and Gran together was strange, but Jo couldn't pinpoint why. Because a new romance between people of their ages seemed strange? Because they were friends for years and suddenly discovered a mutual romantic interest in one another? Or because Gran had found happiness with someone new at the same time Jo lost the chance for a similar type of happiness?

Gran dropped onto the couch, and Jo continued on to the kitchen to get her a glass of water and place her medications on the counter.

Unable to stand the idea of those beautiful flowers rotting in a trash can, late on Friday night, she had brought them into the kitchen and placed them in a new vase. But the dry hours in the garbage had taken their toll. Nearly spent, they were a visual reminder of the state of Jo's love life—wilted and dying.

Her decision to not call and wish Kyle a happy birthday yesterday felt as if she were living her life with Taylor all over, right down to the bitterness.

Thankfully, one person in this house had a chance of finding happiness in love.

She handed her grandmother the glass of water. Gran took a sip and set it on a coaster on the table beside the couch. "When did you plan to tell me about you and Kyle? And don't say you didn't want to upset me. I'm already upset."

"Around the same time that you planned to tell me about you and Bobby."

Gran grimaced. "Touché."

Jo sighed. "I shouldn't have said that."

"No. It was a fair statement." Her grandmother patted the cushion next to her. "Sit down and let's talk."

Jo settled on the couch. "I don't want to discuss Kyle."

"Then let me talk."

Gran folded her hands in her lap and told of the loneliness that comes with being widowed. "No matter how old we are when it happens, children and grandchildren can't take the place of a spouse. It's why I've been concerned about your future, Jo E. I see loneliness in your life that lasts far longer than I've had to experience it, and I don't want that for you." Gran's hands trembled and her eyes grew misty.

Jo wrapped an arm around her grandmother and rested her head on her shoulder. "I don't either, but isn't it better to be alone than with someone you can't trust?"

"And you know you can't trust Kyle?"

"All I can do is ask you to trust me and believe I didn't initiate that kiss."

Why had Kyle asked that of her when her eyes had seen the truth? Or had she seen what experience had taught her to expect?

With Bobby at the house, watching over Gran, Jo slipped over to the shop to relieve Bethany of the management burden.

Jo stayed until the last customer left. She was cleaning when she heard the click of the front door closing. Looking up, her throat vibrated with a growl. She should have locked that door and the back one. Why hadn't she locked the door and turned the sign to "Closed" after the last customer walked out?

Locked the door, pulled the shades, and hid in the bathroom.

Ignoring Sophia Carpenter's entrance, Jo continued to wipe the wood surface of the large table at the side of the room. It was foolish to act this way. She knew it. But knowing of a wrong and correcting it were proving to be two different things for her.

The scrubbing ended when Sophia's clacking pair of fancy heels stopped alongside the table, revealing shapely ankles. As a woman who hadn't worn heels in years, Jo couldn't name the high-priced brand and didn't care to try.

"Can we talk?"

Jo returned to wiping the table, her strokes more intense. "I'm afraid I'm busy right now, Sophia. I'm also closed."

"I didn't come for coffee." The woman bent over to look Jo in the eye. "Please? It's important."

Jo straightened and dropped the rag on the table. She crossed her arms. "What do you want?"

Sophia glanced around the empty shop as if ensuring herself they were alone, like whatever she wanted to say was confidential. Since when was that woman worried about confidentiality and privacy as opposed to kissing someone in broad daylight on Main Street in front of God and everyone else in Hidden Veil?

Jo inhaled a deep breath to calm her temper.

"I heard that you and Kyle broke up. I think I'm to blame."

You think?

Jo walked toward the counter. "I don't have time for

this." The time or the emotional stamina.

"It wasn't his fault."

Jo turned to face her. "What wasn't his fault?"

"That kiss." Sophia caught up to her. "*I* kissed *Kyle*. It wasn't his idea, and he didn't appreciate it." She said those words as though wondering why a man wouldn't appreciate such a move.

Kyle hadn't kissed Sophia. He'd told Jo so. She hadn't believed him and wasn't sure she did now. He might have put Sophia up to this. "It's too late to protect him."

"I'm not protecting him, Jo. When he told me he wasn't interested in me because he was seeing you, I saw red. I figured all he needed was a little convincing." Sophia ducked her head in a rare show of embarrassment. "Since we stood across the street from the coffee shop, I suspected you might see us, so I kissed him. I wanted you to think that he and I . . . that we . . " One slim shoulder lifted.

This was not the Sophia Carpenter Jo knew. She looked more like a middle-schooler than a seductress. And this Sophia reeked of remorse and sincerity.

"Kyle called me this morning."

Ah. Jo had hoped she'd been wrong in supposing Kyle proposed this visit. "He asked you to come here?"

Sophia shook her head. "No. He called to say he forgave me. He also admitted he'd been sick." Her mouth twisted. "I hope I don't come down with anything."

Jo tucked her lips, trying to contain a smile. Not unless food poisoning was contagious.

"Daddy saw us out the window on Friday. He was livid and said I should be ashamed. I am."

Dave Carpenter owned the insurance company across the

street. His office insured both the coffee shop and Gran's home, but Jo knew him well enough to believe he'd want his daughter, spoiled as she was, to do the right thing.

A heavy weight eased off Jo's chest. Although, it was a good thing she didn't still hold the wet rag, or she might lob it at Sophia and dirty that sweet yellow sundress she wore. "Do you enjoy playing with people's lives?"

Blue moon-shaped eyes looked back at Jo. "You aren't making me feel any better."

Was she supposed to? As far as Sophia was concerned, probably. Everything revolved around her.

Those heels clacked with the shifting of feet. "Okay, I deserve your anger. I know it, and I'm so sorry."

Jo wanted to stay angry with Sophia. She really did. Yet, it would only cause both of them misery. "It doesn't matter. Kyle and I have other issues." *She* had other issues. "It wouldn't have worked out."

"Because of Taylor Morris?"

Jo tensed. "How do you know about him?"

Sophia rolled her eyes. "Duh. It's a small town. I overheard my grandparents talking years ago. People say you're afraid to get involved with Kyle because he's another musician."

"People say too much." Including Sophia. Did the woman have no filter?

She laid a hand on Jo's arm. "Whatever your problem, it can be fixed. I mean, turning me down only shows that what he told me was the truth."

"What did he tell you?"

"That he didn't want to lose you." Sophia squeezed Jo's arm. "You can trust him. Believe me, I ought to know. I tried, but he has no interest in me. He only sees you."

Oh, Kyle. She'd been wrong to blame him for that kiss.

Trust. Fear.

All her troubles boiled down to fear that stemmed from a lack of trust. She swallowed against the basketball-sized lump in her throat. Why had she allowed fear to control her life for so long? "Thank you for telling me."

"Are we good?"

Were they? Maybe it was the childlike expectation in Sophia's gaze, or because Jo had reached her quota of grudges and had no room for more. She nodded. "We're good."

For a while after Sophia left, Jo sat at the table, determined to deal with her past once and for all.

She stared up at the black ceiling tiles, her mind replaying Kyle's impact on her life and that of others. His ability to withstand her cold shoulder the night she twisted her ankle. The surprise on their non-date, because he'd learned how much she enjoyed the zoo. His willingness to fix her dishwasher. The church concert where he poured out his worship in song. The quick way in which he'd made friends in Hidden Veil—people like Gran, Bobby, Lane, Sutton. Her list went on. Those beautiful flowers meant to remind her of him.

"God, you've tried to show me Kyle's heart, and I've refused to see his goodness in more than a superficial way. I've also been too stubborn to do what I've known all along that You wanted me to do. You and Gran were right. Without forgiving Taylor, I have no chance of a future with anyone else."

That still left Kyle's career choice to stand between them. He had a point when he said anyone might be unfaithful. So, did it make any sense for her to favor those who chose one career while turning her nose up at those who chose another?

Twenty-nine

Jo carried her phone upstairs to her room. This call required privacy and another prayer. Not that she needed prayer to know she was doing the right thing. She and God had settled that between them at the coffee shop. She'd simply needed the serenity that came from talking over her problems with Him.

Inside her room, she made the call and waited for an answer.

"Jo?"

"Hi, Taylor."

"I'm glad to hear from you. Surprised, but glad. How is Vera? Is she still in the hospital?"

Taylor knew no one in Hidden Veil but Jo and Gran. Who informed him? "She's home and doing better."

"I'm sure you're taking good care of her."

Jo did a double-take at the phone, wondering if she actually talked to the right Taylor Morris. "How did you hear about it?"

"It's what I've wanted to talk to you about. Hold on." His voice turned muffled, as though he held his hand over the phone and spoke to someone in the background. "I thought you should know before it went public."

"Know what?"

"I'm getting married."

"You're—" Her lips parted, but she couldn't find the voice to finish the sentence. Wow. She hadn't expected that news. Then again, why not? It wasn't as though he'd become a monk after their divorce. He hadn't even acted like one during their separation.

"I realize I put you through some bad times, Jo. But I'm not the same man you divorced. For the past year, I've met with a counselor and have learned a lot about myself. I've taken a hard look at my behavior, at my life. I didn't like what I saw. We . . . *I* was too young to marry. Plus, I was full of myself. It was a terrible combination."

"Both of us were too immature for a serious commitment." She'd recognized the truth of that statement long ago, but it was the first time she'd admitted it to anyone else.

"I've also realized I wanted to escape my parents and the family dysfunction more than I wanted to marry."

Because of the constant fighting in the Morris family and his father's heavy-handed discipline, Jo should have shown more wariness going into the relationship. Although Taylor was never physically abusive to her, she had witnessed quarrels between him and his father more than once, and one disagreement that turned into a fistfight.

"It was like I couldn't get away fast enough from Dad's

disappointment in me, you know? I guess I gave him reason to be disappointed. Unfortunately, you suffered from my weapon of choice."

They should have talked long ago. If she hadn't been pigheaded in her unforgiveness, many things in her life might have turned out better. Instead, she'd kept her hurt to herself and acted as though she didn't care. She'd done exactly as her grandmother had done decades ago. Only, they didn't share the same ending.

"It often takes two flawed people to end a marriage, Taylor. I should have been there for you more often . . . been more supportive." Like she was supportive of Kyle's career?

"You had your job, and it helped us through tough months. On some level, I understood that, even though I conveniently forgot."

Jo allowed herself a half-smile she didn't really feel. "Okay, so you were most at fault."

If she could tease him, maybe the smile was more real than she'd thought. Talking with him, here and now, didn't provoke the animosity she'd experienced in the past. She doubted they would ever be friends, but hopefully, they could learn to treat one another with respect.

"I won't deny it."

His marriage announcement didn't explain how he was aware of Gran's heart attack. Unless . . . "Do I know your fiancée?"

"Remember Libby Sims from your high school?"

Libby Sims? "She was a couple of years ahead of me, wasn't she?"

"Yep. She came to one of my concerts last year and said she'd known you. We got to talking, and I asked her out.

Before I knew it, I'd fallen in love with her."

Taylor and Libby? The woman still had family nearby. It answered her question regarding Taylor knowing about Gran.

"Before you ask, I've confessed all my sins. All the big ones."

"I'm glad."

"I was a jerk for looking at anyone else during our marriage, but my counselor has helped me see I feared growing up and taking responsibility. This time, I know it's right. I'll do all I can to make Libby happy."

"That's good to hear, because I called tonight to tell you I forgive you, Taylor. It's long overdue, and I've been wrong to hold back that forgiveness." Honestly, it had been easier than she'd imagined speaking those three words—I forgive you.

"Thank you, Jo. That means a lot to me and to Libby."

Neither of them finished the call with an invitation to keep in touch. Their time together was a shadow in their past. Both needed to move on into a brighter future.

In her room, Gran sat propped against the pillows on her bed, watching television. She hit the mute button when she noticed Jo standing at the door. "How did it go?"

Jo entered the bedroom that smelled of rose potpourri and a hint of baby lotion—of Gran. "Good, actually. We talked about the past. He apologized, and I told him I forgave him." Jo sat on the edge of the bed. "I learned why he wanted to talk to me."

"Oh?"

"He's remarrying."

Gran frowned. "I hope he's been honest with her."

"He said they've talked." She grasped her grandmother's

cool hand. "You were right. I feel better."

Thank you, God, for putting up with me in my stubbornness and disobedience for so long.

Gran placed her other hand on top of Jo's. "What about Kyle?"

Jo sighed. "He's the next one to talk to. I'll go see him tomorrow." Hopefully, he wouldn't take as long to forgive her as she'd taken to forgive Taylor.

"You're going to Nashville?"

A chill swept over her. "Why would I go to Nashville?"

"Oh, Jo E, Bobby said he left Hidden Veil on Tuesday morning."

Kyle was gone? "When will he be back?"

"He didn't say."

He had returned to Nashville without saying goodbye?

But why shouldn't he after the way she snubbed him? After her inability to trust him?

She had let fear ruin her chance for happiness with someone who didn't deserve her doubts.

✳   ✳   ✳   ✳

Jo inhaled a deep, courage-building breath and knocked on the door of Kyle's Nashville apartment. Despite the warm temperature, a nervous chill rushed through her, and a shiver scurried down her spine. What would he say when he opened the door? Would he even care that she came? What if he wasn't alone?

No. Those were questions asked by the old, insecure Jo Ella Ledbetter. Whatever resulted from this visit, she was no longer that woman.

When the door opened, he stood in front of her, his eyes wide. How she'd missed that handsome face.

"Hi, Kyle."

His surprise faded, and he stepped aside. "Come on in."

She glanced around the apartment. A living area to the right, a dining area to the left with a small kitchen behind it, and a short hall with rooms she couldn't see. Overall, it was a nice place, though too stark in decoration for her. No photos or prints on the wall. No knick-knacks or books in the lone bookcase. It looked like the home of a transient, someone ready to move at a moment's notice.

Davey ambled to her side and rubbed his head on her thigh, begging to be petted. She obliged. "Hey, sweetie. I should have brought you some treats."

"I think he'll survive." Kyle shut the door. "How is Vera?"

"She's doing well, getting stronger. She's staying with a friend while I'm gone, and Bobby's taking good care of her, too." Knowing Gran had friends who would look out for her had eased some of Jo's worry over her decision to fly to Nashville.

"Bobby is crazy about your grandmother." Kyle's stare bore through her, and he reached out, then shoved his hands in the back pockets of his jeans, as though he thought better of touching her. "You've come a long way."

It was now or never. Jo couldn't stand the idea of never. "I'm here to apologize for being an idiot."

A slight smile ticked up one side of his mouth. "How big of an idiot?"

"A big one. Giant-sized. The biggest."

"You could have called to tell me."

"This required a personal visit." She grimaced. "Sophia explained and apologized."

His jaw tightened. "I should have called you Friday after it happened."

She nodded. "With my mindset, I can't say I would have believed you. I didn't believe you after you told me."

"It's hard to forget unfaithfulness, and it colors a person's attitude going forward. I should have understood after going through it with the breakup of BC's Posse."

"But you forgave Brian."

"Carrying a chip on my shoulder wasn't worth the effort it took to keep it there."

"I've learned that lesson. I called Taylor." She sensed Kyle holding his breath. "I've forgiven him and finally relegated that part of my life to the past."

He blew out a lengthy breath. "I'm glad for you. Did you ask him why he contacted you?"

"He's getting married to a woman I went to school with."

"Small world. How do you feel about it?"

"He assured me he's changed. I think I believe him. At any rate, it isn't my concern anymore. All I can do is pray everything works out for them."

Kyle grasped her hand and led her to the couch. He sat beside her, his warm hand still enfolding hers. "Jo, I don't blame you for walking away from me in the hospital garden. I've done a lot of thinking and praying about my future."

Her heart sank. Had she made this trip for nothing? Maybe he had planned to break things off with her that day, after all. But that ran contrary to what Sophia said. "So have I. Kyle, you shouldn't worry about me. Whether you form another country band or go solo, I'll support you. As long as we're able to build a life together . . ." Now she sounded desperate.

But it was true. His sudden trip to Nashville had upended Jo's resolve to remain in Hidden Veil. Gran had Bobby now, and as much as Jo loved the little town, she loved Kyle more.

He laid a hand on her cheek, and her heartbeat thrummed like the engine of a race car as she waited for him to say something. Anything.

"I've spent months running from God's call, Jo, and won't do it anymore. I've almost finished the song Brian contracted, then I'll leave Nashville for good."

Leave Nashville? She looked around the apartment again. From her present vantage point, she spotted boxes lined up against the dining room wall. What she had taken for sparse décor was apartment belongings being packed for a move.

"Where are you going?" The question came out as a whisper.

"I thought I'd head to a little town in North Carolina. I miss the coffee shop, my checker-playing buddies, and a little old lady with spit and grit."

Her lips twitched with a repressed desire to smile . . . no, laugh. "That's all?"

"Oh, yeah. I miss the owner of that coffee shop." His eyes rolled upward as if in thought. "What's her name? Hmm . . ."

"Her name is Jo Ella, and I've heard she misses you, too."

Kyle snapped his fingers. "That's it. I remember owing her a private concert."

"You owe her grandmother. However, she can't wait to hear you sing for her." Kyle still hadn't explained his plan going forward. "If you're giving up country music, what will you do?"

"Write songs that glorify God."

"Like 'I Claim You'?"

"Yes, like that one. I talked to Cody Weller and told him he couldn't record the song for his album."

Jo's chest warmed. "I'm proud of you."

"The two of you heard the song in the same way. Cody doesn't want it for a mainstream country album. He's recording an album of Christian country songs."

Jo wrapped her arms around Kyle's neck. "You said yes, I hope."

"Once I got over the shock. I'd forgotten how God can work behind the scenes for our good and His glory."

"Amen to that."

In past couple of days, Jo had taken a good look at Kyle Callahan's heart, and boy, did she like what she saw.

*　*　*　*

This last week in Hidden Veil had flown by. With scouting out homes for rent—Mitch and his family would return in a few weeks—to virtual meetings with Brian, to spending time with Jo, his days were full. This day, especially.

He scanned the area of the park where the mayor had auctioned him to the highest bidder. Now picnic tables, lawn chairs, and blankets covered the grassy area. Even under the deep shade from the tree canopies, his t-shirt stuck to his back.

Friends, talking and laughing, replaced the women who had shouted out their bids weeks ago. Davey sprawled in the grass, soaking up the hot sunshine one minute, and meandering through the crowd to beg for a little love—or treats—the next.

A strong lady, Vera had made terrific strides in regaining her health. She and Bobby held hands while sitting in a pair of old lawn chairs with nylon webbing. The rest of the boys sat behind the older couple, with Bethany and her family on a blanket nearby.

Reagan Hartwell had come, though she avoided contact with Lane Becker. Off and on, Trey sneaked peeks at his vet tech, while Sutton avoided Reagan and her sister Brianna.

Jo had invited Sophia, saying it would show the woman they held no hard feelings toward her. Sophia sat on a blanket with Shaina and Harmoni. Every few minutes, she would glance over her shoulder at a guy about her own age who shot baskets on the asphalt basketball court next to the fire station. She never quit.

No, Hidden Veil was not Utopia, but it was home. His home.

"Are you ready?" Jo sidled up to him, a wide smile on her face.

"Are you?"

"I've been ready."

Kyle laughed. "That wasn't always the case."

"I simply needed convincing."

"Like this?" He leaned down and drew her into his arms, kissing her, because it was what he needed.

Jo sighed. Her eyes closed and an expression of contentment and pleasure settled on that pretty face. "Exactly like that."

He still marveled at the change in her, both of them, honestly.

"Let's do this." Kyle grabbed his guitar and strode to the spot where the stage once stood. "Friends!" His shout brought everyone's attention to him. "Thanks for joining us today. What do you say? Should we get this party started?"

Shouts, clapping, and shrill whistles answered his question, so he strummed the opening chords to a song he'd written years ago and performed with BC's Posse.

Kyle's career path might have diverged to take him in a different direction than he'd planned, but as long as his music didn't dishonor God, he felt no reluctance in performing some of the old songs.

For an hour, he sang a variety of genres—country, Christian, rock, pop. For Davey and Bethany's kids, he added "How Much is That Doggie in the Window." People swayed, some danced, others sang along. Passersby stopped to listen. Performing energized him, but not as much as writing songs for others to perform.

"This has been a great time. I have one more tune in me." He readjusted the guitar. "This one is for Jo." He winked at her. "It's called 'I Claim You,' and it will be on Cody Weller's next album of praise songs."

While the others clapped and "woo-hoo"ed, Kyle's fingers strummed the strings of his guitar. He closed his eyes and swayed, the music washing over him.

"No one could tell me what to do.
No one could teach me, not even You.
I lived my life like I'd never die
Until I learned the truth of that lie.

But You never gave up on me.

No, You never backed off from helping me see
The destructive road I walked.
That destructive road I walked.

So I'll say it once more, since I finally believe,
I claim You, 'cause You've claimed me.
Perfect redemption is what I received
When I claimed You, 'cause You claimed me.
Oh, You claimed me.
Yes, You claimed me."

By the time he reached the second verse, Kyle had forgotten the people in front of him and the ones strolling through the park. He forgot everything but the words and his gratitude that, years ago, God had redeemed him from walking down a road that could have led him to spiritual destruction. More recently, God had shown him He never left Kyle's side, even when Kyle hadn't shown his own faithfulness.

"No one but You could calm my sea.
No one but you could set me free.
You say You love me. My heart sings.
I know I'll love You through anything.

In Your loving arms I'll hide.
When my troubles rain down,
You'll stay by my side
On this eternal road I walk.
It's an eternal road I walk.

The music grew in intensity, as did the strength of his voice.

> "So I'll say it once more, since I finally believe,
> I claim You, and You've claimed me.
> Perfect redemption is what I received
> When I claimed You, and You claimed me.
> Oh, You claimed me.
> Yes, You claimed me.
>
> Oh, You claimed me.
> Yes, You claimed me.

He'd added one more line.

> "And I claim You, Jesus."

The last notes faded. Once the applause and good-natured hoots died down, Kyle glanced at Jo. Like the others, she jumped from her seat in a lawn chair next to Vera, her palms beating together. Their gazes locked. Hers was as soft as the breeze ruffling her hair.

He looked away when his new friends surrounded him, thanking him for the concert and telling him how much they appreciated being invited. Kyle only heard half of what they said as his gaze sought Jo once more. She was gone.

Moments later, Bethany pushed a rolling tray with large pitchers of iced tea and lemonade across the uneven ground. Reagan followed, carrying paper plates and cups, plastic forks, and napkins.

Kyle's eyes narrowed with confusion. Jo hadn't

mentioned refreshments after the concert.

She traipsed through the grass, carrying a large cake, placed it on a gray, age-washed wooden picnic table, and turned to him. "You've sung to us, Kyle. Now it's our turn to sing to you." She faced their friends and raised her hands. "One, two, three . . ."

A choir of voices sang happy birthday to him. Bethany's kids danced in a circle as they sang. Davey added a rare series of barks. And Kyle fought to swallow against the rock lodged in his throat, his face warm from more than the sun. Yeah, he was home.

They sang the last word of the sometimes-off-key song, and he waved a hand. "Thank you. Y'all keep your day jobs."

His friends laughed, and Vera cut the chocolate cake. She handed out pieces, the first going to him and the second to Jo.

Within an hour, and after cleaning up, everyone scattered, leaving Jo and Kyle alone in the park to pack his SUV. He sang under his breath, testing the melody.

> "Why can't you see it?
> Why can't you accept it?
> No one loved you more
> Than I did. Than I do."

Jo stopped on her way to the passenger door. "I haven't heard that before."

"I wrote those lines a few weeks ago. That's as far as I've gotten." Kyle placed his guitar case in the back and paused before closing the rear door. "Have you ever heard God speak to you, Jo? I don't mean inside here." He placed a fist to his chest. "I mean, like a voice as clear as you and I are talking now."

"No. I don't think so."

"You wouldn't forget."

"What did He say?"

"He told me He had something better for me." Kyle swallowed the emotion brought on by the blessing of that voice. "It rattled me and took me a while to understand. I thought He meant my change in career focus. Now I realize it had nothing to do with songwriting or performing. It had everything to do with living for Him."

He planted a kiss on her forehead.

Love lost. Love found. Undeserved love.

He still hadn't put those words together in a song, but now they reminded him of what he'd almost lost. Not Jo's love. One far deeper and everlasting, one he didn't deserve but received through grace.

"Surprised you with the birthday party, huh?" Jo snuggled up against him.

He wrapped his other arm around her. "Totally."

"Happy belated birthday, Kyle." She stood on her toes and kissed his lips, the electricity in the touch zapping right down to the soles of his boot-clad feet. "I love you."

"I love you, too, Jo Ella Ledbetter. Wherever I am, you'll always be there."

Right in the depths of his heart.

Next in the town of
Hidden Veil

Read an exclusive scene as an introduction to the next book in the Hidden Veil Hometown series, **A Horseman's Mission**.
You'll only find this sneak peek into the story here.

A Horseman's Mission

Macie Newman drove down Main Street for the third time in the past ten minutes. If she completed one more pass, someone would call the Hidden Veil police and report her casing businesses in town.

"We've already seen these places, Mom."

"I'm just . . ." *Not sure I know what I'm doing.*

She parked in the nearest space and turned off her car. Peering out the windshield and side windows, she debated the wisdom of her plan. Yes, it was a quaint town, a little larger than she remembered from visiting her grandparents during her childhood. Grandma Peters had grown up twenty minutes away. They passed through Hidden Veil on the way to and from her house.

A move was long past coming. She should have made it after Alex's first panic attack, but she'd let her mother-in-law talk her into staying in Charlotte. This was a chance to start over, to give her son fresh memories and a sense of well-being.

But was this the right town for her and Alex? The right time? Would Alex thrive here? Would she find a job? The questions haunted her.

The Charlotte restaurant where she worked provided a good living for them, but it was closing soon. This town had no comparable restaurant. Truthfully, she hadn't expected it to, but that begged the question: how would she pay the bills while keeping Alex near her? Keeping him safe?

Macie glanced up at the green and black awning. During her drives past the buildings along Main Street, the inviting canvas and bistro tables on the sidewalk had caught her attention. She'd read the name on the awning—Jo E's Java. She could use something to drink and some information.

"Come on, Alex. Let's go inside for something cold to drink."

He stared at the door, his gaze seeming to latch onto the people inside. "I can wait here."

She had done extensive research on this area of North Carolina—halfway between her parents and her mother-in-law—deciding on Hidden Veil for its small size, rural setting, and low crime rate. Despite the latter advantage, she wouldn't risk leaving Alex alone. The stifling June weather pronounced that an impossibility, anyway. "No. You need to come with me."

"I'm old enough to wait by myself." That whiny voice sounded more like it came from a five-year-old, not a nine-year-old.

"The car will get too hot." At least it wasn't raining. She opened the car door. "I'll be right beside you."

Alex tossed aside his drawing pad and colored pencils and met her on the sidewalk. She almost took his hand, but changed her mind. While he didn't seem to mind the idea of a move, lately, he'd shown signs of resisting her attempts to protect him.

A minute later, they stood inside the coffee shop. The popularity of this place that smelled like coffee beans and sugar surprised Macie. But did she imagine the customers had grown quieter with her entrance?

"Welcome to Jo E's." A dark-haired woman in her thirties smiled at her. "I'm Jo. What can I fix for you?"

Macie placed her hands on Alex's shoulders and guided her son past the tables, aware that others watched their movements. Several people nodded a greeting, which she answered in the same manner.

Once she reached the counter, she said, "Hi. My name is Macie Newman." Had she needed to state her name? It seemed polite, since the woman behind the counter had given hers. "I'd like a Caramel Frappe. Iced."

"Good choice."

Macie looked down at her son. "They have smoothies."

He shrugged. "Okay."

"A small orange cream smoothie, please."

"Another good choice." This time, the woman addressed Alex rather than her. "What's your name?"

"His name is Alex." When Jo sent a questioning glance her way, Macie regretted answering for her son. The instinct to protect her shy boy had become ingrained in her.

Macie paid and waited while the woman made her drinks. She looked around at the exposed brick walls, black ceiling, and hanging pendant lights—chic for such a small town. Maybe there were other such eating establishments she hadn't seen. "This is a nice place."

Jo glanced over her shoulder. "Thanks. I've been open about eight months."

"It looks like you get a lot of traffic."

"The summer is busy with people vacationing at the lake, shopping at my neighbor's businesses, and staying at the B & B's." Jo handed Macie a tall melamine glass rather than a disposable cup. "Are you staying in town?"

"No." Not yet. "We're here for the day."

Jo handed her son the smoothie. "Here you go, Alex."

He took the cup and mumbled a quiet thanks.

Macie ran a finger up and down the cold glass. "Maybe you can answer a couple of questions for me?"

Jo's brow creased. "I'll try."

"We're considering a move to Hidden Veil, and I'll need a job. I didn't find anything available online, so I'm hoping someone can point me in the right direction."

"What do you do?"

"I'm a chef." Sous chef, actually.

Jo bit her lip and her head waggled with a slow back-and-forth movement. "Your best chance for that kind of position would be at either Ricardo's or the Red Dog Diner, but Rick has had his cooks for quite a while. As far as I know, he isn't hiring for either restaurant."

Macie wanted to mention being more than a cook. She kept her mouth closed. She didn't want to sound pretentious and had known she wouldn't find the level of position here that she had in Charlotte.

Jo turned to another woman. "Bethany, is the fish camp at Hidden Veil Hideaway looking for a cook?"

Macie asked, "Hidden Veil Hideaway?"

"It's a marina and campground on the lake. Nice. They have cabins and rustic tent spaces and kayaking."

She knew about the lake. It was a few miles outside of

town and not a place she would ever take Alex. Nor would she allow him to kayak. Not that he would ask.

"I don't think they're looking for anyone except waitresses," said Bethany. "You know the McCalls. They like to handle everything themselves."

"True."

Hidden Veil reminded Macie of her hometown. She'd rejected returning there, though. Her parents were great, but they didn't understand the special care Alex required. Maybe she'd find work in a nearby, larger town, yet live here. But what would she do about Alex?

"Well, thank you."

Macie and Alex took their drinks to a table. She had hoped to get him away from the city, with its large public school and the kids who teased him—get them both away from her mother-in-law's influence. Homeschooling her son in a small town and protecting him until he learned to handle his fears had seemed the best thing for him.

Or maybe this was a terrible idea.

"Macie?"

She looked up to find Jo standing beside her table. "Yes?"

"This might not be what you had in mind, but a friend owns a place north of town. He's looking for a cook and housekeeper. The job is on the Becker's Crooked Creek Ranch."

Alex bolted upright in the chair. "A ranch?"

Macie stared at her son, more so at the look of interest and enthusiasm on his face, something she hadn't seen in too long. Housekeeping and cooking for a family wasn't a position she'd considered, and it would send Eva, her mother-in-law, off the edge. However, it might do for a start, until she found something else. Would the owners object if she brought Alex to work with her? Better yet . . . "Is it a live-in position?"

"I can't say."

Then housing might be a problem.

"It's a good-sized place, and there's a cabin on the property." Jo shrugged. "Maybe. You can ask Monte Becker."

Macie and Alex eyed one another. Her throat tightened at the hope she saw in her son's expression.

Actually, a ranch might work out well. Quiet. Few people. A chance for Alex to heal at his own pace without feeling threatened. And a cabin sounded nicer than an apartment.

She'd driven all this way. What would it hurt to check it out? "Where will I find Crooked Creek Ranch?"

She seeks healing for her son.
He's looking for atonement for his brother's death.

Continue the story in *A Horseman's Mission.*

From the Author

I hope you enjoyed Kyle and Jo's love story and look forward to the next book in this new series. Although Hidden Veil is a figment of my imagination, the world is filled with small towns and people who adore them . . . like me.

From the moment Kyle stepped onto the page in the novella, *Lost in Winter's Wonderland*, I knew I had to give him his own story. It works so often like that, meeting a character who demands his own happy ending. (I won't upset Gran by using the term happily-ever-after.)

Then I had to include something that happened to me years ago. Maybe it's happened to you, too. I set out to do one thing, but God spoke to me in a voice as near-audible as it could get. It was as though He stood at my side and spoke in my ear. "Don't. I have something better for you." Kyle was quicker on the uptake than I was. It only took him a few weeks to realize that something better was God Himself. It took me years. Anyway, to God be the glory for the inspiration and direction!

I wholeheartedly express my gratitude for Heidi Chiavaroli's incredible insights and hard work to help me make this book—all my books—make sense.

And to you, awesome reader, where would we writers be

without you? Thank you for your faithfulness in supporting us as we endeavor to entertain while, hopefully, providing you with faith-based encouragement and truth.

One more request of you, though. If you enjoyed *A Musician's Heart*, please take a moment to let others know why. Bless them and this author by leaving a review on the book's retail page, Goodreads, and/or BookBub. Thank you!

Sandra Ardoin

As an author of heartwarming and award-winning romance, Sandra Ardoin engages readers with page-turning stories of love and faith. Rarely out of reach of a book, she's also an armchair sports enthusiast, country music listener, and seldom says no to eating out. Visit her at www.sandraardoin.com. Connect with her on BookBub, Facebook, Twitter, and Goodreads. Stay in touch via her newsletter at www.sandraardoin.com/newsletter.